# Pretty Ugly Lies

By Pamela Crane

*This book is dedicated to all the unsung heroes – my fellow mothers around the world. You're forged with fire but stronger than steel. Embrace the small moments, love yourself each day and always remember you're not alone.*

*I did learn something about insanity while I was down there. People go crazy, not because they are crazy, but because it's the best available option at the time.*

- *Gabrielle Zevin,* All These Things I've Done

# Chapter 1

B lood draped around me like a winter coat, thick enough to taste, feel, wear. My fingers were intertwined with my dead husband's, two platinum wedding bands of regret touching in a soft *clink*. My other hand clung to a knife with the lifeblood of my children smeared up to the hilt. I sat there, crouched in a puddle of crimson, realizing only one thing amid the blanket of fear that suffocated me: this was only the beginning of the end.

It was the beginning of death and the end of life. At least the life I knew. In their last flutter of heartbeats, I was swallowed up into a new life. A widowed life. A childless life. And I had wanted it mere hours ago—to be free of them all. Now suddenly it was more than I could bear.

Rising from my dead husband's side, I dropped his limp hand as I shifted one step away. Other than the bloody ooze crawling across the blond acacia floor, the living room appeared immaculate. Every tasteful knickknack in its place, every sofa pillow plump and lint-free, every toy hidden from view. Even the framed art purchased from Pottery Barn hung perfectly straight on the walls.

All these beautiful things I'd spent a lifetime accumulating, putting in just the right place, tending to with dust cloths and lemon-scented cleaner, suddenly it all felt so meaningless. All of it a waste of time.

Where were my family pictures? Where were my children's stacks of schoolwork spread all over the dining room table? Where were the piles of food-encrusted dishes from a home-cooked family brunch, or dirty cleats scattering blades of grass and chunks of mud all over the entryway?

A museum, that was my home. I lived in a hollow museum—or perhaps a mausoleum was more fitting. No signs of life, no signs of family. Just a sterile block of walls and ceilings and pastoral artwork. This was the lifestyle suburban families like mine slavishly followed—organized and neat, down to the fescue grass in the yard cut to a recommended height of three inches. But darkness hid behind closed doors, climbed up the walls, wove a web that would eventually entrap them in misery.

I'd been caught in that web.

As I heard the distant police sirens screaming, I knew they were coming for me. I imagined the headline: *Mom Snaps and Murders Family.* Such headlines plagued the news more and more these days. Why? Why were we all losing it?

Was it because we felt neglected, taken advantage of, unloved? Were mothers being torn in too many directions, expected to be more, more than *just* a mom? A maid, a chef, a tutor, a breadwinner, a chauffeur, a prostitute. Because that's what we were, weren't we? Expected to give sex in exchange for a husband's paycheck? And if we didn't, well, he shopped somewhere else.

I looked at my husband, a man who a lifetime ago fulfilled me, charmed me, enthralled me. Where had he gone? Where had *we* gone? A part of me wanted to say good riddance; the other part of me ached to breathe life back into his mouth that had wounded me so deeply.

Blinking blue and red lights illuminated the living room. They arrived faster than I expected. I had placed the call mere minutes ago, though to me it felt like grueling hours. I considered going back upstairs to where my children's bodies lay—draped across the playroom sofa and spread-eagled on the floor—in front of a moronic kiddie show on TV I had forgotten to turn off, restful as if they were sleeping. But I knew better. Their last breaths had departed for good. I had checked, just to be sure.

Circling my dead husband's body, a single piece of paper fluttered in my breezy wake. I picked it up, gently rubbing the bruise spreading across my knuckles, then skimmed the familiar handwriting. The first lines captured exactly how I felt, though I would never admit it aloud:

> *Sorry isn't enough anymore. Sorry can't fix what's broken. Sometimes a sacrifice is the only way to start over again. This is one of those times.*

My legs grew unsteady as the stench of blood saturated the room. Exhausted yet eerily calm, I sat on my overpriced Italian leather living room sofa, waiting. From upstairs, the bombastic sound effects from *SpongeBob SquarePants* drifted down to the first floor. The kids always did like to blast the TV volume, no matter how many times I screamed at them to turn it down. No more.

I wondered if I'd ever hear children's programming again.

I closed my eyes to the death, though I could still smell it, taste it. You never expect death to be so palpable until you experience it firsthand. My children's faces flashed through my mind, but not images of toothless smiles or that childish mischievous glow. All good memories were long gone, none left to unearth. Lately it just all seemed to fall apart—all the smiles and giggles and bright-eyed joy vanished in the chaos of our flat daily lives.

All work, no play, as they say.

We had lost the idea of *family* somewhere along the path of work and responsibilities, then slipped into becoming cohabitants.

How could that be? In the catalogue of my mind there was nothing fond to reminisce about. I couldn't even remember the last time our family felt whole, and that painful thought dampened my eyes. Now it never would be again.

Blinking my eyelids open, I pushed away thoughts of the kids. I couldn't stand reliving their vacant eyes and gaping mouths frozen in a silent scream anymore.

I tucked the letter in my pocket, unsure what to do with it. My palms, sticky with blood, were folded primly in my lap as I waited. Waiting for the cops, waiting for the turmoil to settle, waiting to be led out of this upside-down world and into something that made more sense. My thoughts lapped gently over what I'd lost, but also what I'd gained—the ability to feel something again.

Where had it gone for so long?

The tears were streaming now, but I didn't bother to swipe them away. I needed this. I needed to let it out. I'd been fighting to keep my sanity for too long, evidenced by my damnable, throbbing, discolored hand. Eventually every battle must end, but the casualties linger on. My family paid the price for my misery, and I felt their sacrifice. They were my collateral damage. My anguish had bubbled just below the surface for far too long, the silence and anger and fear of losing everything just one sob away. And that sob was now.

I heaved, my shoulders crumbling under the pressure of each strained breath, and I couldn't think, couldn't feel, couldn't do anything but weep. It'd be the last time I'd cry today, if ever again, so I better make it count.

In the recesses of my darkened soul I had thought about this day. I had thought often of what freedom would feel like, no strings binding me, no baggage hefted on my back. No husband, no kids—it was a fantasy I guessed all bored, frustrated wives and mothers imagined now and then but didn't actually want. I, however, almost yearned for it sometimes. But I never told anyone; no, I never showed my true face. It was too horrible a thought to voice, giving it purchase and power in the realm of reality: *I wish I'd never married. I wish I'd never had kids.* I never said those things. Nevertheless, the wish was there, hidden among my inner shadows.

No husband, no kids—now my wish had come true. And yet, it didn't feel liberating. The man I gave my body, my youth, my everything to, who used me and abused me, lay facedown in an endless slumber. I should be celebrating getting rid of this loser, user, abuser, and yet I mourned him.

And the leeching kids. Always whining, always fighting, always screaming, always complaining, always take-take-taking … Shouldn't it feel like a burden had been lifted, to know my time would be mine to sleep in, to eat while my food was hot, to cook what I liked, to clean and know it'll stay clean, to put on music and actually hear it, to watch the shows I wanted to watch, to live a day for myself for once? But I didn't feel relief. I felt a complicated blend of regret and release. I felt an emptiness, as if an appendage had been ripped from my very own body.

Yet I had wanted this, hadn't I? I'd never uttered it aloud, but the daily effort of loving a family that didn't love me back had ground me into dust.

My macabre ruminations were pierced by the sound of my front door swinging open, slamming against the wall behind it as a herd of police officers rushed into my home followed by paramedics who would prove useless.

Just as the barrage of questions floated off the officer's tongue, I regained my composure, wiped away the tears, and prepared to tell the story of the day my soul died and awakened a monster …

# Chapter 2 - Jo Trubeau

*Forest Hills Park*
*Before ...*

My life was the tide. Some extreme lows, some intense highs, but all in all, it was steady and predictable. Even my thoughts drifted like the ocean, ebbing and flowing seamlessly, only occasionally crashing onto the shore of my brain when I realized I forgot to turn on the Crock-Pot or iron my husband's clothes for work.

Yes, my life was a perfect, quiet ripple of water. Until today.

Today my life morphed into a riptide dragging me out to sea. And it nearly drowned me.

You never see it coming when you're in the thick of it, but with the clarity of distance it's easy to look back and know what went wrong.

For me it all went wrong on an otherwise normal Saturday morning at Forest Hills Park, the park that would forever change me, permanently altering my memory. Never again would I look at that place without the accompanying pang of my heartbeat racing, my breath catching, my fear mounting, my world ending.

The metal was cold even through my Guess jeans as I sat on the bleachers, along with two dozen other mothers, watching Preston's soccer team haphazardly kick the ball twenty feet here, twenty feet there, eventually making it down the field before another parent's shining-star soccer player intercepted it. Then the whole process began again heading in the other direction. An exhaustive production of mundanity and futility, at least for those watching.

All of us soccer moms lived in the ideally suburban Oleander Way neighborhood, a long stretch of matching but stately homes that advertised an upper-crust lifestyle. Manicured yards and manicured nails; designer clothes and designer boobs—we were the Kardashians-meet-the-Joneses that everyone else was trying to keep up with. With Mercedes and BMWs parked in every power-washed driveway, Oleander Way families touted wealth, beauty, and perfection.

One of those families was mine.

Time is a harsh mistress. People are always complaining that there's just never enough time to get everything done. I seemed endlessly gifted with Time, so much so that I often lost track of whole days. To me Time was a wonderful maze that I could get lost in with reading, cooking, cleaning, and homemaking. One day blended into the next until Saturday morning arrived, the only difference being the addition of my successful husband Jay, the eye-candy of joggers trolling for a distraction from their workaholic husbands. Notorious for his shirtless gardening, and tanned, muscled chest, if Jay was tending to the yard, you bet there'd be a bevy of bored housewives wanting to tend to him *happening* by. I'd see them circling the block as Jay mulched or mowed, and I'd smirk with pride knowing the sidewalk was as close as they'd ever get.

Not that I minded being the envy of the block. We were unbreakable, impenetrable. Jay and I enjoyed a perfect marriage in our perfect home with our perfect children.

I loved my life. I loved my husband. I loved my children. What wasn't there to love when everything was so perfect?

While Amelia and Abby played at the nearby playground—slipping down the yellow slide, climbing up the red ladders, running across the blue bridge—I held an open book on my lap, its title—*A Secondhand Life*—pressed against my thigh. Every few pages I glanced up to see where on the field Preston had aimlessly wandered. After this season he would have fulfilled his obligation to his father and thus be freed of his imprisonment to the soccer field. I knew the poor boy couldn't wait to toss those cleats in the Goodwill bag once and for all.

As my attention was swept away from Preston and the primary-colored playhouse the girls had been climbing on for the past hour, Time lost any allure for me. One moment I was watching Abby adorning her little sister's hair with bouquets of dandelions, the next moment Abby ran toward me screaming my name—and I never caught the moments in between.

"Mommy," she said breathlessly, running up behind me where I sat in the front row. I always preferred easy access to the ground for a quick escape once the game was over. Not that I was antisocial, but after hours of sitting uncomfortably in the sun while my fair skin freckled and burned, the last thing I wanted to do was *stand* uncomfortably in the sun several minutes more, forced to make idle chitchat about a sale going on at Macy's or where I got those gorgeous earrings. Jewelry always served up conversational fare among these types of women. Occasionally it'd segue into suspected infidelity or someone else's financial woes. As far as I was concerned, gossip should be reserved for during the game, not after.

"Mommy, can I go see the puppies?" Abby finally said after a snatch of breath.

"What puppies?" I asked, expecting to see my five-year-old and three-year-old hand in hand, their matching blond curls swept up off their sweaty necks. I secretly loved that they took after me with their natural golden waves, inquisitive blue eyes, and sprinkle of freckles. But my three-year-old wasn't attached to her sister like she always was. I glanced behind Abby. No sign of Amelia. "Where's your sister?"

"With the puppies," Abby said matter-of-factly, as if it should have been obvious. "Can I go, too?"

Now I was standing—I don't recall doing so—tossing my book on my seat and briskly walking toward the playground, my eyes searching. "What do you mean 'with the puppies'? Where are these puppies?"

"I don't know." The whine in her voice scratched along my eardrums like nails clawing a blackboard.

"You don't know?" Suddenly my voice tensed, a tone I rarely used.

I didn't want to overreact, but Abby's ambiguity was forcing my concern. She knew better than to leave her little sister unattended. Even in our own backyard I had a rule about staying together. An HOA-approved fence—the Homeowners' Association was known for its outlandish rules and was quick to fine rule-breakers—could have easily resolved that issue, but Jay's tightfistedness with a dollar, despite his seven-figure income as a CFO, buried that option before I could build a case for it.

The playhouse and its multitude of colorful hidden compartments were mere feet away, so I figured Abby had left Amelia inside to wait for her. I stooped to peek under and through every nook, expecting to find a chubby three-year-old with a curly ponytail tucked inside as she hid, giggling.

While I came face to face with toddlers galore, none matched my blond-haired, blue-eyed, hot-pink-adorned daughter. After the last section of playhouse turned up empty, panic officially overtook me. I felt my world shifting, quaking beneath weak knees that threatened to toss me to the ground.

"Where is the person who had the puppies, Abby?" This time the question came out in a loud, off-key warble as my lungs clenched up. I couldn't breathe.

"The man over there asked if we wanted to hold them …" Abby pointed an unsteady finger at an empty park bench. "He was right there on that bench. I swear."

A strange man with puppies.

My baby girl missing.

Every mother's worst nightmare come to fruition.

I began freaking out.

Adrenaline kicked in. My body launched into a frantic headlong dash over every square inch of shaded green expanse that led to the parking lot, but still no Amelia.

I heard my heart thrumming in my ears. Strange, because it felt like it was in my throat.

"Amelia!" I screamed as loudly as my parched lungs would allow. Then to Abby I ordered, "You stay put and don't talk to anyone. Just stand here and keep an eye out for your sister, okay?"

She numbly nodded, tears wetting her eyes. But I had no time to comfort her.

"Amelia!" I called again, drawing the attention of several other mothers ambling around as their children played, recognition and fear ghosting their features with traces of relief as they quickly took inventory of their own progeny.

By now too many minutes had passed, and the longer it took me to find her, the more trouble she could be in. I sprinted for the parking lot, glancing back to make sure Abby hadn't disobeyed. As I neared the curb, I couldn't decide which way to start looking. There were too many cars coming and going, too many people, too many children.

I picked the more congested side of the parking lot, figuring my daughter's abductor would have wanted to slip in among the masses.

As I ran, the word sank in: abductor.

My daughter—abducted. Kidnapped. Murdered?

The sequence of thoughts was a train rumbling full-steam, unable to stop in time before it smashed into me.

The sobs and screams for her blended into one frightening, pain-struck chorus. I choked on her name, praying at every car I passed that it'd all been an overreaction. I'd see her chubby little arms wrapped around a squeaky puppy as its tongue lapped at her ruddy cheek.

But as I neared the end of the parking lot with no sign of Amelia, my hope for a happy ending was all but dead.

I needed to call the police. I reached for my cell phone, but my pocket was empty. I must have left it on the bench back at the soccer field. Circling back through the parking lot from the other direction, every empty car turned up more fear.

No Amelia.

And no way to find out who took her.

By now my heart spasmed from the intense workout I hadn't trained for. My lungs felt like they were ripping apart in my chest as each breath grew more constricted. I needed to stop running, try breathing, pull myself off the brink of a panic attack, but my daughter's life depended on me, and the adrenaline pushed my legs forward.

I made it back to Abby and yelled at her to follow me, then sprinted to the bench where I found my cell phone. Punching in the three digits I had never in my life expected to use, the operator answered and through my tears and hysteria I was able to push out the words no mother should ever have to utter:

"My name is Jo Trubeau and my daughter has been kidnapped."

# Chapter 3 - Ellie Harper

I'm not a suspicious woman. I've never been the jealous type. I have trusted everyone with the naivety of a child, and blissfully so. Well, at least until now. Today, however, I became someone I didn't recognize.

The chill of the gray tile permeated through the pockets of my jeans and deep into my marrow as I sat cross-legged on the laundry room floor. The scent of fresh linen wafted around me, offering a cheerful refreshment masking the sweaty-meets-worn-socks odor of overflowing piles of dirty clothes that I had no time to deal with.

Stay-at-home moms don't own the luxury of free time.

After a grocery run in the morning—checking out a brimming cart full of all-organic fruits and veggies and healthy meals planned for the week, while nine-year-old Logan whined for candy as I dragged him from aisle to aisle—I came home to wash, dry, and fold laundry during a DVR'd episode of *The Bachelor*, while Denny watched *SportsCenter* in the bedroom and the kids stayed out of my hair. *SportsCenter* was the reason our sex life dried up. Just the sound bite of the theme song of that show made my libido as arid as the Sahara and made me feel homicidal.

Perhaps I didn't really know what homicidal felt like until today.

Today it felt real.

Today it scalded my brain with thoughts of stabbing Denny, poisoning him, shooting him, burning him, watching him beg for mercy. I wanted him to share the pain he was putting me through—misery, a hateful emotion I had never experienced before.

I've always been the last to admit that I harbor a shallow pool of resentment for giving up my career as a speech therapist so that Denny's dreams could come true—birthing and raising Darla and Logan, now my reasons for living and breathing. Children and homemaking took over my life, were my reason for breathing, leaving little room for myself. And I was okay with that. I loved my family, even if they didn't always show it back. Deep down, they had to love me in return, right? I didn't need a career, though sometimes I wondered why I couldn't have it all.

All that work for my PhD made worthless, except when a telemarketer would call, addressing me as Miss Harper and I'd correct them to call me *Doctor* Harper just for fun. My doctorate was laughable really, since I'd never done anything with it after Denny. We'd barely breached the threshold of the honeymoon suite before he started negotiations about having kids. And in my compliance and sense of obligation, I had agreed we'd start trying right away. Anything to make my husband happy. In fact, it was likely we conceived that very night. As my aspirations of a career fizzled out, I had figured out a new place for me in this world—world's best wife and mommy—and I was okay with it. Well, okay *enough*.

But today I was no longer okay.

Today I poured out what was left of my heart into a puddle of tears on this damn ceramic floor.

I clutched my husband's shirt, analyzing through watery eyes the oxblood stain of lipstick that I knew wasn't mine. I hadn't kissed his neck since too long to remember, and domesticated moms like me didn't wear this shade of whore red, anyway. If that wasn't enough, I could taste the overpowering floral perfume only a tramp would wear that clung to the collar.

I couldn't remember the last time Denny had told me I was beautiful, or that he loved me. Weeks, maybe months had gone by without a hug or passionate kiss, though God knows I had tried to make the moves, since I had needs too. An off-to-work peck on the cheek was all I got these days. Years of marriage had watered down his interest in me, and years of neglect had watered down my hope for rekindled romance.

For about a year we were spiraling headlong into becoming another divorce statistic. And now *this*—lipstick stains and perfume remnants, the proverbial nail in the coffin.

The evidence was too obvious, carelessly tossed on top of the laundry basket. It was almost as if he wanted me to find this to hurt me.

Or maybe it was too obvious to be anything at all.

It didn't make sense that Denny wouldn't have hidden his secret—his marriage-destroying, life-upheaving secret. Unless he wanted to destroy the life we'd built for the past twelve years?

Perhaps I was overthinking the stain. It could have been a saucy spill from dinner. Hadn't we had spaghetti bolognese a couple days ago? Or maybe Logan had dropped one of his markers in the laundry basket, which bled on Denny's shirt.

No matter what excuses I conjured up, my mind circled back to the same inescapable conclusion.

Those were lip prints.

The end was near.

I should have seen it coming. The signs were everywhere. We hadn't gone on a date night in months. Our love life had dwindled into bland missionary-style humping a couple times a month that lasted just as long as it would take him to finish and an occasional birthday blowjob. I imagined a blond, big-haired bimbo's head bobbing up and down as she pleasured my husband in ways I hadn't for far too long.

Did this mean it was my fault?

Where did it go wrong? I remember how in love we were, how he rubbed my back every night as we nestled on the couch, how when we first bought our house, we christened every room, even the laundry room—my personal favorite as the dryer drummed in the background—how we couldn't keep our hands off each other. Now those hands were on another.

Was this the fate of every modern-day marriage?

In the living room down the hall, the television blared an annoying childish melody as the kids laughed at the show. Somehow they had managed to take over the living room television, even though they had their own playroom. Once again my wants, my needs fell to the bottom of the list. I needed to think, but the shrill voices drowned out the monologue that rampaged through my head.

Wiping the salty tear and snot mixture from my heated face with my husband's shirtsleeve, I blinked my eyes dry and rose weakly to my feet. My stomach lurched at the unwanted upright posture and I feared I was going to be sick, but I knew if I didn't make an appearance, the kids would come looking for me. Not because they cared, of course. But because they'd want a snack or a drink, or just to disrupt any peace I might have. God forbid I take a moment to myself to digest losing my husband to another woman.

Right now I didn't feel up to explaining that Mommy was hiding and sobbing in the laundry room because Daddy was a cheating bastard.

I snuck past the children, searching for Denny. After peeking into my empty bedroom, I rounded the corner that opened up into the living room, where afternoon sun flooded through the windows, illuminating a sea of floating dust particles in the air.

"Did you finish your homework?" I asked Darla, as if my world hadn't toppled off its axis and cast me into a perpetually suffocating outer space.

"Shut up," she spat. "You're interrupting the good part."

Normally I'd accept defeat and retreat. I know, it was the worst possible thing a parent could do, letting the child talk that way, grabbing the upper hand. But I'd spent years fighting back, only to have Denny take the kids' side. So my go-to move was robotic compliance. Until now.

"Don't speak to me like that. I'm your mother. Now answer my question or I'll beat it out of you."

With wide green eyes she looked up at me, the shock apparent in the crinkles of her worried brow.

"Geez, what's your problem?" she mumbled. "It's already done and in my book bag."

I thanked her stiffly. Darla, my responsible but bratty eleven-year-old. So organized and on top of things ... including her little brother. On more than one occasion I'd found her with her knees pinned against his back, grinding his head into the carpet. When they fought, they fought hard. Hair-pulling, nails-scratching, feet-kicking hard.

I couldn't remember the last time I had fought with Denny. I wondered if it would be tonight.

"Any tests you need to study for?"

"Already done," Darla replied mechanically.

"Good girl," I praised in a mournful monotone. I wasn't doing such a good job of masking my feelings and I didn't care.

In fact, I wanted Darla to ask what was wrong. I wanted someone to notice my pain. In my life, the world was colorblind and I was the color red. No one saw me for who I really was.

But Darla didn't ask, and I didn't tell. She hadn't even offered another glance as her eyes remained fixed on the show in front of her.

"Do you know where Daddy is?" I asked.

"Nope." Then she went back to numb TV watching as if her monosyllabic answer was enough.

"Darla!" I barked.

She started, glaring at me. "What?" I hated the way her voice rose with a teenage annoyance that she was too young to know about yet.

"You didn't answer me. Where's your father?"

"Am I supposed to keep track of where everyone is all the time?" And there it was again—the insolence, like a sixteen-year-old trapped in an eleven-year-old's body. How did it start so soon with girls?

"I just need to find him. It's important, Darla. Please."

"Sorry, Mommy." Then once again I was reminded that nope, she hadn't quite grown up yet. I was still her *mommy*. A memory lingered of the platinum blond little girl who loved wearing pigtails and splashing in puddles after a storm.

"It's okay. So where's Daddy?"

"He went out on the porch," she blurted, returning to her television entrancement.

I ambled to the back porch, wondering how to act, what to say. I'd been married to the man for twelve years and yet I suddenly had no idea how to *be* around him.

Through the sliding glass door I went, making sure to shut it all the way behind me. Sitting under the veranda nursing a Heineken was Denny, fiddling with his phone, or maybe typing a text to his lover.

I wondered what she looked like. I already knew what she smelled like and what lipstick color she wore while screwing my husband, but other than those vague details, was she prettier than me? Blond? Younger than me? Skinnier than me?

I'd already drafted a picture in my head of a tight-tummied, big-boobed twenty-something slut who could afford those abs because she'd never had children, and whose breasts remained full and perky because she'd never nursed a baby, and whose skin was flawless and tan because she'd never spent sleepless nights tending to sick kids or early mornings rushing around hauling them off to school and on errands. I bet she didn't spend her evenings buying mountains of groceries that her disgruntled children would complain about the next day, then come home to fold countless tiny superhero shirts and glittery shorts and days-of-the-week underwear and mismatched socks while mindlessly watching television alone.

No, Denny's mistress was above all of that, I was sure.

I was dirty laundry and stress lines and gray hairs. She was forbidden passion and sultry breaths and flirty whispers. She was everything I wasn't, everything I couldn't be.

Denny glanced up at me as a pocket of air followed me out of the house. If I were to describe Denny in one word, it'd be distinguished. Although his brown hair was peppered with gray, none of his other features evidenced any indication of his years. It was unfair how men became distinguished and women just became old. He'd maintained a desirable charm with his effervescent smile and sparkling green eyes that I couldn't look away from. As if a tiny finger had molded its imprint on his chin, I found his chin dimple—or *chimple,* as I liked to tease him with—sexy. Darla inherited his eyes, but Logan inherited his smile.

"Hey, babe. What's up?" he asked me.

*I know what you've been doing when you say you're working late,* I wanted to reply. But I didn't. I couldn't. Not yet.

"Nothing much," I said instead. "Mind if I join you?"

"Sure." He pulled out a seat next to him, patting the striped navy and white cushion on the mocha wicker patio set. The overhead tropical ceiling fan lazily wafted a light breeze over us, the palm blades mesmerizing as they circled.

"What are you up to hiding out here all alone?" I made an attempt at playful, but it sounded forced, stilted. Accusing.

"Just playing on my phone." He flashed me a glimpse of his screen where little colorful objects were flying in all directions. Every few seconds it *buzzed* or *dinged* at him. "What's for dinner?"

"Chicken parmesan," I stated with a lift of my lips.

"Sounds great, babe, just be sure not to overcook the pasta again," he said with his eyes fixed on his phone. I couldn't remember the last time he actually looked at me, *saw* me. Something was always in the way, it seemed.

"I bought you that Belgium beer you like—Chimay." I wanted so badly for him to notice me standing there, desperate for his attention. Why was it such a struggle?

"Thanks. You're a doll."

And thus concluded our standard conversation as I grew weary faking it, standing there like an idiot while he ignored and belittled me. I headed back inside, toward the master bedroom where I had picked out every color, every accent piece to portray what I thought our marriage represented back when we first moved in. Deep teals and fuscias, colors of passion. Subtle floral accents and

18

wispy curtains, a Bohemian den of relaxation. Soft chenille blankets to caress our skin to sleep. I wanted our bedroom to be a place of serenity and feverish lovemaking. Time had worn away those emotions for Denny, but not for me. Maybe I loved him too much.

Opening my bedside table, I picked up my worn leather journal and the pen tucked next to it. I needed my outlet. Denny often teased me that it was adolescent to keep a diary, but some thoughts were too dark, too fragile to share with any human, and yet they still needed to be expressed. I wondered if Denny ever picked it up to secretly read, but I doubted it. I wouldn't have minded—in fact, I wanted him to yearn for a peek into my riddled brain, into my secrets, but he didn't care enough to be curious.

*It hurts—my heart, my soul. I think I'm losing Denny. Maybe I already lost him altogether …*

I scribbled. My eyes grew heavy with tears as the words I couldn't speak flowed through my pen.

*How can a marriage survive unrequited love? I want to reach him, but he's so distant. He never touches me anymore. He never asks how I am. He's so consumed with work and his phone that he doesn't see me or the kids. I know the kids sense it too—that we're losing him. But they don't seem to care. He isn't their life after all, like he is mine. He's just their for-now, but he's my forever. All they do is fight and complain. They act like they hate me. Is this normal? It can't be.*
*How can I fix this? How can I restore our family before it's gone? Or is it too late? I want to know—is he cheating on me? Is he in love with another woman? Do I really want to know? I think I need to, but I can't unknow it once it's out there. I don't know how to feel right now. Part of me wants to hurt him, but part of me wants to win him back. Sadly I don't have the guts to do either. I'm a pathetic bystander in my own life.*

I was writing words to Denny that he'd never read. I felt spineless hiding behind my journal, but perhaps it wasn't the right time for confrontation. All he'd do was deny, followed by a series of excuses to combat the evidence I'd present to him. He'd make me feel like a fool, and I'd be forced to accept and ignore the reality. Just like I always did.

Why was I acting so weak? I didn't have to be. I was intelligent, hard-working, motivated. I didn't need to sit back and take the punches.

No, I couldn't let him bulldoze over me, our marriage, our family. I needed to plan this out. Catch him, threaten him. Maybe if he faced losing everything he would come back to us. I needed something bigger to out him, something more irrefutable than a red stain and lingering floral scent. And when I'd dish it all back to him, I swore to myself that he'd be choking every painful, humiliating, life-shattering taste of my overcooked wrath down ... and I'd never let him come back up for air.

# Chapter 4 - Shayla Kensington

Iknew as soon as I said it that the words would come back to bite me in the ass—I mean, *butt:* "I'm going to teach that fucking kid a lesson he'll never forget."

I should have known better than to swear in front of the kids, because a moment later I heard Tenica parroting me from the living room down the hall: "Fucking, fuck-fuck-fuck."

Cringing at my bad motherly example, I didn't bother to scold her. A reprimand would only egg her on to say it louder and more often. Three-year-olds had a way of testing the boundaries—at least mine did.

"Ow!" Arion cried out as I lost focus and brushed the washcloth a little too roughly against his tender nose. He winced at the irritation as I scrubbed away the crusty blood that left a ring under his nostrils. It was the third time in as many months my son had gotten the shit beat out of him on his way home from the bus stop. And more than anything I wanted to kick the kid's ass who kept hurting him. But no, I had kept myself in check, it wasn't the *Oleander* way. I had handled it diplomatically and spoke with the parents; a lot of good that seemed to do. Trent even rearranged his work schedule so he could pick Arion up from school to avoid the bus ride altogether … until his boss demanded longer hours without a cent more in pay.

Cheap bastard.

I wondered how much more bullying I was supposed to allow before pulling him out of school and sending him … where? Our quaint neighborhood on Oleander Way was regarded as one of the best school districts in North Carolina. An unaffordable private school was out of the question. Homeschooling would have been an ironic choice since I was a teacher who hated the idea of educating my own kids. I could handle my classroom, but my own kids? Let's just say that the four hours a day I spent with them after work was plenty for me.

"Sorry, sweetie."

I examined Arion's nose, the cartilage swollen and a blotchy purplish-red, wondering if it was broken again. The last thing we needed was another medical bill to not pay. I still had collectors after me for the last one, no thanks to our shitty insurance that didn't cover a damn thing and hospitals that felt a $15,000 charge to set a broken nose was a fair price for a "surgical procedure." Surgery, my ass! I could have done the same thing at home with a few cotton balls and some tape. The whole health industry was a racket. God bless America.

Unlike most of our neighbors, we could barely afford our house, let alone maintain the lifestyle that was expected of residents on Oleander Way. We epitomized the phrase "house rich, cash poor," a secret we closely guarded from the suburban busybodies.

"So that punk Chris Morrison did this?"

"Yeah," Arion mumbled against the washcloth as I finished up. "But please don't talk to his parents again. It'll just make it worse."

"Worse than this?" I held up the blood-soaked rag. "This is the third time, Arion. I don't understand why he's targeting you."

"Really, Mom? Isn't it obvious? I wear ugly glasses, I'm the shortest kid in my class, I suck at sports, and even the nerds are cooler than me."

"Hey, don't say that. I think you're cool."

"You're the only one who does. Even the girls pick on me. And you don't think it has anything to do with my name—*Arion*? Were you and Dad trying to make my life difficult when you named me?"

"Oh stop. It has nothing to do with your name or your glasses."

Though even I had my doubts.

Almost ten years ago, when Trent and I discovered we were pregnant at last—and by golly, our firstborn would be a blessed baby boy! Hallelujah!—we wanted what all parents want for their unborn child: a perfect, happy life. A life of big dreams and even bigger accomplishments. While picking out blue and gray onesies, and etching sports-themed borders along his nursery wall, his whole life was plotted out. Our son would stand out. He'd excel in sports—preferably basketball—and be the popular kid who ruled over the lunch table. Straights A's for our son, with the occasional B tolerable. And of course he'd be the cutest boy in his class.

His name would be strong and masculine and cool—everything we planned for him to be. But *cool* for us back then became very different from *cool* now. Instead of the symbol of power we had hoped his name would become, it was a noose around his neck. *What kind of name is that?* we heard from family and friends. And thanks to Trent's family name, Leslie, falling back on his middle name didn't offer a better alternative. Add that to his clumsiness and soft-spoken demeanor and it was a recipe for failure. Over and over, with each questioning look and mispronounced spelling, Arion's confidence chipped away until nothing was left but a weak-kneed, battered, and bruised little boy.

Bullies like Chris Morrison smelled the odor of weakness a mile away and stalked their prey.

"Then *why*? Why's Chris hate me? I've never done anything to him—I don't look at him, talk to him, or even breathe the same air as him."

"Maybe that's the problem. He knows you're afraid of him. You've got to stand up to him, defend yourself."

"He's twice my size. He'll kill me."

A likely scenario, unfortunately. The poor kid was cursed with my petite stature—all five-foot-two of me—to go along with his offbeat name, inspired by a Marvel Comics character my husband admired. Only a couple weekends of playing catch in the backyard told us everything we needed to know about Arion's athletic prowess: there was none. The kid was a wet noodle.

I felt horrible. We had done this to him: created a perpetual victim. And if we didn't get him out of this hell of a life, I could envision his face splattered all over cable news reports about the latest school shooting by a disgruntled student that classmates described as a misfit.

"Maybe you can take some self-defense classes, like martial arts. What do you think?"

He shrugged. We both knew his lack of coordination sometimes made just putting one foot in front of the other a challenge.

"I'd rather just change schools."

"I'll talk to your father about it and see what we can do. Now let's get some ice on this and then you go watch some television, okay?"

Arion nodded meekly, following me to the kitchen where I pulled a year-old bag of frozen sweet peas from the freezer. God knows why I even had those in there, other than to act as a makeshift icepack. It wasn't like I could force-feed the kids anything green anyways.

"Here, use this."

"Thanks, Mom." Arion gingerly applied the bag to his eye and ambled to the living room where his little sister curled up in the corner of the slipcovered couch that hid jelly stains and milk blots from years past. In a manic midnight shopping spree, I had ordered a new sofa from Wayfair that was set for delivery any day now. I could already imagine Trent's fury when it arrived, but he'd get over it. One comparison to what my best friend Jo Trubeau's husband let her buy would shut him up until the credit card bill arrived. One thing I loved about Trent was we fought hard, but we made up even harder.

Clutching a sippy cup to her chest, Tenica's chubby fingers hadn't yet lost their dimpled baby fat, and her cheeks still had that kissable thickness that everyone wanted to pinch. I stood there for a moment, watching the two creatures I had given life to, observing their attentive gazes and comfortable silence as they were entertained by whimsical characters and frantic music. It was a cherished moment, basking in the simple pleasures of motherhood, something I rarely enjoyed these days. I never stood still. I never paused to reflect. I never felt … at peace.

Happiness skittered away from me anytime I drew near. I couldn't explain why I felt this way; God knows I tried. But the misery, the mania, the endless emotional roller-coaster cycles haunted me, gripped me like a bear trap sinking iron teeth into my flesh. I wanted to blame it on my bipolar disorder, but was it really just me? Was I the only woman in the world unhappy with life, with no clue what would make me happy? Trent was tired of me, the kids were tired of me, *I* was tired of me. Hell, even my shrink was tired of me. Prescribed me some lithium then sent me on my merry way.

There was only one joy in my life: my little secret.

A dark and forbidden secret that could set my life on fire. It was a danger that thrilled me. Wasn't that always the way of it—security was boring while risks were exciting? It went against the human nature to protect oneself, but I guess that's what made mankind so complex. We were both self-preserving and self-destructive all at once. We ate junk food that spread toxins through our bodies, then exercised to make up for it.

Complicated and contradictory, that was me. I confessed to Trent every stupid thought that bumped along in my head, but when it came to the big stuff, the real stuff that went on in my life, I lied. I hid the lies deeper. I couldn't even tell Jo, my best friend since high school, about the depths of my secrets. It was lonely being me in my make-believe world of lies.

No one knew about them.

And I intended to keep it that way. No matter how much they clawed to get out. Sacrifices must be made.

# Chapter 5 - June Merrigan

The closet was as good a place as any to hide from him. Through the closed door and layers of blouses I could hear his voice, beckoning me, inviting me to join him in hell. It wasn't like there was anywhere I could run. There was no refuge for me. In a few precious minutes I knew I'd be found, and the nightmare would begin.

It was a nightmare I could never seem to wake up from.

The nightmare, after all, was my waking life.

The horrors that awaited me drifted like an aimless ghost, his moaning floating down the hallway toward my bedroom. Beyond his approaching voice I heard shrieks of pain, like that of a child being tortured. The screams intensified, growing louder and reaching pitches that rattled my eardrums. And yet I huddled further into my dark corner, unable to find the courage to come to the rescue.

My face dropped into the palms of my hands as I shrunk into myself, a sob escaping but luckily muffled by my fingers. I tried to reel back the weeping, but it was too late. My body shook under the weight of my tears.

If only I didn't know what I faced on the other side of this door.

If only a glimmer of hope peeked through the slats, into my dark world.

If only, if only … if only I had the power to change everything.

But today I was powerless.

Today I was afraid. I was afraid of what I would do. I was afraid of what I couldn't do.

The sense of helplessness squeezed my lungs closed. I gasped for air between a silent snuffle, praying to a God I had lost faith in two years ago. It was the year I realized that the only logical explanation for my tragic life rested on a cosmic joke some sadistic deity was playing on me—and my daily death was the punch line.

"Where are you?" The sing-songy voice broke through my loathsome reflections, taunting me to come out from hiding.

My breath caught and I wiped my damp eyes against my arm.

"Where are you?" he repeated, his words just on the other side of the closet door.

This was a game to him, but to me it was survival.

If I remained motionless, would he walk away? Or would he investigate every square inch of this room until he unearthed me? It was a gamble, either way a losing hand for me. Because regardless of his choice, eventually I'd have to come out. Eventually he'd find me. They all would. There was no escaping that reality. I could no longer save myself or salvage the thread of sanity that had long ago snapped.

I was no hero.

I was simply the mother of four children—including an autistic son.

Just as silence drowned out the noise of the girls fighting in the living room, I exhaled relief. Maybe Austin had moved on to another room. Maybe I could sit in glorious solitude just a few more minutes, among the quiet shadows. The day had been hell enough already, and I still had dinner and bedtime to trudge through. I needed a moment to myself before I broke. But as the shadows moved and the slices of light played between the closet door slats, it was time to pull myself together.

The light splayed across my face as the door folded open, revealing Austin's smiling face looking down at me. Had he been a normal kid, I would have probably smiled back, but nothing with Austin went as you'd expect.

"Found you!" he yelled before slapping me across the head. His fingernail caught my eyelid, slicing it just enough to startle me backward while I winced in pain.

"Ow!" I reacted, my hand rushing to my eye. And that's when I made my first mistake.

Austin, noting my upset response, began wildly hitting himself in the head, screaming *ow! ow! ow!* with each self-inflicted punishment. Jumping up, I reached for his flailing fists, soothingly reminding him I was okay, it was okay, everything was okay. But he couldn't hear my calming words over his screams, which degraded into an inarticulate screech. His little fists avoided mine, until finally I wrapped him in a fitful hug, careful to avoid his buffeting head, rocking him against the length of my body for nearly ten minutes until his flailing limbs calmed.

Every day I searched for improvements, hoping he'd outgrow whatever held him hostage to a two-year-old's mind in a five-year-old's body. But what he improved on one day he would revert back from two days later and lose something additional in the process. While Austin revolved around a cycle of baby steps forward and leaps backward, I revolved around a cycle of dizzying despair and hardening complacency.

I had discovered a whole new definition of "tough love"—and it had everything to do with finding it tougher to love my family.

When Arabelle was home on break from school it was the hardest, as the next three weeks would inevitably prove. We had the disadvantage of living in a rare year-round school district, an unavoidable added stress. For every other family that might mean more family outings, a mini-vacation, or maybe just extra-long days of boredom. Not our family, though.

Hauling four kids ages one through six was simply too much for me to handle when they ran in different directions. And with Austin's autism, he never responded to his name, making him easy to lose track of.

Only two weeks ago we were at the Museum of Life and Science when he slipped behind a bush during a momentary glance away. While wrestling with my three daughters to keep them by my side, I called out to him, my panic growing as the minutes passed with no sign of him. After begging a stranger to watch the girls while I got help from security, it took us nearly an hour before we found Austin—a mere five feet from where I had first lost sight of him.

While he wordlessly played with a bug he'd discovered, I nearly had a heart attack from my hysteria.

This wasn't the first time it'd happened, and with pained realization, I knew it wouldn't be the last.

Life with Austin was a perpetual state of terror.

Add Arabelle's insistent whining and Kiki and Juliet's irregular nap schedules to that and it spoiled the whole idea of attempting outings. Better to just stay home and die a little bit more inside.

As for vacations—ha! Vacations were for people with extra money. If we could count the couple dollars we cleared after the bills were paid each month, then sure, we had extra money. Our family's first and last vacation was my honeymoon seven years ago—the same week I conceived Arabelle. That week also marked the genesis of my slow death into self-sacrifice and poverty.

All of us being home together turned grueling days into living nightmares. It was a war of wits and endurance. It was a battle for the alpha spot … and I always seemed to lose.

One would have thought Arabelle might show signs of a burgeoning maternal instinct, like other six-year-old girls. But no, Arabelle was a disruptor. She stole toys from her siblings, pulled hair when she was angry, wrestled too roughly with the baby. The family dynamic changed with Arabelle around—from manageably busy to dangerously chaotic. She was the thorn in her siblings' side, and at this rate I wondered if any of us would survive.

It was as if she intentionally antagonized her siblings. A toy light-up piano she hadn't used in years suddenly became indispensable the moment Juliet picked it up. A toddler book years below her reading level, she *was just about to read* as soon as Kiki expressed interest in it.

As I swayed back and forth in a lulling meter with Austin clutched against my chest, fighting my tears from surfacing, my sights rested on the shoebox tucked on the top shelf of my closet … the shoebox that held my gun. I'd bought it two years ago when I found out I was pregnant with Juliet—my fourth child. While I couldn't stand the thought of abortion, somehow suicide seemed a more noble alternative.

Although the plan had been fleeting back then, lately the idea taunted me almost daily. The touch of the barrel against my temple. The cool metal leaving a circular imprint on my freckled skin. The echoing crescendo after my finger squeezed the trigger. My skull welcoming the leaden missile as it splintered bone and ripped brain matter to shreds. Then tranquility.

Not everyone fantasized about shooting themselves in the head. But not everyone harbored secrets like mine.

It'd take every ounce of willpower in my body not to use that gun today.

# Chapter 6

He had always wanted a child of his own. Cherub face, chubby fingers gripping his, squeals of laughter. Everything about children brought a smile to his face, this little girl in particular. Because she was special. She belonged to Josephine. It would be different this time.

"When do I get to see the puppies?"

"What color are they?"

"Can I hold them?"

"Are they fluffy?"

The girl had asked an endless barrage of puppy-related questions in the car, many repeated countless times. The repetition didn't bother him, though. In fact, her persistence delighted him. A good trait in a girl. Determined to get what she wanted, just like her mother.

"We're here," he said with a lilt to his voice as they pulled up to the ramshackle apartment building, the unadorned four-sided brick façade garnished with a variety of archaic window AC units, their only common trait being their degree of decomposition. The remaining unoccupied windows donned security bars and a spattering of corrugated cardboard panels covering broken glass. Piles of refuse scattered the pavement about the building's dumpster, as if the extra distance of placing the waste inside the receptacle was just too much effort for its denizens. It was the cheapest and most obscure temporary housing he could find on such short notice. And they accepted cash. It was the type of place you would never notice unless you were intentionally looking for it. Perfect for what he had planned.

Guiding the girl up the metal stairwell and along the blue carpeted hallway to his apartment's painted front door, he felt a sense of elation being this close to achieving his objective. Everything to this point had transpired exactly according to plan, not one hitch. Attempting to take a child this age presented an array of challenges in and of itself, compounded the variables with conducting the abduction in such a public place, and the likelihood of success seemed nonexistent. One raised voice, one glance his way at the wrong moment by Josephine, one bystander who randomly happened to know this child, and it all would have fallen apart. The Fates were on his side it seemed, almost as if they wanted him to have this child.

Though a part of him wished Josephine would have seen him, seen him taking *her* daughter. He wished he could have stayed to see her reaction when she discovered her baby was gone. But that's how you get caught. No. Must be smart. Must be calculating. He had plans for this girl.

"Are the puppies inside?" she asked, clapping her tiny hands and looking up at him with big blue eyes. Patting her head, he couldn't pull his stare away. She was the picture of perfection with a smattering of freckles across her nose.

"They sure are. We'll go in and feed them. They're probably hungry. How about you—are you hungry?"

"Yeah."

"Do you like ice cream?"

"I love ice cream but Mommy says I have to eat dinner first."

Such honesty. He loved this girl more by the minute.

"Well, at my home you don't have to eat dinner first to get ice cream. Dinner *is* ice cream."

"Can I have rainbow sprinkles too?"

"Sorry, but I don't have those."

"Chocolate syrup?"

"No, not that either."

"How can you eat ice cream without them?" She watched him carefully, like he was about to explain the wonders of the universe, like where a rainbow came from or how the man in the moon got groceries.

"Uh, I just do."

"I don't want it without sprinkles or syrup," she whined loudly. So loudly that her voice echoed down the hall where he certainly didn't want to draw attention.

"Shhh ... please!" he begged. "I'll figure something else out."

And yet the tearless crying continued.

He didn't have sprinkles. Or chocolate syrup. Clearly these were expected commodities amongst children, something he had no clue about. What had he been thinking, that this would be easy? His confidence deflated just enough to make him doubt himself. Perhaps he wasn't as prepared as he thought. From down the hall a woman ambled toward his apartment door, and he felt her eyes watching him. Eyeing the crying little girl next to him. He had come too far for things to fall apart now.

He wondered if the girl's face was streaming all over the news by now, if Amber Alerts were notifying the public of her disappearance yet. If anyone had noticed him at the park, seen his car, given his description to the police. He needed to get inside quickly before anyone else noticed him. Sweat beaded on his forehead as he fumbled with the keys in the door lock. At last the key slid in and he turned the doorknob. Then an idea.

"How about chocolate chips instead?"

Instantly the whining stopped and her tiny-toothed smile brightened. "Can I scoop my own? Mommy never lets me."

"Of course you can, since Mommy isn't here to say no."

Flinging the door open, they stepped inside, quickly closing it behind them. The living room was dark as they entered the sparsely furnished room, consisting of a sofa and television rented under his mother's maiden name. There was no point investing in anything more than the bare necessities, since this was a short-term deal. No one knew he was here, particularly his parole officer. All he needed was a little time to finish what he came for.

He flicked on the overhead light and locked the door behind him, a deadbolt out of the girl's reach. A yellow glow illuminated the room, hidden from daylight by thick brown curtains.

"Where are the puppies?" the girl asked, peeking around the corner into the kitchen.

He hated the excitement in her voice, because he didn't want to crush it. But he had to. It was inevitable. It was part of the plan. He had to stick to the plan, no matter how hard it got. There was just too much at stake.

"I'm sorry to tell you that there are no puppies. But I have something much better in store for you."

As her eyes watered and bottom lip trembled, a tear slid down her cheek. Then he thought sadly of the many more tears that were to come.

That's when he felt it—the battle between his past and present rise within him. He feared if he looked back at the pain behind him it would swallow him whole. But the images wouldn't relent.

Blood. So much blood. Gobs of blood. Her cries as she had cowered in the corner while his fists pummeled her like he was tenderizing a piece of meat. Her skin turning a deep red, then blue, as he continued beating her, kicking her, ignoring the whimpered begging for him to stop. But he wouldn't. Couldn't. The Red had taken him, seduced him, devoured him.

Once his legs tired, he had unbuckled his belt. Dragging it slowly out through the belt loops of his jeans, the leather tip making a faint *fwip* as it escaped each successive denim eyelet.

"No, please, no more!" she had pleaded. But the words were distant and tinny in his memory. It was the fear in her eyes that he now remembered most. It was the fear that aroused him. Gave him strength. Egged him on.

Wrapping the buckle end of the belt around his palm, he had whipped her again and again until her flesh turned raw, splitting her skin, relinquishing the crimson manna he so desired. His thirst for justice urged him on. Show her who was boss. Teach her a lesson.

He was Rage manifested, Fury personified, his perception perverted until all he saw was The Red, not the woman. Not the hole-in-the-wall apartment they called home. Not the threadbare sofa or mismatched chairs. Not the cockroaches clamoring for safety in the walls. Not the flies circling days-old cereal left on the kitchenette table or the overflowing dustbin. He wanted to kill her, needed to, and he couldn't remember why.

She had talked back, hadn't she? They had a fight about money. Again. It was always about money. He had blown her waitressing paycheck at the bar. But it was his money to do with as he pleased, wasn't it? He was the man. He was in charge. Yes, that's what he had told her. And that's when she'd fought back. That's when she made her mistake.

But look who won in the end.

He did. He always did. He always would. He had Always Right on his side.

Something they would all need to learn, starting with this little, inquisitive girl who was the ticket to his future.

# Chapter 7 - Jo

The evening was a tornado of frantic phone calls, confused children, and police inquiries. Sitting on the cream living room sofa, Abby and Preston were sandwiched between Jay and me, while Detective Tristan Cox and his shadow, Officer Dante Buchanan, drilled us for every possible detail we could remember about the afternoon.

What was Amelia wearing? Exactly what time did I notice she was gone? What are the names and addresses of the other parents at the soccer game? All details I knew, but my brain was too muddled to remember. I felt cloudy and disoriented and sick to my stomach.

When the police first arrived, I should have felt comforted that something was being done to find my baby. Instead my fears escalated. Suddenly it was all too real. Wearing an untucked gray button-up shirt, snug black jeans, and Hollywood-trendy hair, one look at Detective Cox and I felt like Justin Bieber was on the case. Clearly younger than me by a decade, what experience could this boy-man possibly have that qualified him to make *detective*? The mother in me wanted to grab him by his unkempt goatee and order him to go home and shave before coming back. He certainly didn't look the part of a professional, in my opinion. But as the detective spoke of Amber Alerts, social media outreach, and canvassing the neighborhoods surrounding the park, my mind slowly changed about him. I'd need to have a little faith if I was going to bring Amelia home.

"Our kidnapper is likely a Durham local," Detective Cox explained, "which means if he goes out publicly with her, someone might spot her. By blasting Amelia's picture all over the Raleigh area, there's a good chance we'll find her."

But what about the chance of not finding her? That was the reality that tormented me.

"Is there anyone you know—maybe someone from your past— who would want to abduct your child? Or a family member who you don't quite trust?" Detective Cox looked at me and I recoiled.

"What? You think a family member took her?" It sounded ludicrous.

"In many cases it's someone related or closely connected to the family. Someone with a grudge?"

"No, no one in our family would do that." I was so certain of this … except for the pinch of guilt that made me wonder if there was indeed someone out to get me. Someone with a motive. Someone I had buried deep in my past, pushing the skeletons into the depths of my closet. But that secret was safe and locked away … wasn't it?

I had taken care of the secret long ago. There couldn't be any connection. At least I sure hoped not. It was a secret that needed to stay hidden. My life depended on that.

"What else should we be doing?" It was the first time my husband Jay had spoken up or shown any concern at all. While his brooding brown eyes and Kurt Cobain hair had won me over at first sight eleven years ago, his quiet nature left much to be desired over the years. I never knew what he was thinking; I wanted inside his head, but he was a locked door that I didn't have the key to.

"Use social media to spread awareness of what happened. Talk to your neighbors. Ask any park regulars if they saw anything. We'll be doing all those things too, but it never hurts to have more people looking."

"Will you be able to have a cop car watch our street in case the abductor comes here?" I asked, glancing back at Preston and Abby.

The detective shook his head. "I'm sorry, but we don't have those kind of resources. We've got a limited number of officers on duty and it's unlikely the abductor would come to your house anyways. He's most likely hiding out somewhere, or possibly traveling with her. But we'll have state troopers on the lookout for a man traveling with a blond three-year-old girl. You'd be surprised how many hits we can get, even with limited information."

Next to Detective Cox, Officer Buchanan looked like a giant. Officer Buchanan's thighs, thick like two tree trunks, hung off the cushion of the catty-corner love seat. He leaned in with interest, a pencil and small notepad in hand. Watching my daughter with eyes as dark as pools of tar, he would have intimidated anyone else with his Army-issue flattop haircut and muscles straining the seams of his uniform. But with Abby he played the part of a gentle giant, his lipless smile genuine and warm.

"Hi, Abby." His skin shined, tight and rubbery, like a car tire. "Detective Cox is going to ask you some questions so we can find your sister. Do you feel like you can talk to him?"

"I think so," she said meekly. I could tell she was scared, overwhelmed, so I rested my hand on her shoulder in a show of support.

"You can do it," I whispered in her ear, then planted a kiss on her cheek.

Detective Cox crouched down at her eye level. "Abby, honey, I'm going to bring your sister home. But I need your help." His eyes searched hers and she nodded shyly. "I want to try something with you. Close your eyes." His voice was rough like gravel, but soothing, as if he'd had plenty of experience drawing shy kids like Abby out of their shells.

Abby did as she was told, squeezing her azure eyes shut.

"Try to remember being at the park. Remember when the man approached you. Can you see him?"

Another nod.

"Okay, good. Now describe for me everything you can remember about him. His hair color, how tall he was, what he was wearing. Can you do that for me, Abby?"

"Yes," Abby squeaked. "Um, he was about as tall as Daddy and had brown hair like Daddy. And he wore glasses."

"Very good," Detective Cox encouraged when she paused. "This helps a lot. How old do you think he was?"

"Maybe my daddy's age."

"Great work so far. What about his clothes?"

"I think he was wearing a green shirt with buttons up the front. And jeans."

She stopped again.

"Did he have any hair on his face, like a mustache?"

"Nooo …" she wavered, as if uncertain.

"You mentioned that he had puppies. Did you see the puppies?"

"No, they were in his car. I went to ask Mommy if I could go see them, but he was gone when we got back."

"Did he have any scars or tattoos?"

"I don't think so. I'm sorry, I can't remember."

"Don't be sorry, Abby. You did great. We're going to find your sister, okay?" He patted her knee and stood, adjusting the badge that hung on his belt beneath the hem of his shirt.

"Mm-kay." Abby's eyes popped open and she looked up at me for approval.

"Thanks, sweetie," I said, kissing her head. "You and Preston can go play for a bit."

"What about dinner? I'm hungry," she whined.

Food—it had completely skipped my mind. No way I could stomach food when my nerves were roiling and nauseating me.

"I'll make some mac 'n' cheese in a minute."

Abby squealed with delight and ran off, trailing her brother upstairs. Irritation at her lack of concern for her sister suddenly bubbled up inside me. How could she be thinking about dinner with her sister missing?

A cocktail of emotions swirled inside me. Guilt. Anger. Fear. I needed to blame someone—someone other than myself. I couldn't be the mother who had lost her child. I simply couldn't.

It had to be Abby's fault Amelia was missing. She hadn't kept her eye on her. She'd left her alone with a strange man who was doing God knows what to my daughter …

Was he raping her as she cried out in pain? Was she chained in some dank basement calling for her mommy? Was she nothing more than a pile of decomposing body parts by now? Every outcome I'd ever read about in the news or watched on a crime show burst on a screen in my head, terrifying me more than if it was happening to my own flesh.

A sob escaped my throat as I shook away the barrage of imagined horrors that my little Amelia was enduring … that is, if she wasn't already dead. All because of Abby, who blissfully tromped around with her brother as if we hadn't just lost a limb from our family body.

Fury began to course through me. Fury at Abby for leaving her sister's side, fury at Preston for having that soccer game in the first place, fury at the man who stole my baby girl, fury at Jay for working so much that he hadn't been there, fury at the cops for not finding her already … fury at myself for being the mom who lost her child.

The truth slapped me back to the present reality: it was all my fault. I had given too much responsibility to a five-year-old. It wasn't Abby who should have been watching her little sister; it should have been me. I should have protected Amelia. This was all on me. I'd never outrun this horrifying truth.

I sniffled and gasped for a shallow breath that wasn't there. My lungs squeezed shut and I bent over as a sob escaped. In a matter of seconds I went from a composed woman asking relevant questions to a panicky mess who couldn't speak through the crying.

My baby girl … gone because of my failure as a mom.

"It's okay, Mrs. Trubeau. We're going to do everything we can to find Amelia." Detective Cox rested his hand on my shoulder. The touch was a small comfort. But it was from a stranger, not from my husband, who I so desperately needed.

I looked into the detective's eyes, beseeching him with a silent plea for a guarantee that Amelia was safe. That she'd be back in my arms soon. My gaze flittered over to Jay, who sat stoic and cross-armed. And that's when I noticed it. It was subtle. Undetectable to anyone who hadn't lived with Jay Trubeau for ten perfect years. But it was a glaring beacon to me, the woman who cherished him, knew him, read between his lines for over a decade.

He blamed me, too.

I felt it in the way he avoided my gaze. I saw it in the cold inches of space that separated us. I sensed it in the tense muscles of his jaw that remained clenched as I wept.

I could carry the burden of self-blame. It was heavy but manageable. But Jay's blame too? No, no, that would crush me. If Jay couldn't forgive me, how could I ever forgive myself for letting this happen to our family? For ripping apart our perfect life? In one neglectful moment I had broken the only thing that mattered to me. And unless I found Amelia and saved her from a deadly fate, I could never repair our lives.

As I walked Detective Cox and Officer Buchanan to the front door where a news van waited to prey on my misery, I caught a glimpse of the growing crowd of neighbors on the sidewalk, like ants feasting on a crumb. While my life fell apart, they enjoyed some fresh drama unfolding on Oleander Way. I'd be their gossip for the next few days, until someone had an affair or got an unflattering haircut.

"You don't have to do this if you're not ready." Detective Cox gestured to the microphones and video cameras lining my driveway. "But the more we get Amelia's information out there, the more likely we'll be to find her."

"Yeah, I'm ready."

I turned to Jay, who stood behind me so close I could feel the heat of his chest on my back. We needed each other now more than ever. I grabbed his hand, weaving my fingers through his, and pulled him toward me.

But then he did something he'd never done before. Unclasping my hand, he recoiled from me. "Jay—" I pleaded.

"Jo, I can't. I can't touch you right now." Taking a step back, he created a schism that I couldn't cross, no matter how much I apologized or begged.

Jay blamed me. I blamed me. And I knew in that instant that if we didn't bring Amelia home, we could never recover, I would never be forgiven. Amelia was the only lifeline we had, our only guarantee of survival. If she ended up dead … we would die with her.

"Go ahead, Jo." Detective Cox turned to me as a reporter stepped up, pushing her microphone in my face. Her hair was smooth and shiny like a wig, her makeup heavy but flawless. She would have fit in perfectly on Oleander Way.

With sobs breaking up my speech, alone, abandoned by my husband, I begged anyone who was watching the news that night to help me find my little girl.

# Chapter 8 - Ellie

S unlight slipped through the wavy sliver between the drapes, caressing the kitchen countertops, then slithering down across the floor where it rested in fractured beams.

*I'm failing at everything I do,*

I wrote, sitting at the kitchen table sipping hazelnut coffee with more cream than coffee.

*My kids are becoming spoiled brats, I'm running myself ragged, nothing I do is ever enough. I'm constantly paranoid and angry … Who am I? I don't want to be this person. But I don't know how to find my way back to who I was—the happier me, the fulfilled me. Was she ever real? Or was that all just a façade? Is this the real me? It can't be. I won't let it. I started leaving notes for Denny around the house, little I love you's and XOXO's. Maybe I can win him back. Can I win him back? I need to try something. Anything. He hasn't mentioned them, which breaks my heart.*

*Yesterday I bought junk food for the kids—God help me, it took every ounce of strength not to toss it out of the grocery cart before I checked out. But I want them to be happy, to love me. If their own mother's love isn't enough, maybe teeth-rotting sugar will do the trick. I feel like I have to bribe my own family to like me. Maybe it's a stage. Maybe I just need to toughen up. Or maybe they need to learn a lesson.*

My hand paused as I heard the scurry of feet pounding down the stairwell. My time was up.

Early morning—the only time of day I truly had to myself, a bite-sized morsel of time for *me*. These were my precious pre-dawn minutes of quiet leading up to the rush to fix Darla's breakfast, pack her lunch, check her book bag, run her to the bus stop, and make it back to my half-drained cup of coffee before it got lukewarm. Of course, by then Logan would shuffle out of his bedroom, his golden bedhead hair sprouting in every direction as he snaked along the floor in his Superman pajamas, dragging lines into the carpet with his heavy steps.

After biting another student for the second time two weeks ago, my nine-year-old son was sent home and threatened with expulsion. It would have been the first expulsion at any elementary school in the district—way to go, son. To save everyone embarrassment, I offered to keep Logan home while I figured out another schooling option. So not only had I become wife, cook, and maid, but now I adopted the role of homeschooling teacher to a boy who could care less about "stupid" things like reading, writing, or arithmetic.

Once Logan was awake, the demands began ... and never ended until bedtime fourteen hours later. "Mom, I want juice. Mom, make me eggs for breakfast. Mom, these eggs taste nasty. I want French toast instead. Mom, clean my favorite shirt. Mom, Mom, Mom ..." And on it went, day after day, hour after hour, an endless cycle of "make me this" and "do that," with the occasional break for an "I don't like this anymore."

Despite the mundanity of parenthood, for eleven years I had dealt with it. Despite counting down the hours before I'd tuck both kids into bed, exhaling relief after that last kiss goodnight, I nonetheless accepted my lot in life. I had a successful husband, two beautiful children, a gorgeous home, the latest gadgets, the fanciest cars, summer vacations, and trendy clothes—what wasn't to love about living on Oleander Way, the epitome of upper-crust society? It had never been my dream life, but over time I slid into its mold. I powerwalked with fitness moms I didn't like, attended

PTA meetings that bored me, mastered nut-free, gluten-free, dairy-free brownies for the school bake sale, hosted baby showers for women whose last names I didn't know, and complimented garish décor while sipping bitter coffee with neighbors who would gossip about me the moment I walked out of their front door. It was the circle of upper-class life, and I had acclimated quite fluidly, if I did say so myself.

But as Denny slumbered blissfully in our bed, curled up in our sheets, probably dreaming of *her,* I realized I wasn't okay with *this.* This boring, mindless routine I lived out. Kids, cooking, cleaning, homework, start over. I had given up a career to make Denny's dreams come true—his *Leave It to Beaver* family and June Cleaver wife. It was a wonder he didn't require me to wear sensible dresses and pearls around the house all day. Meanwhile, he went off and lived his own fantasy with another woman while I ignorantly toiled away, washing his clothes that stank of *her* scent, preparing him dinners that satisfy him after a secret rendezvous with *her* in some crappy motel. I sacrificed and became exactly what he wanted, only for him not to want me anymore.

Flinging open the fridge, I grabbed the strawberry jelly and slammed the door shut. In a haze, I envisioned him kissing her, running his fingers along her skin, whispering "I love you"s in her ear as he nibbled playfully on her earlobe, biting her neck. All moves he used to woo me with many moons ago. Moves I hadn't seen in ages. Banging the jelly down on the counter, my anger began to boil as a tidal wave of scenarios crashed into me.

"Mom, you're gonna break the jelly jar," a tiny voice chirped from behind me.

I turned around, embarrassed at being caught in a tantrum by my nine-year-old.

"I'm just a little frustrated, honey. But I'm fine." I forced a grin and rested a hand on Logan's head, smoothing out his frizzy hair. He shook my hand off and glared at me. "How about we head to the playground after I finish cleaning up? And don't forget to dress warmly—the air's a little cool this morning."

"I don't wanna. I want to play video games."

And already it began—the negotiations.

"It's either math or the park—you pick."

"Fine," he grumbled. "The park."

"Good choice."

Forty-five minutes and two cups of coffee later, Denny headed out the door without so much as a kiss goodbye, while I threw on my everyday yoga pants and oversized sweatshirt before leaving the house with Logan whining the entire way to the car. Maybe some fresh air would clear the web of thoughts that seemed to tangle in my brain. And at least at the park Logan could occupy himself and leave me alone with my worries—the only place I wanted to be right now until I sorted things out.

Forest Hills Park was busy as usual, with a cluster of minivans in the parking lot and scattered strollers packed with snack cups and diaper bags, while moms sat along the outskirts of the playground at the ready to respond to a child's call for help.

As I released Logan into the wild world of public playtime, I found an empty bench just far enough away to soften the playground noise and prevent other mothers from approaching me. I wasn't in the mood for chickish chitchat. I was in the mood for finding out what Denny was up to, for plotting revenge against my cheating husband.

The benches scattered around the park were filling up fast, and as the last open seat was taken, I watched a bedraggled woman in a flowy navy skirt and ugly brown sweater being pulled toward me by her rowdy crew like a hapless dog walker. It was June Merrigan, my best friend since college, the only real friend I had. God help her. I could barely handle my two kids, let alone raise four without losing my sanity along the way. I didn't know how she did it.

"June Bug, I thought you didn't do mornings," I greeted her as I stood and pulled her into a hug.

"I don't. But today I made an exception. I practically had a meltdown at home, so I figured at least here I could put some distance between me and the kids before I did something I'd regret. Plus, too many witnesses."

Once the children scattered, we both sat down on the bench, our thighs touching. June was a hugger, a toucher, a close talker. While other people thought her odd, I found it part of her charm. I guess true friends were blind to each other's quirks. Or in June's case, they made her even more lovable. She wasn't plastic, fake smiles, or oozing perfection. She was vulnerability and hugs when I needed one. She was *me*.

"A meltdown, huh? What's going on? Is it Austin?"

June flashed a grin at me, but I recognized the exhaustion behind her eyes. "That and everything else in my life. They're home on a school break right now, so I'm stuck with all four monsters constantly fighting and crying and screaming. I can't take it anymore. If I hear one more argument about which show to watch ... Guess what? They're all annoying! I swear ..."

Wrapping my arm around her shoulders, I nodded my sympathy, though sometimes June made things harder on herself than they had to be. My mother always told me to pick my battles with the kids. Let some things go. But not June. She was the type who picked every battle—and in the end, she'd always lose the war.

"You're stronger than you think," I reminded her. "You just need to tune it out." Empty advice, I know, but what else could I say?

"It's hard to tune it out when they just keep coming at me. It's always one thing or another. I just want a vacation from my life." She rested her head on my shoulder like a child, and I kissed her hair.

"You know I'll watch them for you anytime so you can get away. I'm practically family, June."

"No, not *practically*. You *are* my family." She sat upright and looked at me. "How are things with you, by the way?"

I considered telling her about my episode in the laundry room that morning—the lipstick stain I'd found, my suspicions.

We told each other everything, after all. But something kept my words in check. With all that June was going through, maybe it wasn't the right time to whine about my own problems, real or imaginary, since at this point I knew absolutely nothing. Why make something of a scenario that could be a misunderstanding on my part? I felt like voicing it would give it life, and that was the last thing I wanted to do. Better to bury it for now.

"Everything's really good," I lied. "Same old, same old."

June sighed. "I wish I had your life. You've always got it together."

I laughed. "No, it's just an illusion. We all have our struggles, June. It boils down to how we cope."

Which led me to wonder, how did I cope? While June poured out her heart and leaned on me for strength, I threw on a mask and hid behind a fake smile. I wondered which was the healthier method. Something told me my methods wouldn't end well.

Our conversation ended when June's kids rumbled toward us like a tornado, each one talking over the next. Austin's eyes were fixated on his hands as he flapped them in the air like he was splashing in the tub.

Once June had passed out packaged cheese crackers and juice boxes, then shooed away the other three kids, she pulled Austin up on the bench between us and sat him down. Still he remained transfixed on his fingers as he flapped them in short bursts in the air. I'd seen him do this many times before, a self-stimulating tactic when he felt overwhelmed or exhausted.

"Austin, do you want to go play with the other kids?" June asked him, leaning down to meet him face to face. But instead of answering, he watched his hands, clearly fascinated and oblivious to his mother's prodding. "Austin, honey, stop playing with your hands. Look at me." But he didn't. "Do you want to go play on the playground?"

His hands held his attention firmly.

June sighed heavily. "He's in his own world today. I wish he would interact with the other kids for more than a few minutes. I can't get a second away from him."

Although lacking real-life work experience, I'd learned more about autism during my doctorate studies than I ever expected to need. Autism and speech therapy went hand in hand, which gave me a leg up when dealing with Austin. Back then I didn't know just how close to home my desired profession would hit—right here in the life of my own best friend.

"Can I try something with him?"

June shrugged helplessness, then waved me on.

"Of course. You're the only one he listens to, anyways."

Sliding off the bench, I dropped to my knees and looked at Austin. "Hi, Austin. Auntie Ellie wants to play. Will you play with me?"

Normally I never would have talked to a five-year-old with such infantile phrasing, but that's where Austin's intellectual development was stalled. I pitied June for having a perpetual two-year-old for the past three years. Once was enough with mine. I couldn't imagine dealing with it every day.

When he didn't glance up, but watched his fingers flitter about, I gently touched his hand, drawing his focus to my touch. The simple contact pulled his gaze up at me and he smiled. "Hi, Austin. How are you?" I tapped my lips with each word, accentuating the speech to hold his attention. Each word was slow and articulated in my best nurturing voice.

"How are you?" he parroted me.

"Austin, say 'I am good.'" This time I tapped his chin as I told him what to say.

Imitating me, he repeated, "I am good."

Thrilled with his response, I applauded him. "Let's try again. Austin, how are you?"

"How are you?" he mimicked again.

Then, mouthing the scripted reply for him, we said "I am good" in unison.

Again I clapped, and his smile widened with pride.

"Would you like to play?" I pointed to the playground.

"Play," he stated, before scooting from the bench and running off to join the other kids.

"You make it look so easy. You need to teach me how to do that, El," June said as I pushed up off the ground and returned to my seat.

I'd worked with Austin many times before, little doses of therapy here and there, but June never seemed to put it into practice at home. It irked me that she couldn't make the time, but I didn't walk in her shoes, so I couldn't judge. She had twice as many kids and half the free time I had, being a working mom, and more pride than an Arabian horse, never taking me up on my offers to babysit or treat her to a spa day. So I was left to impart my wisdom, hoping one day she'd piece it all together and learn how to help her son—and help herself a little too.

"It's not hard. Touch is vitally important for some kids with autism, like Austin. A simple touch can redirect his focus. And sometimes a gesture—like tapping your chin when you want him to talk—helps him understand what you're asking. He doesn't always understand language as it's presented to him. It's just words, and putting the words together to create meaning can be hard for him. So when you practice and repeat the same questions and answers, he'll eventually start making those brain connections on giving words more meaning."

But no matter how much I explained these "tricks of the trade" to June, I knew the reality of parenting an autistic child was much harder than a simple fix and tricks. Daily tantrums, violent overreactions to discipline, emotional detachment … that was just the beginning of Austin's labyrinthine mind and behavior. Sure, I had my hands full with a demanding and recalcitrant boy's boy like Logan, but June wandered aimlessly through this maze of what-to-do and what-not-to-do, tiptoeing carefully lest a landmine explode.

"Thanks. I'll try to remember to practice that at home … you know, when I'm not going crazy with the constant chaos." She laughed lightly, the laughter of guilt.

"One day at a time, that's all we can do, right?"

June looked at me wearily. "One day is all it takes to snap, though."

How true it was. I wasn't doing so well with it, either. A lot could happen in one day. A stress overload. A killer migraine. A harsh word that tears you apart. A death of a loved one. A life-destroying lie. An irresistible temptation. A sinking pit of depression you can't climb out of. Any of those things could make a person snap. My own anxieties flittered through my head as I thought about Denny—what he was doing right now, *who* he was doing right now.

And I realized I couldn't give him one more day to break me more than I already was.

# Chapter 9 - June

Life's cruelty had no end. Its penchant for doling out anguish matchless.

As I arrived home from the park, a slight tug of joy followed me inside. After promising not to wait so long before another get-together—an assurance I didn't have much faith in due to busy work schedules and overbooked kid activities—Ellie had suggested coffee and a play date later this week to work more with Austin. After all these years I hadn't truly seen just how good Ellie was with Austin; perhaps I hadn't been paying attention. Sure, I noticed that he connected better with her than anyone else, but it was more than that. She had a calming influence on him that I had long ago lost. Maybe my patience had worn too thin, or maybe my maternal instincts were failing me. Whatever it was, I vowed to learn how to help my son.

For the first time in weeks I felt a splinter of hope at a chance of normalcy for him—and for myself. In just a few minutes of talking with him, Ellie was able to get more out of him than I could in months. It was amazing—a little miracle that could reshape my son's entire future. *Our* future. And I owed that miracle to my best friend.

A baby step of growth now meant a leap of independence later. Maybe Austin could be "normal" after all—whatever "normal" was these days.

But the euphoric bounce in my step came to a halt when I walked in the house to find Mike—who was supposed to be at work—sprawled out on the living room sofa watching television. His lithe body stretched from one armrest to the other, his feet propped up as he ran out of cushion. His blue eyes darted a glance at me, then returned to the screen.

Avoidance.

Something bad had happened.

"Mike, what are you doing home?" I was afraid to ask. I didn't want the answer that I knew was coming.

"I don't wanna talk about it," he replied bluntly to the television. His unshaved jaw clenched, his blond whiskers catching the sunlight.

As if I would ever accept that answer. Mike always liked to deal with things in his own time, he had once explained to me. Only, his "own time" was never. Run away, hide from problems, avoid. That was his tactic; that was his arsenal to handle problems when they came. Clearly it wasn't effective. I wouldn't accept it today.

"I don't care if you don't want to talk about it. I need to know. What happened?"

I already knew. We'd been down this road too many times. I was in familiar territory, and they were frightening wastelands.

"I got fired today. Happy?" His voice was edgy, and he rolled his eyes as if annoyed, but I knew it was embarrassment buried beneath the grit. No man looked forward to coming home to tell his family he was out of work … again.

"Of course I'm not happy, Mike. Why? What did you do this time?"

"Why you gotta assume I did something wrong?" I cringed as the words bounced off the walls.

"Because you got fired. People don't get fired for doing everything right."

"No, June, I didn't do anything wrong."

As if that was enough explanation.

"Then why?" I needed to know. I was tired of being lied to, of being treated like I didn't deserve the truth. "Tell me why, dammit, or I'll call your boss and ask myself!"

Mike didn't even flinch. Barely looking up from the television, he muttered, "I've been late getting back from lunch a few times. Apparently that's a big deal to them so they fired me."

This couldn't be happening. A layoff, I understood. Cutbacks happened. But getting fired because he couldn't get his butt back to work on time after his lunch break? No, this couldn't be the man I was stuck with for the rest of my life. A man who couldn't even keep a job to save his family.

"Mike, you have to go back and beg for your job back. We need it. We'll lose the house, everything. Go back and talk to your boss. Please."

Only now did Mike bother to sit up and turn to face me. "There is no way in hell I'm begging for my job back. I have more pride than that."

"Put your pride aside for once in your life. Don't you understand? We need your income. Mike, I'm pleading here. You need to get your job back."

He shook his head. "It's too late. I've already had too many strikes against me. They made it clear I was done. It's fine. I'll find something else."

As if it was settled, he resumed watching his show, turning up the volume to drown out any argument I might have left in me. I wasn't done, not by a long shot, so I talked louder.

"Mike, sitting here doing nothing isn't going to find you another job. We have bills already overdue. You have to get back out there, start looking for something else. As in today."

"Can't you pick up more hours at work?" Of course that was his solution—for me to add more to my already-full day.

"Temporarily I can, but if I'm going to work more, you've got to deal with the kids—starting now. I can pick up an extra shift today, but I have to get ready. So they'll need lunch and Austin has to work on some speech exercises."

I stood there, my hands on my hips, watching Mike sit unfazed. I shifted between him and the television.

"Mike?"

"What?" Wide-eyed, he looked up at me as if surprised I was still in the room.

"Did you hear me? I can take an extra shift, but you have to get the kids lunch and work with Austin on his speech."

"Right now?"

Really? Was the exasperation in my voice not apparent enough to register with him? "Yes, now!"

"Fine, fine. Don't get all pissy. You're being a nag."

A nag? Had he really just called me that? I wanted to remind him that he had just come home jobless, that he was watching television while I ran after the kids, that I was picking up another shift at work so that he could "figure things out," that the burden seemed to always fall on me to pick up the pieces of our broken lives.

But I didn't say anything. I didn't want to be more of a *nag*, according to him. Instead I stormed into the bedroom to change into my waitressing uniform, praying that the tips would be good enough to make up for Mike's bad news. But God help the drunk men who pawed at me tonight, because I was in a fighting mood.

Although I hadn't caught up on laundry in over two weeks, luckily my black Jim's Tavern T-shirt smelled clean enough to wear again. I dug through my closet for a clean pair of jeans and also found my knockoff Converse sneakers, hastily dressing before one of the kids spotted me, needing something that Mike was too lazy to deal with. As I scrambled to throw my black hair up in a frizzed ponytail, I spotted several new gray strands that I already knew I would successfully dye, only to have a new crop sprout. I was hopelessly aging beyond my years, thanks to the stress of my daily life.

I called my boss to let him know I'd be in for an extra shift— we were always understaffed during the lunch hour—hoping he wouldn't ask why. *My deadbeat husband can't keep a job to save his life,* I didn't want to say. *My lazy spouse is a loser who can't provide for the family* he *wanted.* I bit the words back, my teeth sinking into my bottom lip. I was so angry, so frustrated, so exhausted at holding everything together by worn strings that would sever at any moment.

My sanity had reached the edge of its threshold and was pouring all over the floor. I was losing it. I couldn't stand the thought of another day of this existence. The voices of four children screaming in the background, slicing through my head; the stress of having to run lunch orders while my feet still ached from yesterday's long shift; the empty bank account, thanks to Mike's never-ending bar tab; the bills, bills, more bills that I couldn't seem to pay down; the perpetual loop of chaos that I was stuck in. I wanted a moment of quiet, just a moment, and I couldn't even have that.

As I breezed past my oblivious husband lounging like it was a Sunday afternoon, like I hadn't just asked him to take care of the kids, his eyes blurry from a nap, only one thought lingered.

I wanted to wrap my fingers around his scrawny neck and choke every last word, every last excuse, every last bit of bad news out of him until it was just me, alone, taking back what little bit of life I had left.

And then I cried all the way to work.

# Chapter 10 · Jo

My bed was warm, but my body trembled with chills. The sun shone brightly, but my world felt dark. My eyelids fell heavily, but I couldn't cross over into sleep. My stomach cramped with hunger, but I couldn't force anything down. Worry was my only companion, keeping me dreadfully cold, awake, and famished.

I didn't care about me, though. I would die if it could save Amelia. Was Amelia being starved? Was she scared and shivering in some tormentor's dank basement? Was she even still alive? These fears pulsed through my brain relentlessly as I wondered where my baby girl was, if I'd ever see her blond pigtails swinging as she chased her sister, if her giggles would ever warm my heart again, if I'd ever feel her stout little arms around my neck. She gave the best hugs.

When I closed my eyes, I could almost feel her near me. In perfect crispness I remembered the night she was born. Barely six pounds, her tiny head full of blond curls, the pucker of her lips. Even after birthing two other babies it was as magical and perfect as if it was the first time. I wept with joy when I first laid eyes on her writhing pink body, her wails a melody that my heart harmonized with. She was so beautiful, so mine. I vowed then and there as I held her close that I would never let her go. From that moment until my dying breath I would protect her. Because that was always the plan—I would go first. A child should never die before the parent. It's unnatural. It defies the circle of life.

And yet here I was, facing that terrifying possibility of losing a child. Where had my promise gone? How could I protect her now?

My perfect life had become a perfect hell.

Tucked in the shadows of my bedroom, the unbearable hours ticked by, each silent minute shredding my heart muscles a little more. Every chirp of my cell phone, every beeping text jolted me like a defibrillator of hope that it was the police contacting me with good news. They'd found her alive, they were on their way home now, she had been untouched, unhurt, my baby girl was coming home. But no.

A knock on my front door an hour ago sent me tumbling out of bed, stubbing my toe as I scrambled to answer. A Girl Scout making her rounds on Oleander Way cheerily smiled up at me offering her usual cookie variety, until her small voice and hopeful eyes sent me into a blubbering heap. I knew Amelia would never wear a Girl Scout uniform, she'd never sell cookies door to door. As I sobbed in front of these strangers, her mother had protectively stepped between us, like I was a nutcase to be feared. I ended up buying ten boxes of Thin Mints to make up for scaring the poor child.

Hope was my focus. I couldn't let the alternative seep in.

Amelia would be all right. In my arms. Soon. She had to be.

But no.

This was not Fate's choice.

Fate wanted nothing but pain for me.

A soft knock at the bedroom door broke into my empty world, but I didn't bid the visitor to enter. I couldn't speak—partly from the dryness of my throat that hurt from all the sobbing, partly from the lack of will to push words out.

Grieving was exhausting.

Despite my silence, the bedroom door swung open. I glanced up to see the cautious steps of Shayla Kensington—a true friend among sparse acquaintances, being the too-busy-to-socialize mom that I was. With soccer games and ballet classes and gymnastics and piano lessons, I barely had time to get my nails done, let alone befriend women who would backbite when given the chance. Some people collect friends, putting them on display as if it was a competition. Not me. All I needed was my family and Shayla.

Despite her penchant for drama, Shay was the one person I could trust. Our shared secrets stayed secrets, not neighborhood scandals. I knew she was here to help, not gather news for the town gossips. As she approached, her eyes watered, her lips trembled; she wore her empathy like a shroud. Then she smiled weakly—she knew I wouldn't want her pity.

"Hey, sweetie," she said. "How you holding up?"

I didn't move. Couldn't speak. Instead I buried my face in my pillow. A muffled sob escaped my lips.

A moment later the bedsprings sunk as she sat next to me, resting her hand on my shoulder, then rubbing circles along my back. I knew she meant to be soothing, but at that moment I wanted to shrug her damn circles off my skin and just be left alone.

"Jay blames me. He thinks this is all my fault, that I let this happen. He hates me. Thinks I'm an unfit mother. Is he right?"

I didn't want her answer, because I already knew what she'd say. She'd tell me it wasn't my fault, that I'm a wonderful mom, that I'd do anything for my kids, that Jay doesn't really think that. All lies. I didn't need lies right now. I needed the truth. And the truth was I had failed my daughter. I had failed my family. Broken it irreparably.

"And before you answer, just tell me this: have you ever lost one of your kids?"

Her sigh brushed my cheek.

"Actually, yes."

"Yes?" I looked up at her, bewildered. She had my full attention now. "You never told me this. What happened?"

"Tenica was a newborn, and I had promised Arion we'd go for a walk outside. Right before we were heading out the door, Tenica blew up her diaper. You know when it goes up the back and they need a whole wardrobe change. So while I'm cleaning her up and putting her in a new outfit, Arion decides to head out without me. I think he was almost seven at the time—definitely knew better. I'm finally ready and he's not in the house. I look outside, he's nowhere to be found. Panic sets in. I'm freaking out at this point. I run all over the yard, down the street, no sign of him. I'm positive someone has taken him. That he's gone forever."

"It's terrifying, isn't it?" I vividly remembered the panic.

"I ended up calling the cops, going from house to house trying to find him. It wasn't until hours later that the cops showed up with Arion. Apparently he had made his way down to his classmate Drew's house, about a mile or so away, and he was there playing video games. Drew's parents didn't even know he was there. That was the beginning of their friendship, so I guess something good came out of the gray hairs he gave me that day."

I wondered how long it would take for the cops to find Amelia … if at all. It had been too long already.

"Why didn't you ever tell me about this?"

"I was mortified, embarrassed. The last thing I want to tell my best friend is that I failed big-time as a parent. But in the end, I had to accept that shit happens. Arion was all right. I could beat myself up about it, or I could forgive my momentary lapse of trying to be in all places at once. Because ultimately, Jo, that's what it was. I couldn't be everywhere at once, and neither could you."

I wished it was the same thing, but it wasn't. Arion wasn't a helpless three-year-old girl. Arion wandered off on his own while my daughter was abducted. The cops found him within hours; Amelia was now two days gone.

"It's just not the same, Shay. Arion wandered off. Someone *took* my baby girl. And I let them."

"I know you're suffering, but I want to help. What can I do, Jo? Please let me help you."

*Find my baby girl.* That's all I wanted, all I needed.

I shifted to my side, cuddling up to her. My best friend since we were sixteen, Shayla and I had spent months sitting next to each other in history class all through tenth grade without exchanging more than a brief grin and hello. Until we both ended up at a No Doubt concert and I had gotten stranded by my date as he drunkenly decided to leave me for a bunch of party girls.

Bumping into Shayla, she came to my rescue and I'd been under her wing ever since. From that day on, we spent high school hitting underage dance clubs, coffee shops, and malls together—growing up but not apart, thick as thieves. Over the years, somewhere along the line we had become like blood kin.

And now she was here for me in my darkest hour, but I didn't want her.

I wanted to wallow … alone.

"How can you help me, Shay?" I exhaled the words. "Unless you know where Amelia is, there's nothing you can do. There's nothing anyone can do."

"So you're just going to stay in bed all day?"

"What else can I do? The police don't have any leads. I'm not a detective. I'm a negligent mother who lost her baby girl."

She huffed at me, shaking her head. "Stop it. This isn't your fault."

"Oh really? She was abducted during my watch, Shay. Who the hell's fault is it if not mine?"

"You know I love you. So I'm saying this with love: shut the fuck up and get off your ass … with love."

She smiled, but today her brusque humor rolled off me. I turned back on my side away from her, curling into a ball.

"C'mon," she coaxed. "Blaming yourself isn't going to find her. Do something productive. Get up, get dressed, and go look for her. I can stay here and watch the kids while you put up posters, or go back to the park and ask people if they saw anything, or whatever you can think of to find Amelia. Anything but lying here torturing yourself, Jo."

In some demented way I wanted the torture. I deserved the pain. No one could possibly understand the panic, the fear, the full-body anxiety, the self-blame unless they had lost a child.

It hurt to move. Every muscle, every brain cell ached. I could feel my own departure, as if my body was shutting down. And I almost wanted it to … if only just to stop the pain.

But what if Amelia was alive? What if she was out there waiting for me to find her?

What if …?

Hiding in bed wouldn't help. I had to keep walking forward. I had to keep searching.

"Maybe you're right, Shay," I said wearily. "Maybe I can bring Amelia home."

"Thatta girl. Think positive." Shayla hoisted me by the elbow and pulled me upright. "No time like the present to get going."

And yet I couldn't muster the energy to move.

I sighed.

"Don't give up. You are a fighter, Jo. Fight for Amelia. She needs you, and you can save her. I just know it."

Shayla had always been a natural cheerleader. Back in high school her verve more than once motivated our basketball team to come back for a win from the most dismal of odds. That same perkiness anointed her cheerleading captain two years in a row.

"Let's make some posters together and we can put them up. I'll do some social media blasts too—you never know who might have seen her or know something. We'll find her, Jo. I promise you, we'll find Amelia."

I needed to hear this. Though the reality was grimly hopeless, Shay's encouragement shattered the darkness that had been sucking me in. I could lie in bed weeping away the days, or I could find my little girl and bring her home.

In a tearful moment of gratitude, I pulled Shayla into a hug and clung to her like she was my life support. Hugging me back, I felt the burden shift off my shoulders, as if hoisting it onto Shayla for us to share. Maybe I'd be okay. Maybe we'd get through this.

"I love you, Shay. I couldn't handle this without you."

"I got you, girl. That's what best friends are for, right?" she whispered into my hair. Then she drew back from me, gripping me by the shoulders. "How about we get started on those posters and bring Amelia home?"

Although I forced a grin for the sake of my friend, I felt my heart tear a little, knowing it would all be futile. It had been too long. Amelia was already dead. I was searching for a corpse.

# Chapter 11 - Shayla

Lies piled on top of lies.

Secrets smothering secrets.

I was beginning to feel bound by the web of deceit I had woven.

Initially the plan was to go straight home from Holt Elementary where I taught a class of rambunctious first graders. Though, perhaps the word *taught* was being generous. Mainly I attempted to keep them in line—and injury free—until the dismissal bell rung at 2:15. On most days I was successful at this job. It just depended on when Isaak Bloomington came to school.

On the days Isaak graced us with his presence, all hell broke loose. After about a month of trying to keep Isaak from picking fights, or throwing chairs, or cussing at the staff, or simply doing what he wanted when he wanted, I looked forward to the days his mother simply didn't feel like getting him to school. Luckily she didn't disappoint me often.

Today was an Isaak day. Following a grueling seven hours of him talking back and slapping a third-grader who was twice his size—Isaak had balls, for sure—I wasn't ready to go home yet.

I needed a smoke and a drink, but I didn't want to drink alone.

After Jo's hourly descent into depression from Amelia's abduction, I let Trent know I'd be stopping by to check in on her again. *I'll be late getting home*, I told him. *Don't wait up*, I said.

Only, I'd hidden a little lie in there.

Okay, maybe a big lie. The best lies were always peppered with an ounce of truth.

I didn't mention where I'd be heading after Jo's.

Jim's Tavern lived up to its Southern roots. Pictures of bygone tobacco plantations and Durham Bulls baseball jerseys lined every square inch of wall space, representing a collage of the town's history. The booth where I sat was made of rough-hewn logs, and above my shoulder a deer's head leered down at me. As unnerving as it was being watched by a stuffed dead animal, the drumming fingers of the man sitting across from me unnerved me even more.

"Kelse, could you knock off the tapping?" I said, irritation edging my voice.

He stared at me, grinning crookedly, his forehead wrinkled with confusion.

"Tapping?"

"Yeah, your fingers. Banging on the table. It's annoying."

"Oh, sorry, babe. I didn't realize I was doing it."

And that was the end of the argument.

Such compliance. I had the man wrapped around my pinkie.

As he returned his gaze to the menu sprawled open in front of him, I felt a teensy bit guilty for snapping at him. Why was I being such a bitch? I couldn't help myself today. I needed to be. And yet Kelsey Gray would suck it up with a smile, like he always did.

"I'm sorry," I added, breaking the awkward silence. "I'm having a rough day and taking it out on you."

Kelsey looked up at me with a charming smile, his teeth so perfect they'd put Denzel Washington's grill to shame. A lock of wavy black hair hung in front of his professionally groomed eyebrows. The man was more put together than me, goddamn him. I often teased him about being a metrosexual, and he'd never quite denied it. He tucked the strands behind his ear, then placed his palm on top of my hand. His cuticles were cleaner than mine, and I was almost jealous.

"It's okay, babe. Let's just try to enjoy the time we have together."

He was asking the impossible tonight, because he didn't realize a fight was in store for us. It had been a long time coming—our inevitable breakup—despite his optimism that we'd be together forever. In his love-drunk stupor, he imagined us eloping on some exotic beach while the wet ink of my divorce papers stained our fingers. For months I'd gone along with it—the dreamy anticipation, the forbidden excitement, the thrill of our lovers' embrace. But the reality was that the fun had worn off. Reality set in, and the reality was that ecstasy lost its potency over time. Steadfast marital love was more enduring than hot monkey sex on the sly.

I had a husband. Kids. A mortgage. Vacation plans. A half-finished herb garden. I couldn't just leave it all behind for Kelsey, no matter how much fun he was on the side, or how pretty he made me feel. Maybe I was a coward. Or maybe I actually wanted my old life and didn't know it.

Once upon a time I had imagined life without my family, my house, my day-to-day existence. In this vision I traveled the world, sightseeing enchanting cities and dining on fine cuisine. But the more I envisioned sharing that journey with Kelsey and his rhythmic fingers, the more I didn't want it. The more I realized I'd rather end up alone than with him.

He annoyed the shit out of me. He was too nurturing, like my mother. He smacked his lips while he chewed. His emerald eyes sat too far apart—his only physical imperfection. He talked about his feelings too much. I damn near hated the man. So why was I dragging this affair out? It could only end badly … and I had a feeling Kelsey wouldn't be as eager to get back to reality as I was.

My reality was my family—Trent and the kids. If I lost them, there would be no exotic travels or extravagant meals. Instead I'd be hibernating in my room and starving myself like Jo was doing right now, because they were my anchor. I didn't want to be alone. Not after seeing what Jo was going through in losing Amelia. I loved Arion and Tenica. I loved the comfortable silence I had with Trent. I loved my job, even on Isaak days. I couldn't give it all up. Not for a man I had grown to loathe.

And that thought set me in motion.

"Kelse, we need to talk."

The dreaded segue.

The beginning of the end.

Just as I mustered the courage to get the conversation over with, the waitress arrived, pen and pad ready. "Welcome to Jim's Tavern. My name's June and I'll be taking care of you this evening. Can I start you off with some fried pickle chips or pork BBQ nachos?"

I glanced up at her, unsure if I should order. Knowing what I was about to do, my appetite was long gone. But the poor woman looked so haggard with her hair falling sloppily out of her ponytail and mascara smearing under her vacant eyes. Stains dotted her black Jim's Tavern T-shirt, and I wondered if she felt this job was as demeaning as it looked. She smiled, but as a fellow woman, I saw the insincerity behind it. June needed this order more than I did.

The most expensive item on the menu it was, then.

"I think we're ready to order."

We placed our orders with the waitress, and I wasted no time jumping into the conversation as she rushed off to another table.

"As I was saying," I began.

"I'm going to stop you right there, Shayla," Kelsey interrupted.

The remainder of my sentence snagged in my throat in shock that this good-looking pushover would dare interrupt me.

"I know what that line is—a breakup line. But I'm not going to let you do this to me. I refuse. I've waited months for you. I've put my life on hold for you. I've given my heart to you. My entire future is wrapped up in you, Shayla. You don't get to just throw that away."

His voice grew firmer with each sentence, and I was afraid to speak. And I was never afraid to speak my mind to anyone. Let's just say I wasn't the most winsome personality, but I was a force to be reckoned with.

Clearly I had lost that force with Kelsey.

"You're going to get a divorce like you said you would," he growled. "We're going to get married. We're going to travel to the places we talked about. You're going to fulfill every damn promise you made to me. Or else, be prepared for war."

"War?" I scoffed.

"Shut up!" he yelled, banging his fist on the table. A spoon clattered to the floor and my glass of water trembled. I felt curious eyes watching. "If you think you can just walk away from me, you're wrong. No one walks away from me. I will take you down. Your husband, your children, your co-workers—they will all know about what you've been doing with me in your free time. I will ruin your life, like you're trying to ruin mine. So before you say another word, think on that."

I sat in stunned silence. Kelsey had never been rough with me, aside from in the bedroom. He had always seemed to go with the flow, letting me call the shots. But clearly not anymore.

I didn't know this man who sat before me, and I didn't want to find out more about him. All I knew was that I believed every word he said. The threat was real; the threat would devastate my life. This wasn't going to be as easy as I hoped. I'd need a plan to get rid of him—one that would allow me to walk away free and clear. If any such hope existed.

Kelsey's green eyes bore into me and I knew what I had to do. It would be ugly, it would require sacrifice, but in the end it was the only option. He left me no choice. I'd make Kelsey regret that first lustful gaze eight months ago, the moment he approached me across the bar offering to buy me a drink. I'd ended up ordering a shot of Johnnie Walker blue label, even though I didn't like scotch, just to see how much he'd spend on me. Every steamy early-afternoon sexcapade after this would be a burning brand on his skin that he'd never forget and always regret.

Because I was going to take Kelsey Gray down, and I knew exactly how to do it.

"Well then," I said, my voice quavering and my stomach wringing itself sick as I contemplated my next move, "how about we order a drink?"

# Chapter 12 - Ellie

*I* never expected to find myself the victim of unrequited love by the man I've married. How can it be that someone I've given all but a sliver of my heart to doesn't love me back? How can twelve years of devoted for-better-or-worse, in-sickness-and-health love boil down to absolutely nothing to one half of the union and yet hold every ounce of meaning in life for the other half?

Sure, I've always thought it possible that one of us loved the other just a little bit more—that person being me, of course. It was obvious from the beginning, evident in the way I hung by his side while he shifted slightly away. In my longing gaze while his attention was elsewhere. In my need to talk to him in bed about anything and everything on my mind when he just wanted to fall asleep. I never discounted our love over those small details, though. It was simply me being an emotional, attached woman and Denny being an unemotional, detached man. But the depth of our love I never doubted. The security of our relationship I knew was strong.

Oh, how wrong I was. I loved him too much, and he loved me too little … or perhaps not at all. Maybe I was a prize to be won, only to be regifted to someone else. Or a conquest where the thrill faded, and being the macho man that he was, a new victory must take my place.

This wasn't how marriage was supposed to be. One couldn't simply give up on it without the consent of the other, right? We were bound together. But what I saw as cupped together in a delicate oneness, Denny saw as constrained by chains. While I delighted in our gentle drawing together, Denny pushed to break free from his bondage. What is left for me to do but fight for a marriage Denny has already

*surrendered, or walk away as years of love wither and die? What kind*
*of choice is that?*

\*\*\*

I hadn't meant to find it. But there it was, slapping me like a cold
wind. A receipt for a $184 dinner for two at Ruth's Chris Steak
House, a fancy-pants restaurant Denny had never treated me to in
all our years of marriage. And paid for with cash. How perfectly sly
of him. The receipt told me all I needed to know—two surf-and-
turfs, one bottle of wine, one dessert. There was nothing corporate
about this meal. It was clearly romantic.

The receipt had slipped out of his pocket while I was prepping
a load of laundry. It seemed innocuous enough, until I uncrumpled
the wad of paper and read it.

Denny's dress pants glided from my hands to the floor. As
I clutched the thin, wrinkled paper, all I knew was that my
suspicions were confirmed: Denny was a cheating bastard. And
Denny was going to pay for his mistake. I couldn't decide if I was
heartbroken or angry … or maybe a bit of both. The line between
love and hate was a thin gray haze, making it easy to slip between
the two emotions. As much as I loathed my betraying husband at
this moment, my heart still belonged to him. It always would; he'd
been the only man I ever truly loved, and that wouldn't change. It
couldn't change. Because I'd split my heart in half the day we got
married, gave him that part of me, and entrusted him with it for
life. Why did he have such a firm grip? Why couldn't I take my
heart back? Why couldn't I shake him off?

Suddenly I knew the answer. Because deep down I was no one
without him. He created me back before I knew who I was. I based
my personality on what Denny liked in a woman, focused my
dreams on Denny's dreams, built my identity on Denny's picture
of what a wife should be. Without Denny, who was I? I didn't
know because I'd never bothered to find out.

I liked what Denny wanted me to like. I read what Denny
recommended I read. I cooked the meals Denny savored most.

I raised the kids the way Denny demanded they be raised. I cleaned the house the way Denny preferred. Denny was the sun I revolved around. And yet he had left me in a sunless void while he found a new galaxy to explore—the woman he ate $184 surf-and-turf with.

A tear slid down my cheek. The realness of my findings couldn't be explained away anymore. The lipstick stain and lingering perfume on his shirt was circumstantial evidence. This was exhibit A. It was true. It was clear. There was no legitimate reason for this receipt to be in his pocket. Especially on a night he told me he was working late.

I suspected she was a co-worker, but it was only just that—a suspicion. I needed to know who he was screwing. If she was prettier than me, younger than me. Did I even have a chance to compete against her? Did I even want to?

I felt the pull of obsession as I read the receipt again … and again, wondering if they held hands across the table, if candles illuminated the space between them, if they shared kisses between each bite, if they fed each other dessert, if they split the bottle of wine until they were tipsily flirting and touching. While I sat at home cooking *him* dinner and washing *his* laundry, he was spending *our* money on my younger, sexier replacement.

I hadn't seen any unusual expenditures from the bank account—and I checked it almost daily online—so Denny was being extra careful when treating the home-wrecker to dinners out by using cash. Were there other meals? Or—God forbid—hotels?

A gasp choked me as I imagined my husband checking into a hole-in-the-wall hotel with a giggling skank by his side. Or was it something classier? Was she footing the bill? If she worked with him and made good money, there was no way I could compete with beautiful *and* successful.

Heading into the bedroom, I rifled through the dirty clothes hamper, searching every pocket but turning up empty-handed. I wondered if he had tossed any evidence in the bathroom garbage can, so with careful fingers, I pushed aside used tissues and sticky pieces of floss in search of crumpled receipts. Again, nothing.

Denny covered his tracks well.

I'd become the prey of deceit. While Denny's manipulation tore at my flesh, horrid visuals sunk their teeth into my brain. Was he with her now? What did they spend their time doing? Did they talk? Or just bang each other's brains out? The thoughts crackled and fizzled without mercy. No one wanted to be that woman—the bitter, suspicious wife who rummaged through her husband's clothes and watched his bank account and checked his car mileage looking for clues to his secrets. Obsessive jealousy wasn't becoming of anyone, certainly not me. I was above that … wasn't I? Of course I wasn't better than this flux of emotional turmoil. Any woman who discovered she'd been made a fool of by the love of her life would go a little crazy. It was my right to breakdown.

And that's when I knew there was only one way to make the stabbing pain in my chest stop.

Find Denny and his mistress and hurt them like they hurt me.

# Chapter 13 - Jo

Sixteen.

That was the number of sexual offenders listed who lived within five miles of Forest Hills Park, according to the online registry.

Sixteen men hiding perversions that would make your skin crawl.

Sixteen monsters who raped or preyed on children, still roaming free.

Sixteen predators who could have stolen my little girl.

Sixteen was a large number to look into, and I had no idea where to start. I'd skimmed over their profiles, but they all looked so … eerily normal. Like someone I'd pass in the grocery store aisle and maybe even offer a friendly grin. And how would I know when I'd found the man who took Amelia? I doubted he would just confess, or be holding a sign saying "I kidnapped your little girl." Would my heart split with pain? Would my brain sizzle with subliminal recognition?

As I paged through each criminal, I felt nothing. Just an empty space in my head, a vacancy in my heart. Maybe it was too much at once. I needed to focus on one at a time, letting my maternal instinct guide me.

Adjusting my search criteria, I decided to narrow it down to a one-mile radius from the park, and this gave me three hits. One was a nineteen-year-old charged with indecent liberties with a seventeen-year-old minor. My three-year-old wouldn't have been his target. Also, based on Abby's description, he was too young.

Another perpetrator was charged with sexual battery of a fifteen-year-old girl. A teen victim. Again, an unlikely match.

The third, though—his record caught my attention:

Description: INDECENT LIBERTY MINOR
Victim's Age: 7
Offender's Age: 42
Primary Name at time of Conviction: GUNNER, MAXWELL

His charges specifically dealt with exposing himself to a minor. His victim wasn't quite as young as Amelia, but he sounded like the kind of pervert who might take indecent liberties one step further into molestation, I thought with a cringe. Then one step more by abducting a child—perhaps my child. Each progression was a baby step into darkness. With his red hair pulled back in a stringy ponytail and sporting a wiry goatee, the image of my daughter's kidnapper was born.

But based on Abby's description, this man didn't fit at all other than his height, approximate age, and build. Had he shaved his goatee, dyed his hair brown, and thrown on glasses as a disguise? It was possible, maybe even likely. I couldn't risk not checking him out.

I jotted down his address, grabbed my keys, and headed out the door. Within the forty-eight-hour window of her disappearance, there was a chance Amelia could still be there.

Ten minutes later I pulled up to a white brick ranch-style home straight off a *Better Homes and Gardens* cover. Whiskey barrel planters, placed at precise intervals on either side of the stepping stone walkway, overflowed with colorful petunia blossoms, and neatly trimmed boxwoods and nandinas followed the brick around the corners, where they continued toward the fenced-in backyard. Not a piece of mulch was out of place as I walked up the sidewalk, wondering what kind of sicko tended to his garden so meticulously.

Perhaps a soft, feminine type … a child molester type. What better diversion for passersby than to distract from the old well in the basement where he kept his victims like a real-life Buffalo Bill from *Silence of the Lambs*. Was I as dumb as Clarice for coming here?

When I rang the doorbell, I felt a pinch in my palms and glanced down at my hands. I had been clenching them so hard that my fingernails bit into my flesh, marking it with angry pink semicircles. My jaw began to ache with the tense bite of anticipation.

I was a mother lioness ready to pounce and claw at whoever answered the door.

My little girl could be on the other side. My little girl could be waiting for me to rescue her. I wondered if I should just burst in, or manipulate my way inside. Should I call the cops? Or just play it cool and hopefully catch him off-guard? I had no idea how to handle it, but I knew—I just knew—that my baby was here. We would be reunited in mere moments. I could feel the hope surging as the door swung open.

And then just like that, my hope sputtered to a stop.

A woman who looked to be in her mid-seventies answered the door. Her short white hair was perfectly coifed, but her plump, wrinkled lips, painted a garish red, were comical—like the wax lips I used to buy at the dollar store as a kid. Her friendly smile revealed dentures that could have used an Efferdent bath. I caught a whiff of old-person smell mixed with a hideous floral perfume, a combination my waggish father used to describe as dog shit in a flowerbed. For all that, she looked like a doting grandmother ready to hand out home-baked cookies to trick-or-treaters. Not the sinister creature I had expected.

"Can I help you, dear?" Her voice creaked like old joints.

"I'm looking for a Maxwell Gunner?" I said, my voice lilting with a question.

"Oh, he's at work, honey. And you are—?"

"My name's Jo…y. Joy. I'm a … friend of his." I'd almost forgotten what I was doing here.

A smile widened her floppy cheeks. "How wonderful! Would you like to come inside to wait for him? He should be home soon. I've got a pot of lavender tea I'm steeping as we speak."

I fumbled for a decision. Would a creepy man who lived with his tea-drinking elderly mother be harboring a victimized child in his house? I suppose anything was possible, so I nodded. At least I wouldn't need the cops to help me handle this woman if the need arose.

"Thank you. That's very kind."

She opened the door wide and waved me to follow her into the living room. "Have a seat and I'll bring some teacups. It's not often I get visitors, so this is a treat."

The house was quiet. No sounds of crying children or fingers clawing behind a bedroom door. No flies buzzing around weeks-old leftovers or lonely light bulbs swinging from a stained ceiling. This wasn't at all what I expected from a child abductor's residence. Everything in perfect order—the mark of a woman with too much time on her hands and a touch of OCD.

I wandered to a well-polished upright piano with neat rows of framed pictures perched on top. Grainy pictures of a ginger boy in a crooked, shiny party hat blowing out birthday candles. Sepia pictures of a young mom version of Grandma Gunner holding the same boy in her lap, both smiling giddily. A young bearded man cradling a baby in a flowing white christening gown. An older version of that same man hefting a little girl on his shoulders on a beach outing. All so normal. All so family-like.

What could have possibly turned this average man into a child-molesting monster?

"That's my Maxy—so happy, once upon a time," a voice whispered behind my neck, startling me. Her sigh tickled my skin as she hung at my back. "You know, before all that stuff with Fiona's mama."

"Fiona's mama?" I echoed.

"Didn't he tell you? About how his ex tried to run off with his little girl and accused him of doing something unspeakable to little Fiona. Poor girl hasn't seen her daddy since. Such a shame."

Unless what the mother said was all true. It often started in the home—the tragedies.

"I'm sorry for what he went through." Except I wasn't sorry at all. The son of a bitch had my daughter.

"So handsome, isn't he?"

"Um, very," I replied. Bile churned in my stomach. I felt its sickly sweetness rising slowly to my throat.

Turning away from her collage of memories, we headed to the sofa.

Handing me a thin china teacup, Grandma Gunner sat primly on the floral sofa still wrapped in plastic. My rear glided back along the slippery cushion, making an embarrassing flatulent sound. I'd never understood the purpose of stripping a sofa of its purpose—to be comfortable—all for the sake of *protecting* it. Protecting it from what—being used?

"So how do you know Maxy?" she probed.

I couldn't tell her what really brought me to her house today: *I think your son may have abducted my daughter.* And now that I was here, I wasn't so sure he was behind Amelia's disappearance. But he had to be. He was the only lead I had.

"Oh, we met at the store." As generic and safe a response as I could create.

"That's nice. He's a good boy, Maxy is."

"I can tell. He's got a good mama." I smiled warmly, and I noticed a sparkle in her eyes at my forced compliment.

"Oh you hush, you sweet girl," she said, dismissing my compliment with a humble wave. "I try, Lord knows I have."

I sipped my bitter brew, sucking it down quickly to get it over with.

"When does Max get home from work usually?"

She glanced behind her, where a floral-painted porcelain clock ticked its hands toward one o'clock.

"He usually gets home by noon, but he must be working late today. He called in sick two days in a row, and without paid time off, he usually tries to make up the time the same week."

"So he was home the past couple days?"

"Down with a cold something terrible. I just hope I didn't catch it. At my age it's hard to recover from viruses. I ain't no spring chicken no more."

If Max was home when Amelia was taken, then that eliminated him from the suspect list. There was no point sticking around only to get caught in a lie.

"I'm sorry to hear he wasn't feeling well. But I don't want to keep you. I can stop by another time."

I rose from the stiff cushion and set my cup down.

"Are you sure, dear?"

"Yep, it's not a big deal to pop by later. I really should get going, though. It was nice meeting you."

"Pleasure was all mine, Joy. Come back soon."

"I will," I called behind me as I trotted to my car. While backing out of the driveway, I imagined the confusion on Maxwell's face later that evening when Grandma Gunner announced that his good friend Joy had stopped by. I felt bad about my deceitful intrusion, since Grandma Gunner seemed so eager for company and I almost wanted to offer that to the lonely elderly lady.

Although I hadn't gotten the answers I hoped, I couldn't stop looking. There were clues out there. I just needed to find them.

Forest Hills Park was less than a mile away, where I planned to put up flyers on every square inch of hangable surface. By the time I arrived, the parking lot was practically empty as a handful of mothers dragged their fussing children home for after-lunch naps and pre-dinner television. As I stuck posters to trees, streetlights, garbage cans, and anything that would hold the flimsy pieces of paper with Amelia's rosy cheeks and sunny smile, my eyes kept roaming back to the playset she was lured away from.

In the briefest of moments my world was torn from me.

In a single absent glance I never saw Amelia walk away, out of my life and into danger.

One backward look could have saved everything. And I hated myself for missing that chance.

It was all just too overwhelming. Everything began to spin. Like all the air had been sucked out of the world. I was going to faint.

I quickly sat on the nearest bench, head down between my knees, gasping for breath where there was none to be had. Choking on my memories, playing again and again in an unending loop, in a relentless game of what-ifs and could-have-beens.

Every panic-filled, guilt-ridden moment came crashing back upon me. Running through the park, screaming her name, hope dying with every passing moment and every failed endeavor. Every empty car and every discovered child who was not my Amelia, another rend on my soul. Until that final moment of defeat, where I became resigned to my fate, any hope for a "close call" perished as I punched in those fateful numbers. 9-1-1.

My finger hovered over the green "call" button on my phone. I hesitated. I didn't want EMTs to rescue me. In fact, I wanted the pain, the panic. It was what I deserved.

Slowly, agonizingly, the moment subsided. A pinprick of oxygen was allowed back into my world, just enough for a trice of relief. My starved lungs attempted to gasp great gulps of air. Too soon. My pulse first crescendoed from the lack of sustenance, then diminished to a horrible conclusion.

I needed to calm down or I was going to die right here on this park bench. Part of me just wanted to let go. Maybe this was what I deserved for losing her. Jay certainly thought so. Maybe this would show them, prove to them that I wasn't unfit.

No.

I couldn't let go yet. Not while she was still out there. Not while she still needed me.

Through sheer force of will, I pulled a rivulet of air into my aching bronchi and compelled my heart to beat once … twice … thrice …

As the darkness subsided and I regained the use of my faculties, I realized I might never be able to set foot in this park again.

# Chapter 14 - Shayla

While Kelsey sat at our table sipping his room temperature Bud Light, I hunched over the bathroom sink grimacing at the mess I'd made of myself. My eyes stung from the tears I'd cried as I emptied my stomach into the toilet bowl five minutes ago. I washed away the runnels of mascara tumbling down my cheeks, the water cool against my hot skin.

My intestines bubbled and churned as I sipped lukewarm water from the faucet, hoping to wash out the taste of bile. I had a bad feeling it wasn't the barbeque I'd eaten that sent me rushing to the bathroom. Perhaps it was nerves over what I was about to do to Kelsey, but I doubted it.

Then a thought crossed my mind. It crept slowly at first, hanging on the outer rim of my brain. My body shook with dread.

No, it couldn't be right.

I counted the days.

Shit. My period was late. By at least a week. How could I have not noticed?

Maybe it was nothing. Maybe it was a simple case of bad food. Maybe I was hitting menopause early. That had to be it, because anything else would be the death of me. I couldn't handle another child; I could barely handle the two I had. And then there was the looming question of whose baby it was. Chances were a 50/50 split. Oh, God ... I couldn't be one of *those*. Better book my spot on *The Maury Show* now.

No, I couldn't entertain the possibility of pregnancy. I needed to quash that fear right away. An unplanned baby tossed a wrench in the plan to destroy Kelsey ... or maybe not. Perhaps it could work in my favor.

Rifling through my purse, I found my cell phone and dialed the most advantageous three numbers a violated woman could dial.

"9-1-1. What is your emergency?" the operator stated.

I inhaled a breath, prepping my voice for a convincing performance.

"I'd like to report a rape."

***

While the police escorted Kelsey Gray into the back of a squad car to take his statement down at the Durham Police Station, I was given the okay to go home while Kelsey pondered who he was up against. I was no wilting flower that he could pluck out of its pot and toss away. I was a fucking redwood tree, stronger than steel. I'm unmovable, you bastard, and my roots are deep.

I averted my eyes as he passed me in the parking lot, afraid of what I'd see in them. Him being pissed, I could handle. But his creepy calmness as the cops showed up asking him questions gave me shivers. Something wasn't right about a man with no reaction to a rape accusation. His smirk said it all: this isn't over. Bitch.

I'd be ready for whatever he brought. I was ready for war.

Certain I'd made my point to him, firing the proverbial warning shot across his bow, all I wanted now was a hot bubble bath and a good book. But there was one stop I needed to make on my way home to Oleander Way.

It was the longest two minutes of my life. While the twenty minutes leading up to it were excruciating—searching for the fastest pregnancy test, then waiting in line to buy it, then sitting in the drugstore restroom stall peeing on the stick—the post-pee wait was even worse. Any woman could tell you that two minutes felt like two hours when watching those blue lines form. A plus or minus—what would it be? A roll of the dice—pregnant or not? Life or death? A woman's fate rested in such simple symbols. Those 120 seconds would redefine my entire life with a make-me-or-break-me finality.

I exhaled, not realizing I had held my breath the entire time.

It was the moment of truth. I stood and turned back to where I had placed the pregnancy test on the back of the toilet. My fingers trembled as I picked it up, looking away to prevent the inevitable just a little longer. Secretly hoping to catch it off-guard with my sudden glance in an effort to decree my desired outcome.

I held it in front of me, eyes closed, mumbling a fervent prayer in case God was listening.

And then I opened my eyes.

# Chapter 15 - June

My toes pinched in my too-tight sneakers.

My legs ached from running orders.

And my head throbbed from the weight of the world crushing it from all sides.

As my impromptu shift ended, I couldn't find the strength to go home. I couldn't muster the energy to console Mike, depressed and jobless yet again, as if his life was so difficult and mine so easy. I couldn't referee another Austin breakdown, or Arabelle chastising Kiki and Juliet for messing with her stuff. My hell continued well past the doors of Jim's Tavern, shrouding my home, my family, my very existence. There was no haven for me.

I had taken a roundabout route to Forest Hills Park, burning up the gas that was supposed to last for the week. Right now I didn't care about gas or money or making it home. A moment to myself, a pinch of quiet was my only focus. After parking in the same spot I always parked in—a habit I saw no reason to break—I stepped into the chilly air and headed for the dusk-dappled trails, inhaling the clean, earthy scent of pine trees and honeysuckle vines. I followed the smooth concrete path through a copse of trees, nature tugging me into a reverie. There was something calming about the thicket of a forest, the expanse of a flower-mottled field, the trickle of an unbridled creek. It was just what I needed. This could be my haven.

As I rounded a curve in the path, I bumped into a woman, sending her reeling backward and the stack of papers she carried flying.

"Oh, I'm so sorry!" I said.

"My fault," the woman replied. "Should have been looking where I was going."

"Here, let me help you pick these up."

"No, really, it's—"

"I insist."

"Thank you," she said. I detected genuine appreciation in her voice, and something else—barely masked pain.

As we both stooped to collect the papers, I came face to face with a picture of a little girl with a baby-toothed smile and dimples. Two curly blond pigtails jutted out like sprays from a water fountain.

MISSING CHILD was printed across the top in red Helvetica Bold type.

And then it hit me. One mother to another, a sudden anguish coursed through me for this total stranger who had lost a child.

"Is this your little girl?" I asked, afraid of what my question might spark. Afraid she'd break into tears and I'd have no idea how to comfort her.

"Yes, this is my little Amelia. She's only three." The woman's voice trembled and I imagined how hard it was to speak.

"What happened?" I asked before I could think.

"She was … abducted from this park two days ago." A tear slid down her face, and I felt a lump rise in my throat. I hated watching the misery plague others like it did me. But this—this was a whole new level of pain I'd never understand.

"Two days ago?" The wound must have been so fresh, still bleeding. "I'm so sorry." My consolation sounded flat against the mountain of hurt she was climbing. I didn't know what to say. What could I possibly offer this grieving, broken mother whose child was missing while mine were safe at home?

"Do you come here often?" she asked me. The question indicated something other than mere friendliness; she was fishing for a lead.

"Yeah, I'm here almost every day with my kids."

Her eyes widened with hope. "What time were you here two days ago?"

"Um, around one-ish, I think. It was after lunch, I remember, so yeah, about one."

"Then you might have seen him—the man who took her! It happened at one thirty. Do you remember seeing my little girl?"

I still had a stack of flyers in my hand. I studied the cherubic face.

"Let me think." I needed my memory not to fail me. For the sake of this woman and her child, I wanted to remember something, anything that could help her. I closed my eyes, concentrating on the details. I remembered sitting on the wooden bench, watching while the children scampered across the grass. But most of the time was a numb haze as I zoned out of my life into another world—a world where I didn't have kids screaming or fighting or melting down for no reason at all.

I was useless.

"I'm sorry, but I can't remember anything unusual." Handing her back all but one of the flyers, our fingers grazed, her hand quivered. This poor woman was falling apart right there in front of me. "I wish I could be more help."

"Please! Try harder. You must have seen something. Anything?" An edge of hysteria to her voice. Mania. This I understood all too well.

"I'm so sorry …"

She wiped at her wet cheeks, reigning in the cavalcade of emotions plaguing her. "Well, if you think of anything or remember something, please call me or text me on this number." She tapped a pink painted fingernail against the paper in my hands. "Thank you."

As she began to walk away from me, I touched her arm. "I'm truly sorry for what you're going through. I really am. I hope you find your little girl and bring her home safely."

"I appreciate that," she said.

Smiling wanly, the woman strode purposefully toward a pine, stapled a flyer to the trunk, and rounded the corner.

Her plight gave me a dose of perspective. I was worried about money woes while she worried about her child being murdered. I fumed over Mike's laziness while she dreaded a kidnapper's machinations. We'd lost a second income while she lost her baby. I suddenly felt so immature, so childish, so self-centered and absorbed with my two-bit problems when others suffered losses I couldn't imagine.

I wondered what it felt like to be her. To have a child vanish. To never see her face again. To never hold her tiny hands in mine. To never hear her voice or run a comb through her hair. What was the unknowing like? What would it feel like to remember a life before—when that tiny person blessed every moment and everything was whole—but knowing that only a fragment of it would remain?

What if my own children were unreachable, but somewhere out there? What would life be like if they were suddenly ... *just gone*? Would I yearn for the fights Arabelle instigated with her siblings? Would I miss Austin's self-inflicted assault when telling him no? Would I suddenly find Kiki's incessant whining a sweet melody? Would the absence of Juliet's all-night feedings keep me up at night?

Would the things that caused me such grief become nostalgic memories if they were taken away?

It was hard to imagine the terror, the worry, and perpetual panic that this woman felt. So hard to imagine, in fact, that I didn't feel anything at all. And for a startling self-realizing moment, I saw myself for what I was. A woman whose heart had been tapped dry. An exhausted, empty shell. A person who could no longer appreciate the little moments in life, because life was simply too heavy. A mother who didn't love her own children anymore.

I could feel for this woman, for the loss she had suffered. I just couldn't turn the mirror back upon myself and feel the same. What kind of monster had I become? Did I even care?

It was then that I wept.

# Chapter 16 - Ellie

*I*'m suffering from a perpetual case of nausea, this urge to curl up in a ball on the bathroom floor waiting for my entrails to spill on the tile. It's like my body is being torn to shreds and I'm helpless to stop it.

*I'm the walking dead. A decaying zombie, shuffling along and grasping for food to nourish my soul … and yet my soul is gone. I'm just a shell. There's an emptiness where my essence used to be. I'm no one. Nothing. A vacant ghost wandering the earth, unseen and unnoticed.*

*Denny doesn't see me. Doesn't want me. Desire me. Love me. To Darla and Logan I don't exist, unless they need something. And only then do I become a pair of serving hands and scurrying feet to heed their every beck and call. My life's purpose for the past decade—taking care of my family, adoring my husband, raising our children, building a safe home for us—it's all char and ashes. I wish I could be a phoenix strong enough to rise from my scorched life, new and beautiful, but I simply don't have the drive to start over. I must find the courage, though. If I don't, I fear what I will do.*

\*\*\*

There's a sense of empowerment that comes with knowing something that no one else does. A little secret that you carry, clutch close to your heart, ready to use at just the right moment. A secret is like a loaded gun—it can protect you when cornered, or win you a war. It can kill, if necessary.

My secret was my ace in the hole. But I was one card short of a royal flush.

I needed one last piece of evidence before I went on the offensive.

Denny thought he was so smart. So careful. He thought I didn't know about his mistress. While I played dumb, happy wife, he thought he was playing me. But his starring role as lying, cheating husband would soon end. I'd see to that personally.

When Denny called to let me know he'd be working late— "I'm sorry I have to work late again tonight," he had said, "but I promise to make it up to you, babe"—I wanted to scratch his eyes out through the phone. But instead I checked my anger and replied coolly, "Aw, we'll miss you, honey. I'll save a plate of dinner for you."

I didn't mention that there would probably be poison in his meatloaf.

He had called me from his office phone, probably to ward off any suspicion, so I knew he was still there—for the time being. I'd need to hurry if I was going to get there before he left to meet *her*. His whore. The kids grumbled as I packed them into the car when instead they should have been starting their bedtime ritual.

"Where are we going this late at night?" Darla asked as I sped toward the office, keeping my eyes peeled for any cops with radar guns. "Aren't we supposed to be in bed?"

"We're taking a little trip to Daddy's work," I explained stiffly.

"Now? Mom, this is stupid." She continued to gripe, but her words hid behind the buzzing in my brain.

"Darla, just please stop talking or I'm going to lose it!"

"Okay, sorry," she whispered.

My patience was on a short leash that threatened to snap. I didn't want to take my pain out on my kids, but I'd lost all control of my impulses. I wasn't behind the wheel; some strange, dark creature had taken over my body, forcing me to claw my way to the truth. I was the marionette of some deranged puppeteer. Maybe I was holding the strings; maybe the rage was. I couldn't tell where I ended and the rage began. Maybe we were one and the same.

An uncomfortable silence held Darla and Logan captive in the backseat, so unlike their usual bickering. I sensed that they were scared of me. Hell, I was scared of me at this point. I hadn't wanted it to be like this. I wished that they could understand, but this was an adult situation that I couldn't explain. Or could I? Was there a way to tell your children that your family was falling apart without causing them intense psychological harm? I wondered if I should say more. Certainly at age eleven Darla had enough understanding to know that Daddy wasn't supposed to spend time with women who weren't Mommy. Would that even register to her young mind? My goal wasn't for understanding, though, was it? I wanted to turn the kids against Denny. I wanted them on my side. I wanted him to see their disappointed faces and decide to fix everything—if not for me, then for them. For his flesh and blood. If he couldn't love me enough to stick it out, could he make the sacrifice for his children? I hoped so.

Instead, I pocketed my thirst for vengeance … for now. I'd need to know for sure what was going on with Denny before I set the kids against their father.

Minutes later I parked several spots away from Denny's car. He was still at the office—I hadn't missed him. I wasn't sure if this was what I wanted anymore. My stomach roiled as I could hardly stomach the thought of watching him flirt with his mistress. I wasn't ready for this, my body screamed for me to turn around, go home, and return to blissful ignorance. But I'd already seen too much. I already suspected too much. I couldn't stop now. The impulse was too strong.

Shutting off the engine, we waited in silence—me clutching the steering wheel as my knuckles whitened, the kids staring out the window in the backseat and grumbling.

"Are we going in?" Darla asked after several soundless minutes. I could hear the wariness in her voice.

"Not yet," I muttered, watching for Denny to come out the red brick building's revolving front door.

"Can we stop for ice cream on the way home?" Logan chimed in.

I sighed, my emotions thawing. The last thing I wanted was to turn this into a fun family outing, but perhaps I owed it to the kids after dragging them into my drama. "If you're patient while we wait, I think we could do that."

"Yay!" Logan cheered.

"That's my boy," I said, trying to keep up the mood.

"You're so dumb, Logan. I can't believe you care about ice cream while we're forced to sit here in the dark. Daddy would have taken us for ice cream without making us do this." Clearly Darla's fear had dissipated and her allegiance to Denny was firm. It was with this thought that I realized we had already divided, Denny and I. His side versus my side. A growing schism that we couldn't seem to bridge. And the worst part was that the kids were stuck in the middle of a twisted game of Pick Your Favorite Parent. Who would they choose? I already knew the answer to that. It wasn't me.

"How much longer? I'm bored." Logan's voice stretched out the words in a whine.

"We'll be heading home soon. It's a surprise for Daddy. Just hang in there for me, okay?" But it was too much for me to ask.

"This is stupid," Darla complained, and I felt my patience wearing thin.

"What is your problem?" I spat back. "Why are you acting like a brat?"

"Why do we have to sit here at night when it's bedtime? I'm tired. Daddy's probably working so he doesn't have to spend time with you anyways. And I don't blame him."

My jaw dropped. My ears hummed. Was that what my own children thought of me? I couldn't believe what I was hearing, after abandoning a career for them, carrying them for nine months, pushing their fat newborn bodies out of me, nursing them while my body deteriorated, wearing their poop when their diapers exploded, catching their spit-up on my shoulder, losing sleep to tend to them, cooking for them, cleaning up after them, giving everything of myself to them. After all of that, they simply saw me as a useless robot whose only value was what I could give them. God forbid I try to discipline them, teach them values, or ask for a little patience. Their father was ever the hero while I was always the villain.

And that was when I felt it: the snap.

I swung around to face her, grabbing her by the chin. "What did you say?"

"Nothing." Darla's jaws clamped shut, but I would pry that hurtful little mouth open with a crowbar if necessary. She wasn't getting off the hook that easily.

"No, I want to know what you meant by that." I released my grip but watched her carefully.

"Just that you're never fun and that's why Daddy works so much—to get away from you."

I couldn't respond at first. To hear this kind of news from my child … "Did he say that about me?"

"Sorta. When I asked why he works so much he said it's easier than coming home to you."

I couldn't believe he had said those words to our young, impressionable daughter.

"Do you agree with him?" I didn't want to hear the answer, but maybe I needed to. I wanted the truth more than I wanted the comfort of lies.

"Kinda, yeah. You're boring and you always tell us no. Sometimes I wish I had a different mom—a cool mom."

"A cool mom? What's uncool about me?"

"I dunno. You don't let us watch scary movies, you always have to schedule everything, you don't let me dye my hair or dress the way I want. You have to control everything, Mom. Even Dad— you control him too."

I had no defense. My eleven-year-old child was right. Wise beyond her years. I did have a complex—an addiction to structure, order, perfection. I'd dedicated my life to fitting in with the fitness moms, the PTA, the beauty pageant parents, the trophy wives with their luxury cars and landscaped yards and honor roll students and star athlete kids. This had been "the dream," but it was never *my* dream. This was where Darla was wrong. It had always been

Denny's dream, not mine. His wish, enforced by me. I couldn't care less if Darla's hair was blond or blue, or if she wore trendy or goth. I only wanted them happy, and I had failed. In trying to please my husband, I let my kids down. Was this the plight of wives everywhere? Were we all just obeying orders in an effort to hold our marriages together? Or was I the only one?

It was in that moment that I knew there was no point to any of this. To catching Denny in his affair, to confronting him, to threatening to take everything from him if he didn't break it off, to reminding him of what we had and what he risked losing ... because I had already lost it all. My husband didn't want me. My own children didn't want me.

What else was there to lose?

What else was there to gain?

Absolutely nothing. I mucked my hand. There was no reason to play. No reason to fight. The war was over without a single shot fired. The only casualty: me.

# Chapter 17 - Shayla

Her voice was muted and remote, like she was calling me from a dream. Though heavy with sleep, my eyelids fluttered open, then squinted shut at the white light above me. Beneath me, cool tile pressed against my back, forcing me to shift on my side. Everything blurred into a haze, and I had no idea where I was.

"Ma'am," the girl said, her hand soft, but firm, on my shoulder. "You passed out. Are you able to get up?"

As I forced my eyes open and pushed myself halfway up, that's when the fog lifted. Every last painful detail slammed into me.

The pregnancy test.

There it lay, on the dirty restroom floor beside me, the glaring plus sign mocking me. I remembered now … seeing the results, my heart trying to shove its way through my chest. Then standing up off the toilet seat, making my way through the stall door clutching that goddamn pee stick … but everything after that was a blank.

What stood out to me now wasn't the red-shirted employee hovering over me, or the severe restroom lights, or the grimy floor pressing against my tailbone. The baby growing inside me—the baby whose father was a huge question mark—that was the only thing I could think about.

I needed to talk to someone, to figure out what to do. But who? Confessing everything to Trent was a death sentence for my marriage. Telling Kelsey about the baby was a death sentence to my sanity. I couldn't be with Kelsey because I didn't love him. And I couldn't tell Trent the truth because I did. I was in a no-win situation.

Since high school Jo had always been my go-to conscious, the person I could count on to set me on the straight and narrow path of redemption. Jo understood me, loved me regardless, and accepted me no matter what. Like when I lost my virginity to Dougie Rollins, the STD king. While everyone else called me a whore, Jo hugged me through the tears—and penicillin. Or when I got high in the girls locker room and made a pass at our math teacher, Jo rescued me from a lifetime of embarrassment—and a guaranteed suspension—by lying to the teacher that I had taken one too many pain pills for a cheerleading injury.

For years she had supported me through every mishap and mistake. She was my lifeboat in the storm. Except for this. This storm I couldn't weather with her.

She'd never forgive me. Jo, on her perfect pedestal, with her perfect husband, with his perfect job, and their perfect house, with their perfect kids, could never understand something of this magnitude. Devoted, honest, passionate about Jay, she could never understand the urge to cheat. The compulsion I lived with every morning, every afternoon, and every evening for something more, something exciting. While I lay in bed next to my husband, who I loved, the thoughts plagued me that it wasn't enough. I felt so utterly empty and I didn't know why.

I'd never be able to tell Jo about Kelsey. I didn't know why I couldn't tell my best and only friend in the world that I had been having an affair all this time. Maybe it was her look of disappointment that I dreaded. Maybe it was her admonishment I didn't want to deal with. I knew how it would unfold. She'd tell me to stop instantly, then insist on me confessing to Trent … or else. I knew what her "or else" would mean: she'd threaten to tell if I didn't. Jo was honest like that. I both respected and despised her for it.

All I wanted was to go back to my life eight months ago—just me, Trent, Arion, Tenica and our blissful drama-free family. Was there any path back to that? Even if I lost the baby, Kelsey wouldn't let me walk away—not after what I'd just done, accusing him of rape and all. Only one journey to freedom came to mind … and it was unthinkable.

"Thank you," I said as the girl helped me to my feet.

"Congratulations." She smiled at me, picking up the test and handing it to me.

If only she knew …

"First one?" she asked.

"No, my third," I replied, hoping this was the end of our chitchat. My claustrophobia began closing in on me as I felt the floor shifting, the walls creeping in on me.

"You sure you're okay?" The girl sounded as uncertain as I felt.

"I will be once I'm home." But I wouldn't. Not until this whole thing was over.

"Well, make sure you take care of yourself, okay?"

"Yeah, I will. Thanks."

I grinned stiffly through the nerves that rumbled in my belly. My chest tightened, lungs constricting. I needed to breathe. I was sure I was having a panic attack … a suffocating, blinding fear verging on hysteria. My heart strained to pump blood, and a dizzying blackness tunneled my vision. The stark walls began leaning in on me, soon to crush me if I didn't leave right now.

I pushed through the restroom door, feeling the eyes of drugstore lurkers watching, wondering who I was—the crazy lady who passed out on the toilet. Heading straight for the front doors, I ran the rest of the way to my car, fumbling with the unlock button on my keychain until I heard the click.

Crumbling into the driver's seat, I counted rhythmically. *One, two, three, four, five …*

Inhale.

*Once I caught a fish alive …*

My brain unwittingly conjured the nursery rhyme song that Tenica was currently obsessed with singing.

Exhale.

As my chest deflated, the pungent stink of my stress breath mixed with the stale car air, nauseating me. The sounds of wheels screeching and horns honking thinned into the lull of rushing blood in my ears. The winking lights and stretch of parking lot narrowed into a spot of bare space in front of me. My head felt woozy, and I suddenly had the urge to climb out of my skin.

I needed help, but who could I turn to that wouldn't judge me? Who would keep my secret? Who would be honest with me? Who would tell me what I needed to hear? There was only one person I could bring this kind of news to, and I was pretty sure she would kill me when she found out.

# Chapter 18 - Jo

Another hopeless day passed. After talking to a couple dozen people strolling through the park, not one had anything helpful to offer. No one had seen anyone suspicious. No one recognized the man fitting the description Abby recounted—which basically described every white, brown-haired, middle-aged male in America. With every passing minute I was losing my daughter a little more, as if I was feeling her fingertips slipping out of mine.

Detective Cox had just finished fingerprinting the men's restroom at the park along with the playset where Amelia was approached by the kidnapper. He was outside the restroom packing up his equipment when he turned to me.

"Jo, I want to be straight with you, because that's the only way we can find Amelia." He frowned and continued. "But I'm probably not going to find anything from these prints. There's a lot of partials, too many people touching everything. If he used the restroom, he was probably smart enough not to leave a calling card behind. But any usable prints I'll run through the system to see if something comes up. Who knows? Maybe we'll get lucky."

"I appreciate it. I just wish there was more I could do."

"These posters are great." He held up the stack I had given him. "We'll make sure every Durham resident sees her face, okay? We'll saturate the media—TV, radio, newspapers. And there's always the possibility that he'll return her ... when he's done with her." He stuttered the last part of his sentence, and I wondered what that meant.

"When he's done with her?" I yelped.

His chest rose and he avoided meeting my glare. That's when I knew the worst was coming.

"Some men will abduct children for short-term purposes and then drop them off somewhere when they've gotten what they wanted. I don't think you want details, but the important thing is the children are returned alive. Most child abductors don't plan to kill a child. They usually have an ulterior motive. So it's very possible Amelia is alive. We just need to find the clues that will lead us to her."

I wasn't sure if this was good or bad news—that Amelia had been raped and would have to live with that for the rest of her life. Having her innocence stolen so young would change her, wouldn't it? Could she ever be the sweet, silly girl she once was? Would she remember every horrible evil committed against her chubby little body, or was she young enough to forget? I shook the thoughts away before the visuals overtook me.

"You think she was sold into a sex-trafficking ring?" I'd read about this happening, local to my very own town. Children and girls abducted and sold for a few hundred dollars to people who would hold them captive, selling them for sex. Just the idea of my daughter … going through *that* … no, I refused the thought. I felt bile rising up my throat.

"No, I'm not saying that. But if that's the situation—and that's a big if—we've alerted police to keep an eye on all highways and interstates for a girl matching Amelia's description. If whoever took her is traveling with her, someone will spot her. Her face will be on every phone, on every social media site, on all the news stations. Her kidnapper won't get far, Jo."

He sounded so sure of himself, so positive that she would be like a majority of missing children and returned safely home. But I feared the reality of that small percentage of victims who were never found … or who never made it out alive. Thanks to the media, those were the only stories I could bring to the forefront of my memory. Not the survivors. No one could know for sure how this would end, but not all little girls escaped a deadly fate. The question was: would mine?

"You mentioned clues—how do we find them?" I asked, knowing that if he had the answer, he would have already found my daughter.

"Keep asking people if they've seen her. Keep putting her picture everywhere. If there's anyone from your past that might have reason to take her, any secrets we need to know about—that's often a clue."

I didn't have secrets, no skeletons to hide—except for one. One that couldn't possibly be linked to Amelia's disappearance. That secret had been from another lifetime, and no one knew about it except for me. Certainly that blemished moment in history had nothing to do with Amelia. There was no reason to unearth a lie that had long ago died. But what about Jay? Was he hiding something? A sin that might have attracted Karma's destruction of our family? I knew my husband, adored my husband, trusted my husband—at least I *did* ... but most wives did until something changed. Until a lie unraveled that proved why we should trust no one.

I didn't want to live like that—untrusting and suspicious of everyone. But my daughter was stolen, my life upturned, and whoever did it watched from the shadows. Someone picked my Amelia out of the thousands of other little girls out there, and he did it for a reason. That reason was connected to someone we knew. I could feel it crackle through my body.

"You're assuming her kidnapper is out running around town with her. But what if she's hidden in his basement somewhere, never exposed to the public? What then?"

Silence. My question had stumped the know-all wunderkind detective. It was the dead end we both dreaded.

"We'll cross that bridge once we've exhausted every other option. For now, let's focus on seeing if anyone saw them the day she disappeared. Maybe we'll get a hit on where they were headed. We'll find her, Jo. We will."

But no matter what empty promises Detective Cox offered, one fact would always remain: my daughter, whether alive or dead, would not be returned to me the same as she was before. Trauma always left an ugly imprint, marring the soul. How damaged would her innocence be when—or if—we found her alive?

I sighed, trying my damnedest to keep my tears in check. It was getting harder and harder not to spill my fears all over myself. "So what should I do now?"

"Go home, Jo. Go home, make some tea and a sandwich, put on a television show, read a book, try to sleep—anything to distract yourself for just a few minutes from this." I opened my mouth to protest, but he held up his hand to stop me. "I know you're in pain. I know you want to do something to help us, but there's nothing you can do right now. I need you healthy. I need your brain functioning. And you can't function without sleep or food. Please, take care of yourself and your kids and let us do our job."

I shook my head, kicking a patch of dead leaves at my feet and scattering them. "You don't understand. And I hope you never have to. But I won't rest until she's in my arms." I left him standing there, trudging back to my car. I fell into my seat wearily, my eyes glancing in the rearview mirror where the pink butterflies decorating Amelia's empty car seat caught my eye. Another reminder of the emptiness in my heart.

Minutes later, as I pulled up to my house, one of the Oleander Way Powerwalkers, as I called them, waited on my front porch holding a Tupperware dish of a casserole I was sure I wouldn't eat. Marcy Grayson—the alpha dog of the pack. Her painted smile never faltered, her white teeth always sparkled, her tight body always stole men's glances, and her voluminous hair never grayed. She was a beautiful phenomenon that every woman hated and yet wanted to be.

Her piteous smile greeted me as I parked and walked up the walkway to a house that no longer felt like home.

"Hey, sweetie," Marcy said, patting me on the back like we were old chums. "How you holdin' up, hon?"

"How am I *holdin' up*? How do you think I'm *holdin' up*, Marcy?"

Her eyes, blue like a cloudless day, widened like I'd just slapped her. "Not … good?"

"You think?"

"I'm so sorry, Jo. I really am."

I looked at her, assessing her artificial frown caked in pink lipstick. She knew nothing about me, other than that I hosted bake sales for the elementary school and cheered on the sidelines at Preston's soccer games. She didn't know the depths of my broken heart, or the fear that feasted on my flesh. How dare she act like she was a friend, comforting me in my time of need? I wanted to scream at the top of my lungs that my life was destroyed, my heart ached with every excruciating moment that Amelia was gone, and it would be nice if for one second Marcy and her minions could step down from their pedestals and actually care. I wasn't a person to them; I was full-course gossip, and we both knew it. That was why she was here. Never once had she shown an ounce of interest in my life—other than my husband—until drama beckoned her like a moth to a flame. But before my anger spewed out, Jay opened the door, rescuing Marcy from an ear beating as he guided me inside with a firm hand.

"Marcy, so nice of you to stop by." Jay always had a matter-of-fact way about him—genuinely nice with a subtle professionalism. I had always liked that about him, because it left little room for misinterpretation by predators like Marcy.

"I can't imagine what you're going through. But I thought your family might need a home-cooked meal during this tough time." She handed Jay the dish while I rolled my eyes behind the cover of the door.

"You're so thoughtful, Marcy. Thanks, and we appreciate it."

"If there's anything else I can do, Jay, let me know. Me and the girls will help in any way." *Me and the girls.* It was fitting of the pretentious clique that they were.

"Just tell everyone to keep looking for our little girl. That's what we really need."

"Of course, Jay."

They exchanged goodbyes, and a moment later Jay shut the door and turned on me. "What the hell, Jo? Our neighbors are trying to be nice and you looked like you were about to bite her head off."

"Oh!" I scoffed. "Don't be fooled. Marcy just wants the scoop on the latest drama on the block to talk about at her weekly hen gatherings. She doesn't give a shit about Amelia."

"Whether Marcy's being sincere or not, does it really matter? The more people who know what's happening, the more likely someone might find her. We need every set of eyes and ears we can get. Even Marcy's."

He had a point, but I wasn't in the mood to concede.

"Maybe it's not just Marcy's sympathy you're interested in?" I shot him the glare I only reserved for our harshest of fights.

"Excuse me?"

"You heard me. Maybe you want to *dig in* to more than just her casserole."

He rolled his eyes. "You're insane."

"Am I really? Am I? Don't think I don't see you out there, showboating for the reject cast of *Desperate Housewives*, doing your *yard work*." I didn't know why I resorted to accusations, because I didn't really believe this, but I couldn't stop the venom from flowing.

"Showboating?"

"Showboating! It's 50 degrees out. What earthly reason do you need to have your shirt off? And don't try to feed me some bullshit line about you not wanting to get your nice shirts dirty, because you sure as hell had no problem wearing the brand new jeans I bought you to play soccer with Preston. Grass stains all over the knees." It had taken three washes and a bottle of stain remover to clean them, and I could still see a green remnant.

"Knock it off! Don't you try to turn this around on me."

"Turn what around?"

"*This.*"

"And what's *this*?"

"What *you've* done to our family."

And there it was. The colossal finger aimed at yours truly. The flashing neon sign above my head pulsing GUILTY in alternating crimson and clover, over and over. I knew it was coming, but it was more than I could bear. My own husband against me when I needed his support the most.

"What I did?"

"Yes, what you did! You lost our daughter! She was your responsibility. Yours. Not Abby's. Yours. You were supposed to watch her. Protect her. Keep her safe. That was your *only* job."

"You have no idea what it's like trying to keep track of three kids at once."

"Don't give me that. Preston was on the soccer field. I've seen him play, so I'm not going to believe in some enthralling performance you couldn't peel your eyes from. That just leaves Abby and Amelia, and they were together. So that's one … one place you needed to keep your attention. But no. You couldn't do that. You were off in the clouds, in your own little world, detached and unaware of everything around you."

"That's not fair." It came out a whimper. I could feel the tears coming.

"Fair? Don't give me fair. How is you losing my daughter fair? I work and slave to provide for this family, give you everything you could ever want. Your only responsibility is the children, and you let some stranger just walk off with one of them."

"And where were you? The only reason we were at the park was because of Preston's stupid soccer game. A sport you forced him to play."

"I was working! Providing for this family. Keeping you in your Pradas and Guccis, and your valets, and your Whole Foods …"

"I never wanted any of this. I never asked for any of it. I never gave you a salary requirement when we first met."

Life had been so simple back then. Money was tight, but we got by paycheck to paycheck—together. We may not have thrived, but we survived. Not all the money in the world was worth the death of our marriage.

"*Right*. Well, you certainly seem to have no problem spending it."

"Do you think this is my ideal life? To be raising three kids basically on my own with an absentee husband, who periodically graces us with his presence and leaves heavy canvas sacks full of money marked with cartoonish dollar signs on occasion?"

"Isn't it?"

"No! I don't give a shit about any of this! The cars. The clothes. The house. The money. I don't fucking care. All I want is you. The man I married. The man I fell in love with. The man I shared a shitty one-bedroom apartment with, way back when. Just you, and the family we made … together."

Was it too late to go back to that?

"I know I screwed up," I continued, my voice softer now. "And I can't fault you for blaming me, because I've been shouldering my own guilt more than you could ever assign me. Something you would have seen if you had even looked at me since it happened. It's tearing me apart. Tearing us apart, and I know it's my fault. If I can just find her, fix this, I know I can save the rest."

Silence.

As I pushed past him, he wrapped his arms around me and pulled me to his chest. I had forgotten how soft his lips were as he pressed them to my forehead, hugging me tighter.

"I feel like I'm losing you."

"That's just it, Jay. I'm lost without Amelia. We're lost."

"But you have us, babe. Me, Preston, Abby—you're not alone in this. We need you, just as much as you need us."

His lips trailed down my cheek to my lips, soft and tender and passionate and greedy. Closing my eyes, I felt our shared need as he slipped his tongue in my mouth, tugging on my lower lip with his teeth. For a moment I let myself be swept away in a hunger for affection, and I kissed him back. Until an image of Amelia, hunched in a dark cavern, entered my mind and drained the connection. The moment fizzled out as quickly as it had ignited and I pulled away.

"I'm sorry, Jay. I just can't."

I turned and left him standing there with a dull sadness in his eyes that once sparkled. I simply couldn't bring that sparkle back, not until Amelia was safe. Heading into the bedroom, I crashed onto my bed, my own little world of torture as I waited to die a little more each hour.

I didn't need or want anyone but Amelia. I don't know how the rest of my family got lost in the dark, but I couldn't see them, feel them, hear them anymore. All I heard were Amelia's cries for her mommy. All I felt were her fingers reaching out for mine. All I saw was my baby drifting away from me. I had become a ghost, wandering aimlessly, searching for a way to come home. But I couldn't come home until I found my little girl. She was my only redemption.

# Chapter 19 - Ellie

When I saw *her* I knew my life was over. She was perfect in every way. But not the short-term-fling dumb-bimbo kind of way. The gorgeous-new-trophy-wife kind of way. Long honey chestnut tresses framed a flawless face, her smile white and sparkly as she laughed at something Denny had said. Her bare arms clung to my husband in flirty possession. It was a casual grip, like she was saying, *He's mine, but I don't need to hold on too tightly because he's not going anywhere.* Her silver dress clung to her in a silky embrace, running down her perky breasts and tight butt like cool water. As I admired her taste in high fashion, I glanced down at my own oversized sweatpants and baggy T-shirt. I'd become a bum. How did this happen? It was no wonder he went looking for something more.

His new lover dressed in Neiman Marcus while I dressed in Target. Her skin was soft and supple while my creases grew deeper by the day. Her hair curled in natural wavy tendrils down to her waist while mine hung limply in a frizzy ponytail. Her laugh echoed in the streets while my sobs bounced off the car's windows.

She was light, spicy, exotic. I was dark, bitter, plain Jane. I couldn't compete. It was over.

"Who's that with Daddy?" Darla asked from the backseat.

"That's his new lover."

I hadn't meant to be so blunt, but the toxic pain slithering through me overcame any sense of discretion. The kids might as well know the truth. The end was inevitable, so I should prepare them for it.

"She's pretty. Why don't you ever look like that?" Darla asked more casually than I could handle.

"Is she going to be our new stepmom?" Logan added.

No sense of outrage. No indignation at witnessing their father's betrayal firsthand. Just a *blasé faire* acceptance.

The bite of their questions branded all-new fears on my flesh. I couldn't win Denny back no matter how hard I tried. I couldn't even win my own children back. My existence had been trampled under $2,000 Manolo Blahnik stilettos.

"It looks that way," I finally answered after a long beat.

From behind the glass, I watched Denny guide my replacement from the office door into his car, my breath steaming up the window. I wondered what life would look like as a divorcee: arranging holiday kid swaps, picking up the kids every other weekend with that twenty-something woman greeting me at the door in a sexy kimono and skin-tight tank top that my flat over-nursed boobs would never fill. And what if they had children? Their new family would gradually push me out as my children spent more time with Denny than with me, and I would become obsolete, disappearing into nonexistence.

It was the curse of motherhood—when the children turned against the one who raised them, the one who gave up everything for them. I couldn't let that happen. I would rather die than become nothing to them. But why should I be the one to die when they're the ones who abandoned me?

I became a snake shedding its skin as I fed on my anger. I dropped the mask that I hid behind, letting my inner monster loose. In a hot moment of bubbling rage, I imagined killing them all, giving the thankless leeches what they deserved. I wanted them to writhe in suffering, to drown in their tears, just like me.

It was only a fleeting thought ... that hung on just a little too long.

\*\*\*

*My emotions hop, skip, and jump from one extreme to another. One minute I want to watch the life bleed from Denny in a long, drawn-out, painful death so he can feel a fraction of what he's putting me through. Another minute I'm sobbing into my pillow, desperate to win him back.*

*I'm currently in a strategizing how-to-repair-my-marriage moment.*

*I can't give up. Not yet. I blame myself for the state of our marriage. I haven't been as attentive as I should have. I haven't met Denny's physical needs. I'm sure this is only about sex; it usually is. One look at his mistress tells me everything I need to know: midlife crisis. Denny wants strange, new, exciting. I'm stable, predictable, endearing. But I have a prediction. After one nibble of new, he'll realize his tastes haven't changed after all. It's me he's always savored. He'll come back, I know it. Because sex eventually gets old with anyone, and it's always about sex. It has to be.*

*I can't think about the alternative—that if it's not about sex, then it's about me specifically, and I just can't accept that. I've done everything for him, so how could he possibly stop loving me? No, it has to be the sex … or lack of it. This, I can fix. I'll do anything he needs for fulfillment. I just hope it's not too late to pry her claws out of my husband's flesh. If it is, I don't know what I'll do. Go crazy, I guess.*

\*\*\*

Three hours passed before Denny came home. Three hours of graphic scenes playing out in my mind, scenes of them touching, tasting, whispering, fondling, sucking. I felt my pulse quicken and my vision blur and my stomach cramp as my brain went wild with scenarios, like I was watching an amateur erotic film. It also gave me three hours to contemplate what I should do—or could do. As angry as I was with my husband, I still wanted him back. I know—stupid, ignorant girl that I was, but when you spend a lifetime with someone, when you build a family and a home and plan your future and happiness around that one person, it's not so easy to let go.

In a blink I was taken back to our wedding day. An intimate affair with only forty guests on a deserted North Carolinian beach. The lowering sun had sent most sunbathers home for the evening, casting an orange glow as our pastor wedded us, me in my $70 white gown I had found off the rack, Denny in a linen button-down shirt and drawstring pants. So young, so free-spirited, so effortless.

June had spent hours curling my hair just right, touching up my makeup to cover the sunburn I'd acquired earlier that day, and I felt like a princess marrying her prince. We had written our own vows and afterward I had stolen Denny's handwritten copy from his white pants' pocket that you could see through when the sunlight hit them just right. I had kept that folded piece of paper in my wallet ever since. Every anniversary I read it back to him while we fed each other white cake with raspberry filling and buttercream frosting, frozen and saved from our wedding reception.

Out of all the memories we'd created together, that was my favorite. And I clung to it now, wishing I could recreate it.

I dare anyone who truly feels the burning brand of love to walk away without turning back, without some last-ditch effort to regain what was lost. There is nothing simple or matter-of-fact about it. The heart wants what it wants, and mine wanted Denny, cheater or not. Love always has a cost, whether it be vulnerability or pain. Right now it was costing me both. As far as my love was concerned, his sins against me melted into the background, even though my brain saw them as flashing neon warnings about the danger that was to come.

Knowing that it could only end badly, I still needed to try to win him back. And I knew one way to do that. One irresistible, magical, heady offering that Denny would never turn down.

A streetlight set our bedroom curtains aglow when Denny walked in well past dark. Candles and fabric rose petals that I'd had since our honeymoon led a path to the master bathroom, where I had prepared a bubble bath in the Jacuzzi tub. It'd been eons since we last used the tub, a novelty that always sounded better than the effort was worth. But tonight would be different. Tonight I would wine him and win him with relaxation and overdue sex. Scenting the bathwater with drops of lavender essential oils that I had impulse bought at a neighbor's essential oil party, I finally put the purchase to use. Those damn oils would save my marriage tonight.

I heard the bedroom door close and Denny call out, "Ellie? You in here?"

"Come find me," I toyed. The bubbles nearly overflowed the tub as I pushed myself up out of the water just enough to give him a peek of bare skin. Closing my eyes, I exhaled the weight of vulnerability that pressed down on my chest. I was petrified he would reject me. But he was still my husband, still a man, still ravenously sexual.

"You taking a bath?" he said as he popped his head around the doorjamb.

"No, *we're* taking a bath—together. Come join me." I playfully splashed at him, luring him closer.

"What's gotten into you? We never take baths together." He looked at me with a crooked grin, his eyes narrowly scrutinizing me.

"No reason not to start now. C'mon. Get in. I'll massage your back—and maybe some other parts, too." I held up a bottle of massage oil and winked.

He leaned down and kissed me on the forehead. "It's sweet, but there's no room, babe. Just enjoy yourself. I'm tired anyways. Gonna watch some SportsCenter then hit the hay."

"I'm not taking no for an answer." I grabbed his wrist before he could walk away. "Please, I want to have some fun together. I promise to make it worth your while—name your fantasy." At this point I was willing to do anything—even requests I would have otherwise never even considered—to keep him. Yes, even *that*.

Denny roughly pulled his arm away from me. "Seriously, Ellie, I'm exhausted and not in the mood. It's been a long day. Maybe some other time. Okay?"

As Denny walked away, the drum of his polished dress shoes treading across the floor, I realized it was too little, too late. I had lost him, and his heart was nowhere to be found.

# Chapter 20 · June

"That'll be $23.42," the familiar girl at register nine told me while a kind, disabled man who often chatted with me started bagging my groceries—just the basics to get through the rest of the week until payday. That's how we lived, from paycheck to paycheck, but with Mike out of work, we'd be living from credit card bill to credit card bill.

In the shopping cart seat Juliet squealed to get out, while Kiki, whose hand I gripped so she wouldn't wander off as she was prone to do, wriggled free. I'd lost sight of Austin and Arabelle, then found them playing with the broken stuffed animal vending machine. I breathed a sigh of relief.

I slid my credit card through the payment slot and waited.

It buzzed angrily back at me.

"Sorry, but the payment was declined," the girl said, clearly embarrassed for me. "Do you have another form of payment?"

"Oh, uh, yeah, sorry about that." I smiled crookedly, feeling my cheeks redden. The line behind me grew as I searched through my purse for another credit card, my fingers frantic and trembling under the eyes of the growing crowd.

I pulled out another card and swiped it.

Another irritating buzz.

"Um, that one got rejected too," she said, trying to be sweet about it but annoying me nonetheless.

"Yeah, I heard the sound. It's pretty obvious," I muttered. A quick check of my vacant emergency cash pocket and my last hope was eradicated. I was out of credit cards, out of cash, out of patience, and now out of groceries. "I'm sorry." I shrugged. "I'm just going to go. Can someone put these back for me?" I waved at the bagged groceries and pulled Juliet out of the cart.

"Sure, ma'am. I'm really sorry ..." The checkout girl didn't know what to say.

I didn't know what to say either. It was utterly humiliating. I'd never be able to show my face there again.

I fumbled with the cart, trying to push it out of my way, until I was stopped by a hand on my shoulder.

"Wait, honey. Let me help you." The voice was syrupy sweet and Southern, with a hint of belittlement.

I turned around, coming face to face with Eloise Benson. To put it mildly, I detested Eloise with every fiber of my being. She wasn't just some girl Mike dated before me. She was "the one who got away," his dream girl who broke his heart and left him battered and bruised. I was Mike's rebound from Eloise, though I'd often wondered if he dreamt of Eloise while lying in bed next to me, or on top of me, for that matter.

I only recognized her from old pictures I'd found of Mike with his arm around her at a fancy Christmas party, them kissing in the Virgin Islands, her sunbathing on a Floridian white sand beach, Mike hugging her while they hiked through the Appalachian Mountains. All funded by her well-to-do parents who spoiled her with gifts and trips because they believed love could be bought. Maybe it could.

I burned every last picture I found, gleefully watching the flames lick the colorful prints as they curled up, then fell into a heap of gray ash. But the memories were still buried somewhere in Mike's brain, memories I could never disintegrate or replace with our own.

I'd found myself wondering why Mike and I never did the adventurous things he did with her, but he'd always reassure me that he didn't need that kind of entertainment with me. I was "enough," he'd say. But I usually walked away from those conversations thinking he simply didn't want it with me because he'd already given up on us.

"No thank you," I stated coldly, shrugging her manicured fingers off of my shoulder. "I'm fine."

"Oh. My. God. June Merrigan. I can't believe it's you! It's me, Eloise Benson."

I couldn't force a grin no matter how hard I tried. "Yeah, I remember."

"How's Mikey doing? And look at you—four kids? You look amazing for pushing out that many. Me, I'm still living wild and single like always." Her lips parted in a sparkly montage of condescending smirk and pitying frown.

"No kidding." I felt the pleading stare of the register girl wishing me on my way as the line behind us grew restless. "I gotta go."

"Oh! Of course. But I saw you were having card trouble. I insist on helping you out." She handed her credit card to the checkout girl. "You can put her groceries on my card."

Thrusting my arm out, I knocked her hand aside. "Absolutely not. I'm not a charity case, Eloise." There was no way I was letting this bimbo buy my children anything.

Popping her hip out, she rested her knuckles on her jutting hip bone visible beneath her cropped top, which was way too indiscreet for a woman her age. "So you'd rather keep your pride than feed your children? Oh, hush."

The blood rushed to my head so fast I swayed. How dare this woman who knew nothing about raising children accuse me of negligence! "Excuse me? Are you saying I can't take care of my own children?"

"Not that you *can't*. That you *won't*. But whatever—it's your family, not mine."

"Exactly, it's *my* family, so back off."

My adrenaline was boiling by this point, and I had no idea what I was doing or saying. With Juliet in the crook of one arm, I leaned forward and pushed Eloise with all of my frustration and resentment and jealousy and fury, smashing my hand into her big, fake boob, sending her stumbling backward into the man behind her, which then created a domino effect of bodies slamming into bodies all the way down the line.

No one said anything as I collected the kids to leave.

As I muttered a hasty thanks to the handicapped bagger for his wasted time and practically ran out of the grocery store, I wondered if that same future awaited Austin. At age five he could barely put six words together. A decent job or a wife was probably out of the question. It was inevitable I'd be taking care of him for the rest of his life, for the rest of *my* life. The dismal thought followed me out of the automatic doors and through the parking lot to the van. As I loaded the kids but no groceries to carry us through the week, I realized we had hit an all-time low and I didn't know how we could ever recover. No, we hadn't hit rock bottom. Rock bottom was high above us now.

*\*\*\**

With four kids huddled behind me, I knocked on the door of the one person I could fall apart to. The one person who knew me and *got* me. The only person who could help me push my stuffing back inside when my life was coming apart at the seams.

Ellie Harper was my eye in the tornado, my anodyne in a world gone mad.

She answered, took one glance at me, and dragged me into a hug. With arms limp at my sides, I stood there, allowed her tenderness to wash over me, then puddled into tears. I sobbed into her shoulder, my chest heaving, shoulders quaking, nose dripping for a good, long minute, until she let go and pulled me inside.

As the kids scrambled up the stairs to find Logan and Darla, I slumped onto the sofa.

"My poor Juney. Let's get some coffee in you. What's going on?" Ellie asked as she puttered around the kitchen, clinking dishes as she gathered two mugs.

"My life's in shambles, El. Mike lost his job."

"Again?" I could almost hear her eyebrows rise.

"Yeah, and I couldn't even afford groceries today. Twenty-three dollars. That's all I needed and I didn't even have that. Maxed out all my credit cards, no money in the bank. It was so embarrassing. And to make matters worse, that slut Eloise was there, rubbing my nose in it."

"Oh, Mike's ex? Yikes! How'd that go?"

"I practically took a swing at her. I think I'm losing it. I'm in a really bad place, El."

"Aw, sweetie, how much do you need?"

"No, I don't want your money. You have a family, too."

"Juney, stop. That's what friends are for—to help in times of need. Let me help you. Please. What do you need? Groceries? Give me your list."

"I don't know …" I hated to accept a handout from anyone. It meant I failed as a wife, a mother, an adult.

I thought back to my childhood, when me, my sister, and my brother grew up with a single mother—and no one else—to raise us. No father to bring in the money. No grandparents to babysit. No neighbors coming to the rescue with a bag of groceries. My mother, a hero of a woman, singlehandedly raising three children and never once accepting aid. I couldn't compete with the legacy she had created, for no matter how hard times got, she always found a way to provide. She was my blueprint for motherhood. I was supposed to stand on my own two feet, somehow make everything work out on my own. Yet her work ethic also killed my mother too soon, wiping out her life by age fifty-six.

While other grandparents lived out their golden years doting on their grandchildren, my mother slipped into an early grave. She'd carried too heavy a burden for too long, and it eventually broke her heart. Literally. I found her in her crappy apartment already dead. Cause of death: heart attack.

"No, I really should figure this out myself. I'm a grownup. It's what grownups do."

"Just because you're a grownup doesn't mean you have to be alone in everything. Sometimes being an adult means accepting help from those who love you. If you don't accept my money then I'm just going to drop bags of groceries off at your house when you're not home. Don't make me do that." She grinned and I laughed.

I couldn't turn her down. Ellie's insistence, along with her generosity, knew no bounds. I'd lost track of the number of times she had dropped by with casseroles or toys or garbage bags full of brand name clothes that her kids had outgrown— or in most cases never wore, as I cut tags off of them. She was the Giving Tree that I unknowingly kept taking from, and yet she found purpose in it, not resentment. No words could express my gratitude, though I often tried. I just didn't deserve her.

"Fine, if you insist. But I don't know when I'll be able to pay you back."

"Don't worry about it. My treat. It's actually good therapy for me to do something nice—to help someone else. See? You're reciprocating by getting my mind off my own troubles. Getting me out of my head."

Troubles—in Ellie's life? As far as I knew, she was a goddess among women, though she was oblivious to this fact. Men wanted her, women wanted to be her—envying her beauty, her lifestyle, her gorgeous home, her normal kids, her handsome husband, her stable and perfect life. What could possibly be troubling Ellie? Was her private jet out of style?

"Let me guess. Did your famous chocolate chip scones turn out too dry?" I winked, but her face remained stoic.

She averted her gaze, staring at some faraway object, telling me it was something far worse. Something real.

"Denny's cheating on me."

"What?" I couldn't have heard her right.

"With a woman half my age and twice my beauty. I'm pretty sure he's going to leave me for her. Even the kids are on his side. I can't blame him. She's gorgeous, elegant, fun. All things I'm not. I'd leave me for her."

"No, that's not possible. You must be imagining things. Denny would never cheat on you. And your kids—they adore you! You're Mom of the Year every day."

Ellie shook her head, sadness etched in tiny wrinkles I had never noticed before now.

"It's not my imagination. I have proof: receipts, lipstick stains on his shirts. I've even caught them together."

"Oh, El. I'm so sorry." I grieved with her, pulling her into a comforting embrace, a stifled sob escaping her lips.

"It's all a lie—my whole life. I never told you Logan got kicked out of school—permanently. I played it off like it was just a temporary suspension, but he's done. Stuck at home with me and hating every minute of it. And now Denny doesn't love me anymore. The kids tell me they want a new mom, saying how beautiful and cool Denny's mistress is and how I'm not. I have no job, no worth in this family. I can't compete. And I don't want to compete. I just want … I want to die, Juney."

I couldn't believe what I was hearing. All the secrets, the lies— why would she hide this from me?

"Why didn't you tell me this stuff? Here I go thinking everything's perfect and meanwhile you're going through a rough time and I haven't been here for you. This is what best friends are for, so we don't have to go through it alone."

She shook her head. "I don't know why I was secretive about it. I guess I didn't want you to think I was messed up."

"You mean like me? Hey, at least we can be messed up together." I chuckled, but we both knew the truth behind the joke. Both of us had left our families to follow our husbands to a place where we would end up isolating ourselves from the only people who cared about us. We were fortunate we at least had each other, but it was hard to feel lucky when life continued to crumble.

"I just can't deal with Denny, with the kids anymore. I'm done. I'm just tired of feeling unloved, unwanted, unappreciated. I just want it to be over."

Ellie, in all her glorious flawlessness, was giving up. If Ellie had no chance of happiness, what did that mean for the rest of us? What hope did I have?

"Don't you dare say that! You'll get him back. And your kids are just … kids. My kids say stupid things all the time."

"It's not just kid talk, though, June. They really seem to despise me lately. They were with me when I caught Denny in the act, and they were happy for him."

"No. I'm sure that can't be it. Maybe they're hitting puberty early. I hear the teen years are a bitch." I forced a laughed, trying to lighten the mood, but Ellie remained silent. Contemplative. Sad.

Ellie picked at the shredded seam of her Target yoga pants, a new look for her. Normally she dressed Ann Taylor Loft; even her workout clothes were Victoria Secret sexy. The wrinkled shirt and scruffy pants reflected the state of her soul—tattered and worn out.

"I don't think I want him back. It's over. And the kids—they've never liked me. They tolerate me because I'm their mother, but they don't love me. We've never had that connection that other moms have with their kids. It'd be better if I just left the picture."

"Just because you're not a warm and fuzzy mother doesn't mean there's no love there. Look at me and my hellions—it's constant chaos and loudness and tears. But we still love each other." As I said this, though, a dark cloud hovered beneath the words. Sure, there was a pool of love somewhere inside me, but it had grown awfully shallow lately, and hard to find. With Austin's autism struggles, Arabelle's defiance, and the two little ones who constantly vied for attention, my well of love was tapped dry. What was once a lake—I'd never quite felt the ocean that other moms did—was now a stagnant puddle, the source having been insufficient for the constant siphon until it fully desiccated. Now with each subsequent draw, the shores receded further and further, with nothing to replenish it. Some days I found it impossible to face them. Almost daily the urge to flee chased me. Or worse. But I couldn't escape them; my children had become my prison, my husband my jailer, and my life the executioner of my soul.

It was a horrible, unthinkable feeling as a mother, but it was as real as the conversation I was now having.

"I don't know how you do it, Juney. With all the burdens you have to carry … I would have given up long ago. You're a tough *chica*."

I smiled feebly. I wasn't tough at all. I crumbled a little more each day as my edges became sharp crags. I don't know how I hid it so well. "I've got you. You're my strength. And I'll be your strength, okay? We'll get through this crap together."

"But what if I don't want to get through it?"

Ellie left me lingering on that thought as she got up to refill our coffee cups. The scariest part was that I had no idea what Ellie's ominous question meant. Could my secret be hers as well?

# Chapter 21 · Jo

Detective Tristan Cox had fed me lies. "We'll find her," he had told me. "We'll do everything in our power to bring Amelia home," he had promised. Three days had passed and my baby was still missing. Though no one said it, I knew what that meant.

There was little chance I'd ever see her again ... unless it was at the morgue.

It was early afternoon when Detective Cox knocked on my door, sending me running to answer it. When I saw it was him, I wasn't sure whether to be devastated or elated. But he was empty-handed, which couldn't be a good sign.

"Let's sit down," he said as he sailed in, leading me into my own living room like I was a lost puppy.

And yet I obediently followed him, a sense of dread flowing in my wake.

We both sat on the sofa, him next to me, slightly turned to face me. I appreciated that he didn't try to distance himself from me, though I wasn't sure why it mattered.

"Do you have news?" I asked. I wanted news. And yet I didn't.

He sighed before he spoke, a heavy groan that meant no. "Nothing yet. We couldn't pull any prints from the park, but we hadn't expected to turn up anything from those anyways. We've sent out an Amber Alert with her picture all over the news and social media. We'll need to wait and let that gain some traction, then hopefully we'll hear something."

"*Hopefully?*" I choked on the word. "*Hopefully* isn't good enough, Detective. *Hopefully* isn't going to bring my daughter home."

"Everyone's looking for her. There's only so many resources at our disposal. But we've contacted every police department in the area, and we'll all keep looking until we find her. Please don't give up hope, Jo."

I didn't know what to say or feel anymore. Was a part of my past linked to Amelia's abduction? That possibility gnawed at me—especially after the letter I had received earlier that morning. It was nothing, yet maybe something. I hadn't told anyone about it. It would destroy my already devastated life. But the timing couldn't be ignored. I hadn't even known his name and suddenly now, amid Amelia's disappearance, he contacted me. Was it coincidence? Or was it a clue?

The silence between us lengthened as I pondered the significance of the letter. The postmark was three states away—a Pennsylvania zip code. If he was eight hours away, how could he have orchestrated a kidnapping? And why? It didn't make sense that he was involved. Yet I knew, I just knew I needed to tell Detective Cox, but if I did … I couldn't fathom the aftermath of the truth coming out.

"Are you okay?" he asked me.

I nodded numbly. I wasn't okay. Not even close to okay.

"Is there something you need to tell me?" he probed. The guilt must be written on my face. I wondered if Jay had seen it too.

I shook my head, felt my tear ducts swell, ready to gush. As if looking down from above, I watched myself unravel. My skin felt clammy, and I was one breath away from sobbing on this man's shoulder. I was alone in this battle for my child. I couldn't face my demons and I couldn't save my child.

Jay hadn't even bothered to call off work today—he'd already taken too many days off this year, he claimed—and I was left to deal with cops and flyers and press calls on my own. And naïve Preston and Abby—they had no idea what to think of all this. At age seven Pres understood a bit of what was going on, that his sister was missing, but he didn't recognize the evils of the world. He just thought she'd gotten lost.

Abby, only five, didn't comprehend much of anything. She knew her little sister was gone, but she kept thinking she'd just show up at the front door. How do you explain rape and murder to a child? Even my own stomach couldn't tolerate it.

So I was left to digest the reality of my worst fears on my own. Every day I fought for Amelia alone. Every night I tossed and turned with visions of her being tortured, alone, in the dark. Here I floundered, on my own isolated island of anguish. I yearned for a comforting embrace. A tender kiss. A man's touch.

"Do you have children, Detective?"

He shook his head. "No, I don't. But I've seen this scenario enough times to sort of understand what you're going through."

"And do you find most of the kids who go missing?"

With a shrug he said, "Most of them, yes. It's often a family member who kidnaps a child."

I couldn't keep from asking the unaskable. "Do you think Amelia is still alive?"

He rested his hand on my shoulder. The warmth of his touch tingled my skin through my shirt. "I hope so."

I looked up at him, mere inches away, and saw genuine caring in his eyes. He wanted to find my baby as much as I did. I was sure of this. Our connection buzzed, and I closed my eyes against it. Yet I needed to feel alive. The motion happened before I knew what I was doing—my subtle lean into him, my hand rising to cup his chin. I couldn't pull back until my lips met his with just a whisper of a kiss … and then it was too late.

He jerked back, startled by my advance.

"Jo, I understand you're hurting, but—" He stopped, unable to put words to what just happened.

Embarrassed, my cheeks flooded with a warm blush that spread down my neck. "I'm so sorry. I don't know why I did that."

"You're hurting. You're just trying to find comfort. I'm not upset. I just can't, y'know?"

I was mortified, speechless. "I don't even know what to say. I'm not myself." I turned away from him, hiding the tears that welled in my eyes. What was happening to me? Who was I without Amelia?

"Hey, Jo," he soothed, approaching me from behind. "Go easy on yourself. You've got to stay optimistic, okay? Don't fall apart on me."

"It's been over three days now. I've seen the stats on finding her alive after two days. It's not good. What hope do I have, Detective?" I turned to him, searching him for the truth, no matter how harsh or ugly.

He looked at me with pity and shook his head. "I don't know."

All along I had sensed my daughter's life force, knew she was out there waiting for me. It's what drove me with an obsession to do anything and everything to find her at any cost. But then comes that moment a mother feels the soul connection to her child dissipate. In this moment Amelia's presence lifted from my heart, and I knew the worst was done. I felt her departure, and I crumbled to the floor.

# Chapter 22 - Ellie

*M*y body aches. My head throbs. My brain is exhausted. All day my thoughts circle round and round, wondering what Denny is doing now, if he's with her, what she's like, whether she makes him happy, what he plans to do with me, what about the kids, what about our home, what about our future. The cycle is grueling, and yet I can't stop its centripetal force.

These thoughts, they torment me. I'm pretty sure my own mind is out to get me. Am I crazy for still loving him, regardless of all his abhorrent behavior? Or is he the crazy one, picking some cheap slut over a wife who adores him and would do anything and everything for him? I suppose it doesn't matter who's crazy, does it? In the end I'm going to lose everything while Denny saunters off into the sunset with that fake-boobed charlatan draped on his arm. Over my dead body.

I've decided to end it. I can't stomach the idea of him leaving me, a husk I don't recognize anymore. Like a vulture picking at a carcass, he's consumed every last shred of my identity and left me with nothing but brittle bones. I can't let that slide.

We'll be together once more tonight. It'll be special, romantic, passionate, vulnerable, intense, purifying ... and it will mold us as one for eternity. We've lived together, now we'll die together, and we'll be remembered together. I didn't want it to come to this, but I'm weak. Oh, I'm painfully weak. I had no idea how pathetic I was until now. My life value clings solely to a man who loathes me, resents me, doesn't give a crap about me. How could I let this happen to myself? How could I wrap myself so tightly around him that I suffocated my very own existence, leaving me dead without his breath through me? He did this to me.

*I'm ashamed of what I am—his puppet. Once upon a time I had dreams, personality, passion, ideas. Now my dreams have become nightmares. My ideas are insanity. All I can think about is putting this lie of a life out of its misery, razing this toxic marital badland. And I'm not going alone.*

\*\*\*

The sting of rejection hung on me like cheap perfume. For the entire day I'd managed to plaster a pleasant smile on my face. "Sweetie pies" and "love yous" dripped from my lips like honey. Behind this mask was a grotesque caricature of the dutiful wife and mother I used to be. I didn't recognize myself anymore through the haze of anger and the lust for revenge that twisted in my gut like a knife.

Outwardly I was as placid as a country lake. But in my murky depths lurked a beast that time forgot, secret and savage, with a thirst for blood. No one could see it, no one could sense it, but it was there, patiently waiting for the right time to show itself, to feast.

Tonight was that time.

I had planned it all out. As painless as possible, but final. I'd spare the children this fate, though maybe that was the greater reprisal. Let them understand loss, sending them off into the system, make them appreciate what they had. But no, not Denny. And not myself. I'd give us a death scene worthy of Romeo and Juliet to commemorate our twelve years together. It was hardly anything compared to the marriages of many others I knew. Some celebrating twenty years, others forty. And yet Denny could barely surpass a decade with me. Now it was out of his hands. We'd be together for eternity, whether he liked it or not.

Out on the veranda he waited for me. I'd nearly begged him to come home on time tonight, to which he finally agreed after a brief debate. When I saw his car pull up the driveway, I ushered the kids upstairs to watch a movie and eat candy and popcorn, which immediately put a stop to their fussing over what I was making for dinner. Then I fluffed my hair, touched up my lipstick, gulped two glasses of liquid courage, and waited.

I had lined the entryway with scented candles and rose petals that led to the sliding glass door—and me on the other side of it in a saucy little pose. More candles illuminated the space with a soft glow while jazz played from my iPod. For dinner, filet mignon, sour cream mashed potatoes, and grilled teriyaki Brussels sprouts—Denny's favorite, and the kids' least favorite—followed by an almond cream cake topped with honey-roasted almonds. As the kids happily settled into their playroom sofa, each holding a tub of buttered popcorn with a side dish of M&Ms, I led Denny to his seat on the veranda for a night of fine dining, seduction, and our last goodbye.

The poison was the hard part to figure out. After a little research, I discovered the oleander tree in our very own backyard was the perfect weapon. Named after the trees that grew wild in our neighborhood, Oleander Way was brimming with them. I was amazed our HOA hadn't outlawed them due to their poisonous properties. Crushing a handful of leaves and flowers into a paste, I let them soak in the wine bottle, along with a dose of antifreeze for good measure. All day the bottle sat, taunting me with the inevitable closure it would give me.

We were now mere moments away from the grand finale.

The table was set with our fine white china trimmed in silver, crystal glasses of poisoned red wine poured, meal steaming hot and meat perfectly cooked—Denny's medium, mine medium-rare. With knife and fork in hand, he glanced up at me and smiled. Oh, the power of his smile! I melted like butter under a hot sun when he looked at me like that. Even now, brooding with hatred toward him, I found myself slightly wooed.

"You've outdone yourself, gorgeous."

Damn him and his charm.

"What's the occasion, babe?" he asked, savoring a mouthful of steak. "And you look amazing, by the way."

It was an afternoon-long process perfecting my hair and makeup, picking just the right dress that looked appropriate for a dinner at home but sexy enough to make him want me again. The sleek green silk matched my eyes and complemented my shiny auburn hair. I looked as good as I felt, which was a new sensation for me.

"Thanks, honey. No occasion—I just wanted a nice dinner together. I felt we were overdue."

He leaned over and kissed me, a tinge of my lipstick staining his lips.

"Well, I'm glad you did. I wanted to talk to you about something."

"Oh?" My nerves sizzled at the cryptic tone. Was he about to confess everything? Was he planning to officially break up? I couldn't let him say it. I needed more time. I only wanted one good last memory. Why was Denny so insistent on stripping that from me?

That's when I realized it was all a fantasy. I wouldn't get the last date night I had wanted. It was over before it had begun. Skip to the end—that was the only choice I had left.

"Before I say anything, I want to make a toast." He hoisted his wine glass and I lifted up my own.

It would only take a few minutes for the poison to work its way into the bloodstream, delivering a deceptively pleasant tipsiness and slurred conversation. That was when my plan to have one last night together would begin. We'd suffer together throughout the night as the headache set in, then the cramps and nausea and dizziness. By early morning we'd experience delusions as our heart rates slowed to a deadly lull. In a seamless crescendo we'd both fall into an endless sleep, together, dying as one. A perfect end to a perfect misery.

Denny's eyes glossed over, and I saw raw emotion in them.

"To the most beautiful woman I know. I haven't treated you the way you deserve, Ellie, but today I want to change that. I want to be the man you married—the man you fell in love with."

I sat in shock, uncertain about the changing tide of the evening. It sounded as if he was recommitting himself to me, to us. If he'd ended the affair, I could move past it. I loved him more than I loved myself. Was everything better? Or was I misreading him?

If Denny still wanted to salvage our marriage, I would forgive him. I could get past the cheating, the lies, the deception. Together we would figure it out. Maybe there was hope for us after all. Maybe it wasn't too late. Or was this all just more lies? Was I letting myself be duped yet again? Just for him to hurt me for another round? I had to decide. Now. Continue onward to this final goodbye, or fall back and try again. There was really only one true answer in my heart of hearts.

Denny clinked his glass against mine, but as he tipped his glass up to sip the poisonous concoction, I dropped my glass to the patio floor, the glass shards scattering at our feet.

"Oh shoot!" I yelped.

Denny set his glass down and jumped up. "It's okay, hon. I'll clean it up. You sit and enjoy the amazing meal you cooked."

"Are you sure?" I cooed.

"Absolutely. Sit tight while I get something to clean this up."

Denny ran into the house while I sat there, relieved I had stopped him in time. While Denny was inside, I heard his phone chirp. There it sat, on the table before me, with a new text. I wondered if it was *her*. I'd never found damning evidence on his phone before since he deleted his text history almost hourly—a suspicious act in itself. Maybe it was a small mercy. The thought of subjecting myself to the sexting and sickening endearments between my husband and his whore stayed my hand. Not to mention, Denny zealously guarded his phone, never letting it out of his sight. Until now.

Checking behind my shoulder, I figured I'd have enough time to take a quick peek while Denny found the broom, so I picked up his phone and swiped across the screen to unlock it. A message from a mysterious "JW" scrolled across the screen. The phone immediately opened up the text history, so I scrolled up to the top to read it from the beginning of the conversation:

Denny: I'm sorry, but I need to end things. I can't keep doing this. Please forgive me, but I want to fix things with Ellie. She doesn't deserve this. Goodbye.

JW: Are you kidding me? You are NOT going to break up with me over a text! You talk to me face to face like a man.

Denny: There's nothing more to say, Janyne. It's over. Don't contact me again.

Gotcha. So her first name was Janyne. I mentally catalogued it for future use. And then the text that had just come through:

JW: If you think you can avoid me, just wait until I show up at your house and introduce myself to your wife. You can't just walk away from me like we didn't share something special. If you try to end things, I will take you and your whole family down with me. Choice is yours. See you tomorrow … or else.

What did that threat even mean? Was she really planning to confront me with her husband-stealing, home-wrecking confession and expect me to just give up? If that was the case, I'd be ready for her. I wasn't afraid to pull her hair, slap her face, or bite her. If Janyne wanted a catfight, she'd get a catfight. I couldn't guarantee that Denny would end up picking me, I couldn't ensure my children would ever think I was hip, but one thing I knew deep down in the marrow of my bones: I would go down fighting.

I clicked on her name and revealed her cell phone number. Maybe I could even have a little fun with her. I grabbed my phone and typed in her number to text her. I hit the letters so fast and hard it was a wonder I didn't crack my screen:

Ellie: I know who you are, Janyne. Absolutely no one. You think you have Denny's heart, but you're wrong. He doesn't love you, never has, never will. Save yourself from looking foolish and walk away while your kneecaps are still intact.

I hit "send" and watched the message zoom off into cyberspace. It was the first time I'd ever done anything so confrontational, and it felt exhilarating. Or it could have been the two glasses of wine I'd already chugged before Denny got home that made me feel like I was on top of the world.

My elation ended with an abrupt *beep*.

So you're the bitch he's always complaining about. If anyone's been the fool, it's you. Your own husband cheating on you and you just take it. How noble. It sounds like you're threatening me. If you want to play rough, you have no idea what I'm capable of. But I'll be happy to show you.

Suddenly I regretted instigating a war with an enemy I was not prepared to fight.

# Chapter 23 - Shayla

I had called in sick, still buried beneath my 500-thread-count Egyptian cotton sheets and turquoise Pottery Barn comforter that I'd bought two hours and six hundred dollars ago. Alleviating my turmoil with a home décor shopping spree and maxing out my credit card on wall art and more baskets than I knew what to do with, I figured what the hell. I deserved something nice for once—my internal excuse I used any time I bought something I shouldn't have.

Trent would have a fit when he got home from work, his black, oily eyes narrowing into angry slits when he saw what I'd splurged on this time—especially after a new sofa had been delivered only yesterday. But I didn't give a shit. I was going to ride out this storm in style.

After tossing the incriminating pregnancy test in the across-the-street neighbor's trashcan by the curb, I decided to live in denial for the rest of the day … or maybe the whole nine months. I couldn't deal with the bastard child of an affair growing inside my belly. I needed it gone, but the nausea that sent me to the toilet every couple hours reminded me that it wasn't going anywhere … unless I terminated it. It was an option, wasn't it?

Pulling my blanket up to my face, I inhaled the sweet fresh linen scent. It reminded me of when I'd first brought Arion home from the hospital. A tiny, dark baby with jet-black hair swaddled in freshly laundered baby blankets. I hadn't put him down for two straight days, as if he was a new limb I had grown. I'd never felt such love, like my heart would burst with it. I could never find the words to explain it to Trent, that sense of awe and pride and bliss you feel when you push the baby out and hear that scream that tells the world he's alive. Men could never understand it, after carrying a baby for nine months, finally meeting that newborn face to face.

I had spent months imagining what those tiny fists that pummeled my bladder looked like, or what those skinny legs stretching from my pelvic bone to my ribs would kick like once outside of my womb. For nine months I planned, imagined, felt every moment of the baby's life. And here I was, pregnant with another. I couldn't go through with giving it up, no matter how much I hadn't wanted it five minutes ago. Because right now I wanted this baby with every fiber of my being. But the cost … I couldn't begin to calculate the cost of keeping it.

Up until now I'd been able to hide my trysts. But this was a secret that I'd have to confess with each month of my growing belly. This baby was a nail in my marital coffin.

A roiling in my stomach sent me running for the toilet, where I dry-heaved for several agonizing minutes until my body was too weak to purge the dry cereal I'd eaten an hour earlier. As I hung my head over the ceramic bowl, the doorbell rang.

Who could that possibly be? If it was Kelsey I was going to kill him. He was very possibly the reason I was in this condition, putting murder on my mind.

Again the bell rang, a chipper chime that zapped my nerves.

I shuffled my way to the front door, wondering what doom awaited me on the other side. I opened it and gasped.

"Bev?"

My sister, Beverley Hopper, both my friend and enemy. We were so different yet so alike. Her the goody-goody, me the rebel. But both of us stubborn as mules. She whisked past me, nearly spinning me off my axis.

"You didn't have to come over," I mumbled. Of course she had to—it was in her nature to get involved. If there was drama, you could bet Bev was sniffing around nearby to help, in her own high-handed way. She fed on drama like a mosquito on blood.

"Sure I did. You called me. You're in trouble, so here I am."

That was Bev—matter-of-fact and to-the-point. A diamond in the rough with a heart of gold and entertaining quirks out the wazoo. Despite our sisterly rivalry, I loved her more than anything. I owed her my life. I even respected her, a sentiment I didn't dole out often.

Bev raised me when our alcoholic mother couldn't. While Mom slept off another drinking binge, Bev cooked hotdogs to fill our grumbling tummies. When Mom missed another shift at work due to a hangover, Bev skipped school to stock shelves at the local Food Lion to cover our rent. Through good and bad we carried each other, though the bad seemed to surface more frequently than the good.

Bev knew me too well to leave me alone right now. She'd seen the worst of my bipolar disorder, when the meds mellowed out my manic episodes but also zombified me when I felt depressed. My sister was the calm but firm hand on my shoulder.

Her short wavy hair appeared freshly trimmed and styled as it shined a chocolate brown. Her cheeks were rosy red as if she'd run all the way to the door. Pushing her wire-rimmed glasses up, she plopped her overstuffed purse to the floor, swung her beige coat off her shoulders, and hustled me to the sofa.

"Tell me everything." It was more a demand than a request as she shoved me onto the cushion, then dropped down next to me.

"There's nothing more to tell. I told you the situation—I was having an affair, I got pregnant, I'm not sure who the baby's daddy is, and now I gotta deal with it."

"Jeez, Shayla, you act like this is no big deal. You're ruining your life and sitting here talking about it like it's a grocery list." Bev's brow furrowed as she pursed her lips at me.

"What do you expect me to do? Bemoan my crap-ass decision-making skills? You can thank Mom for passing that trait on to me, by the way."

Her eye roll told me what she was thinking. "Don't blame Mom for your stupidity. You learned that all on your own."

"You're not making me feel better, you know."

"I'm not here to make you feel better about cheating on your husband. I'm here to tell you to get your act together and fix this."

"This is why I didn't want to drag you into it. I should just deal with it on my own."

"You don't have to deal with it *alone*, Shay."

Bev stood and bustled to the kitchen, her hands quickly grabbing mugs, teabags, and creamer. After setting a kettle of water on to boil, she fell back into the sofa, tucked her legs up under her, and stared at me.

"What?" I grumbled.

"I'm curious what your plans are. You cheated on your amazingly perfect husband and now you're pregnant. What now?"

I groaned irritation. "I don't know. That's the whole reason I'm freaking out. Should I tell Trent? Should I tell Kelsey?"

"It would be a good idea to let your home-wrecker know, just in case you need a paternity test."

I had forgotten to mention to Bev that I had accused Kelsey of raping me, so I doubted he'd be interested in fathering a child with me. Even if he did, the feeling wasn't mutual. I wanted him as far away from me as possible.

I knew he was pissed when he called me after leaving the station to say they let him go and he wasn't going to let my little game go unchallenged. I wasn't sure what that meant other than I knew it wasn't the last I'd see of him. But it was a minor detail I'd keep to myself. I had enough on my plate to deal with, and anything more would only send Bev into an overbearing frenzy.

"And by the way, Trent isn't as perfect as you seem to think he is."

"You wouldn't know because you're blind to how incredible he is."

"And how would you know how incredible *my* husband is?"

Bev sat in uncomfortable silence. I watched as she glanced away, chipping at her peeling nail polish.

"Bev?" I said again, trying to break through her avoidance. "Do you … love Trent?"

She coughed, and that's when I caught a glimpse. Her eyes moistened with emotion. I recognized that look. I used to look that way at Trent, long ago. Back before a house mortgage and full-time jobs and kids. My own sister was in love with my husband.

"Answer me!" I demanded.

Sorrow flooded her eyes as she finally looked up at me. The whistle of the kettle jarred us both, and Bev beat me to the kitchen to pour mugs of steaming chai. She scooped heaps of sugar into each cup, a drizzle of milk, then carried them over to the living room. She sat one down in front of me and nursed the other before speaking.

"I'm sorry, but yes. I've loved Trent since I met him. But you got to him first. You won, I lost, and now you're treating him like garbage. I just don't get it. You have no idea what you have."

I remembered the day we'd met Trent. We'd been on a girl's night out, karaokeing at the local bar. There Trent sat, dressed in black, his charcoal hair slicked back in a sexy pompadour like a James Dean throwback, his face smooth and his grin mischievous like a boy's, but his charm well cultured like a man's. That night Bev and I flirted, teased, and eventually invited him to buy us drinks all night, which he generously did.

The liquid courage led from one thing to another, and within an hour I was Olivia Newton-John to Trent's John Travolta as we belted out a *Grease* medley. By early morning the three of us found ourselves at his apartment—a total bachelor pad with a few pieces of mismatched furniture and nothing to eat—chatting about life, love, and dreams.

That night Trent picked me, not Bev; he kissed me, not Bev. And while she hadn't shown the bitter regret then, it came pouring out now.

"You found the most amazing man. How could you ever let him go? How could you betray him? If only he'd have picked me … I would have never hurt him like this."

Bev hadn't found anyone worth marrying after that night, though the dates lined up for a chance throughout the years.

She was beautiful, passionate, intelligent, and any man's dream woman. But she was picky—too picky to settle for anyone who wasn't Trent, apparently.

"I didn't mean for things to turn out this way," I pleaded. But how did one capture a marriage steeped in disappointment in words? "It wasn't something I set out to do. Trent and I have been growing apart; Kelsey filled in the gaps. Sometimes shit just happens."

"Getting pregnant by another man just *happens*?" she retorted.

"First of all, I don't know that Kelsey is the father. Trent could be. Which is why I don't know what to do."

"Whatever." Bev rolled her eyes.

"And secondly, if you'd actually commit to a man for more than three seconds, you might actually know what it's like for a relationship to decay. To become just roommates. Strangers that pass in the hall on the way to the john. It's always new and exciting for you because you never settle down. Try living with the same person day in, day out and have kids and chaos and financial stresses and months on end without a night out, much less a good banging, and rushed dinners and falling asleep in front of the tube nearly every night like two fossils in an old folks' home … You have no idea!"

"Oh, I feel so sorry for you," she scoffed.

"I'm not asking for pity. I'm just tellin' you how it is. After a few years it gets hard, especially when you're never in the same place at the same time, and you've said all there is to say to each other. The kids make it so you are both so drained caring for their constant, incessant needs, you can't fathom meeting another's in that one hour of downtime before sheer exhaustion drags you into a restless slumber. And then it starts all over again. Day after mind-numbing day."

Bev watched me with skepticism, because she had no idea what I was talking about. How could she? She never lived it.

"Then a cute guy tells you you're beautiful and amazing— something you haven't heard in years—and it's easy to fall for it.

It's new and exciting and mysterious. And suddenly you're desirable again after so many years of just feeling old hat. But you wouldn't know anything about that because you've never been in the trenches with another person. You've never been to battle with someone—which I've done for years. For you, it's always new. It's always special. Did I mess up? Yes. But you could never understand why until you're in my marriage, in my life, in my battle."

Nothing but crickets.

I had shut her up, something I had thought was an impossible feat. We both knew there was nothing left to say. But Bev wouldn't leave without getting the last word.

"I'm just warning you because I love you, but if you don't start being honest with Trent and yourself, you're going to lose it all—Trent, the kids, everything. You've been warned."

And with that cryptic threat hanging in the air, my sister stormed out of the house, taking my breath away with her.

# Chapter 24 - Jo

*M*y darling Josephine:
    *I must have tried to write you a hundred letters over the past ten years, and yet I could never figure out how to start them. I miss you. I never got over you. And yet I hate you for holding my heart captive for all these years.*

*You're probably surprised to hear from me after a decade. You may not even know who I am. I doubt you can even recall my face. No matter. I've remembered for the both of us. While you've moved on to play house with the man you never should have married, having children that should have been mine, I've kept your little secret. I've protected your little fantasy life, which should have been with me.*

*It may sound crazy that our one night of passion has lingered so long for me. Maybe, just maybe, it's lingered as long for you too. I can hope. It must. Maybe you remember seeing me across the bar, one week before your wedding, desperate to get out of your marital obligation. Your eyes were rimmed with tear-smeared mascara. Even in your pain I found you hauntingly beautiful. I can close my eyes and still picture you—the way your black top hugged your breasts, your curly hair framing your face, your cheeks flushed with the warmth of alcohol. You swayed in my arms that night, and you've been swaying in my memory ever since.*

*Maybe it was the postcoital conversation in the back of my car that hooked me. As you cuddled in the crook of my arm, we shared laughter and life stories. Our dreams for the future. Our future. The unspoken agreement that we would find a way to be together. Or maybe it was your incredible mind that has kept you in my thoughts. Or maybe it's because I've spent seven lonely years in prison filled with regret over letting you go so easily. Whatever the case, I haven't forgotten your smile, your laugh, or the way it felt to be inside you.*

*You told me that night that you'd never before felt the passion and connection that we had. I felt it too. It took me a while to recognize that's what we had, but I finally understood. I hope it's not too late to reclaim our destiny together. Do you remember the way our bodies melted into each other, blurring the lines of where you stopped and I began? I do. I relive it every night as I fall asleep. Memories are all I have to keep me going some days. But the memories we created are worth living for.*

*I've often wondered if you miss me too. Do you even know my name? I don't know if we'll ever see each other again, but I hope to someday. Even if only to lay eyes on your face one last time and hold you in my arms again.*

*Thinking of you forever and always,*

*J*

I refolded the letter for the umpteenth time and shoved it in my underwear drawer, where I'd kept it hidden for the past month after I'd gotten it. My name and address scribbled messily on the front, no return address. Just a Pennsylvania postmark from a town I couldn't remember anymore.

If only I had been more lucid that night ten years ago, maybe I would have remembered J's name, maybe I wouldn't have slept with him in a cold-feet self-destructive moment of panic mere days before my wedding. Maybe I wouldn't have been crying after the silly fight I'd had with Jay about the wedding flower arrangements getting mixed up because he hadn't called to confirm our order like I asked him to.

Odd how I clung to the memory of that fight when it really didn't matter. Who cared what my bouquet looked like? No one would remember. I couldn't even remember. And yet I could remember every detail of the ensuing argument. I couldn't ignore the irony of how angry I was at him about it in the moment, when it was such an insignificant detail compared to the bomb I would detonate that same night in the arms of another man.

For years I hated myself for that night, the night I became a fraud, and I often teetered on the verge of confessing everything to Jay simply to alleviate the guilt. But I always came back to the same conclusion—that destroying my family wasn't worth a free-and-clear conscience. This was my burden to bear in order to keep my family whole. Yet it wasn't whole anymore, was it?

I hadn't realized it a month ago when I pulled the envelope out of the mailbox, curious who would be sending me an anonymous letter. Then I read it, and now the words changed everything. Clearly our drunken tryst wasn't as meaningless for him as it was for me. What if he had something to do with Amelia's disappearance? Although he sent this from three states away, what if he was here now? He clearly knew where I lived, and knew way more about my life than made me comfortable.

I had to confess—no matter what it cost me. If there was a chance he was behind the abduction, I had to find out. But I had nothing—no last name. No first name even, just an initial J. He had mentioned doing time in prison. I wondered how hard it would be to search for prison records for everyone whose first name started with J, to see what information popped up; maybe I'd recognize his name if I saw it. A ridiculous thought, I know. Of course, he might not have used his real name that fateful night, and damn if I could recall if he'd even mentioned it. Still, I might remember him from his mug shot, but that whole night was such a rum-induced blur, and I doubted he looked the same as he did ten years ago. Right now the idea of blindly searching through inmate records felt too daunting to deal with. Reliving the past was exhausting.

I shut the drawer and shuffled to the window.

Rain spattered against the windowpane, dropping like tears from the eyes of God above. If there was even a God watching. How could there be, with everything He was letting happen to me, to my little girl? There couldn't be.

I had always been spiritual—thanking God every Sunday morning, every night during prayers, every dinnertime meal. I'd even talked to God in the spare quiet moments while in the shower, or while power-walking in the evenings through the neighborhood in my Victoria's Secret leggings and oversized T-shirts, my ear buds cycling through my iPod workout playlist. My neat ponytail swinging merrily while I tossed a friendly wave to every neighbor I spotted or car that passed by.

That was life before.

This was life now:

I hadn't slept in four days. My hair was so matted I couldn't run a brush through it, nor did I even try to, giving a whole new meaning to the term "dirty blond." My toothbrush sat in its ceramic holder, unused, for days, but my teeth weren't collecting tartar because I wasn't eating anyways. But never-ending mugs of coffee left behind a subtle brown tint, and I was pretty sure I felt a cavity taking over my back molar. I couldn't tell the freckles on my nose and cheeks from the grime. The same sweatshirt and sweatpants I wore for the past four days were stained and reeked, but I didn't care. My daughter was out there—dirty, scared, and hungry. Why should I deserve anything more?

I kicked God to the curb along with all the other crap I no longer believed in. Like myself. Like living.

Hiding in the bedroom, I couldn't stand the sound of Preston and Abby playing and giggling as if their sister was there with them. How could they even smile during a time like this? Anger frothed up inside me, popping like little bubbles of fury. I didn't want to be angry with them. In my head I knew they were just kids—only seven and five, what could I expect?—and they didn't understand the magnitude of what Amelia's disappearance meant. That she could be dead. Gone forever.

I loved my kids, but their callousness poked at me. I reminded myself again and again that they didn't understand. They were just children, unaware of the horrors their sister was facing. I spent their lifetimes shielding them from such truths, and yet here I was, needing them to suddenly face the world's atrocities for my own comfort.

What was wrong with me? Why couldn't I handle this? Why couldn't I save Amelia? Why couldn't I nurture Abby and Preston anymore? My brain was no longer navigating my actions; instead, a primal urge to find Amelia controlled every thought, every impulse, even at the neglect of my other children. I knew this, and yet I couldn't stop it. There was only one way I could see to save *all* my children.

My stomach lurched with bubbling bile. I needed fresh air. I needed quiet.

Grabbing my keys and cell phone, I headed to the garage. Maybe just a quick ride around the block to help me think. Abby and Preston would be fine alone for five minutes.

I pulled out into the downpour, wipers swiping the patter of droplets away. I turned out of the driveway, with no direction in mind. After circling the block once, then twice, I began to feel aimless, restless. Fifteen minutes later I found myself sitting in the car in an empty parking lot, engine running, staring through a rain-soaked windshield at the spot where Amelia was taken from the park.

For the first time in my life I was utterly helpless. I had no way to control this. Nothing I did would give me my desired outcome—to have Amelia back in my arms. I'd done everything— posted missing child flyers, worked with the police, made daily rounds at the park pursuing every person I saw, begging for any information that could help, blasted Amelia's picture all over the Internet, prayed. What else could I do? How could I fix this?

I couldn't.

And that lack of control was frightening.

What if Amelia was dead? At least right now I had hope. But if her tiny, lifeless body was found … then what? I might as well be dead too, because I couldn't recover from that. Maybe a stronger mother could, but not me.

My kids were my only purpose in life. They were my breath, my strength to wake up each day. Without them I was nothing. No one.

Our family was worthless without Amelia. We needed all the parts to be whole—Jay, Preston, Abby, Amelia, and me. If one part died, the rest of us went with it. That was what family was about. All or nothing.

The melody of my ringtone sang out from the center console. It was Jay. I answered hurriedly, hoping it was good news.

"Please tell me Amelia's home," I sputtered.

"Where are you?" he spat. His voice was terse and angry.

"What's wrong?" I asked.

"What's wrong?" His volume rose. "You left Preston and Abby here alone, Jo. Where the hell are you?"

"At the park. I just needed to drive around to clear my head."

"You can't do that, leaving two little kids at home by themselves! You're lucky I came home early. God only knows what could have happened if I didn't get here."

"They were just playing in the living room. They're fine. I'm on my way home now."

"Don't bother. I really can't stand to deal with you right now."

"What's that supposed to mean?"

"It means that you're not the only one dealing with losing Amelia. We're all scared. We're all in pain. But you can't neglect your other kids, and me, and yourself because of it. When was the last time you bathed or ate?"

I couldn't answer him.

"You can't shut down like this, or you're going to lose us all." Jay's words rammed into me, physically hurting me, and at the same time paralleling a familiar resonance with my own budding realization. "And quite frankly, I can't deal with your obsession. Let the police do their job. Your job is to take care of the kids who still need you—here, at home."

"Amelia needs me!" I cried.

"You can't help Amelia. But you can help Preston and Abby by being their mom." He paused, his exasperated sigh filling in the silence. "Maybe you should stay with Shayla for a few days until you're emotionally ready to handle this better."

"It's like you don't even care, Jay. How can you be so detached about this?"

"I'm not detached, Jo. Amelia's my baby girl—I love her more than anything. But I can't neglect everything and everyone else over this. Neither can you. So here's your choice: come home and be a part of this family, or find somewhere else to wallow."

Jay had issued an ultimatum in the midst of the darkest days of my life. It was at that moment that I knew I hated my husband's goddamn guts.

# Chapter 25

Ten long years. That's how long it had been since he'd seen Josephine Lively, or Jo Trubeau, the name she went by now. He liked her maiden name much better. It suited her. More befitting her lively spirit.

It had been three days since he had taken her daughter. After much tears from the lack of promised puppies, he had been able to placate Amelia with bribes of sweets and treats. But still, three days is a long time to spend with a three-year-old, especially for someone not experienced with children.

By the end of the first day, after the umpteenth epic toddler tantrum over apparently nothing at all, he came to the conclusion that there had to be something very wrong with this child. This could not be normal behavior.

He also discovered the unexpected, undesired side effect of his pacification tactic: sugar rush, inevitably followed by its equally enjoyable younger sibling, sugar crash. One moment Amelia is sprinting through the apartment, squealing, doing backflips off the sofa, the next she is laying on her back in the middle of the kitchen, wailing inconsolably at the ceiling.

Wash. Rinse. Repeat.

After a sleepless night tending to the aftermath of the candy-induced mania, he decided to employ the help of Big Pharma. A quick trip to the local drug store and he was stocked with every drowsy-causing liquid medicine available—just to be sure he got the right cocktail—and an oversized bottle of melatonin gummies.

From the first dose, this seemed a much better alternative than his previous method. Amelia was much calmer, and a bit lethargic. No running. No screaming. No crying. This parenting thing wasn't so tough as everyone made it out to be, he mused. Unfortunately, it didn't last.

He didn't realize that concentrated levels of antihistamines, like diphenhydramine and doxylamine succinate, used in Benadryl and Nyquil, respectively, could actually cause hallucinations, especially in young children. A reality he was forced to endure at two in the morning while he tried, unsuccessfully, to assuage this frantic *cherub* that the puppies were in fact *not* going to *get her*.

Day three dawned following yet another sleepless night, and his body ached for rest. In an exceedingly rare moment of peace, while Amelia colored the pages of the Cinderella coloring book he'd bought for her, he sat sipping coffee at the kitchenette table across from her. Coffee—a luxury he'd forgotten about during his prison time, and his sleep-deprived lifeblood. Savoring each drop on his tongue, he let himself indulge in the moment.

Right now was perfect, even if only for a short while. Because after he was done with Amelia, most certainly everything would be thrown askew. But it was a gamble he had to take. A means to an end.

He watched Amelia drag the crayons across the paper in vivid streaks. Apart from her bouts with what he could only explain as demonic possession, she was a beautiful little girl. So sweet. He hated that he'd used her to get to her mother, but seven years hidden from polite society had eroded what few ethics he had. When you had to fight for your life—for your food, for your shower, for basic commodities, for your "virginity"—you couldn't help but indulge the animal within you. Prison life had left him hollow and angry, and there wasn't room for much else. Only his undying love for Josephine kept his thread of humanity intact.

The long stream of redundant days hadn't tempered his memory of her. If anything, time had eternally preserved that special night like flowers pressed between the pages of a book. That angora cream shawl soft to the touch. Those bangle bracelets that clinked as she talked alluringly with her hands. The low-waisted jeans that offered a glimpse of her naval and advertised the shape of her hips. Her blond hair hanging in loose curls, tickling her shoulders. It was instant attraction—her beauty only emphasized by the dingy walls and dark atmosphere of the bar.

Every moment clung to him like fragrant oil. Their sticky stools scraping against each other. Her furtive glances. His nervous smile as he mustered the courage to say hello. It had been foreplay for nearly half an hour before he dared make eye contact.

He had noticed the hulking engagement ring on her finger from the first moment and felt a shudder of disappointment. She was taken, of course. How could she not be? And then she grinned at him. An invitation. He accepted. Why not, if only for a fling?

They spent the next two hours talking, flirting, and drinking. He was mesmerized by her involuntary seductiveness. The way her fingers ever so softly grazed his as she reached for her drink, or how effortless her palm fell to rest on his thigh.

An abundance of rum and Cokes led to his suggestion that they "get out of here." She numbly followed him to his car, where the spark ignited. Giving in so easily, she allowed him to take her fully, their heavy breaths steaming up the windows.

He remembered how she kissed the sweat off of his forehead, and he licked the salt off of her lips. They continued kissing long after the sex was finished, groping and grabbing and touching and tasting each other with frantic urgency, like they were attempting to devour the other. It was intense and powerful, sweet and sensual. He'd never been with a girl like this before, and he'd come to realize he would never find it with anyone else again.

After the sizzle faded, and sheer and utter exhaustion took hold, she rested against his chest in the backseat, their chests heaving as she confessed her cold feet about getting married. Too young. Too many unrealized dreams to live. Worried her fiancé might not be *the one*.

"Then don't marry him," he had said, inhaling the passion fruit scent of her hair.

She had looked at him sarcastically, as if the logic had never occurred to her.

"Oh, let me guess. I should marry you instead?" The alcohol had slurred her words and she laughed.

But in that moment it didn't seem all that funny to him. She was perfect in every way. The type of girl he could imagine himself house shopping with, having kids with, growing old with. She wasn't the typical bar skank that most of his evenings resulted in. She was intelligent, pure, funny, genuine.

"Hell no, I'm not the marrying type," he said instead, feigning machismo. "But you shouldn't get married if you have doubts. You'll end up with a lifetime of regret."

He could almost see her brain working as she contemplated his words with a cute nibble of her lip. Damn, she was adorable.

"Maybe you're right. Maybe I shouldn't marry Jay. But what if he *is* the one?"

"Out of the billions of people in the world, you think there's only one person out there for you?"

"I dunno. Maybe. I think that anyone can find a spouse they can live with, connect with even. But then there's that epic love— that soul mate kind of love. A one-in-a-million kind of love." Her eyes had gone all dreamy as she spoke, and her words were so delicious he throbbed to taste them. "That kind of love, that's what I want, but I don't believe you can get that with just anyone. It has to be someone special, someone created for you and you for them. The hard part is finding that person."

"How will you know when you do?" he had asked with genuine interest.

She shrugged and looked at the ring on her finger. "That's what I'm trying to figure out."

"Well, until you do ..." he chortled as he pulled her back on top of him for another round, her legs sliding so perfectly open, enveloping his pelvis, swallowing him inside her.

He later realized just how right she was. He could feel the vibrations in the air between them, could sense the unique connection they shared. Josephine was his one and only, but it took her slipping between his fingers for him to realize that truth.

He'd gone through many women after that night of backseat passion and whispered dreams. Drowned his misery with sex and booze. Then got himself into trouble after one particularly drunken night when he'd beaten a chick half to death after she mocked him for being so sentimental. At the root of all that wretchedness was Josephine. She had left her imprint on his heart and it stopped beating after she said goodbye.

One night of confessions, of unfettered passion.

One night of waking a slumbering love that hibernated deep in his heart.

All it took was one night to fall for Josephine Lively and to decide he'd do anything to get her. Absolutely anything. Even at the cost of her child.

The plan was ready to execute. It was time. With his latex gloves on to ensure he left no trace of himself, he held the ballpoint pen and touched it to the paper. Not one to make empty threats, he hated the idea of hurting a child. Especially her child. But some sacrifices were necessary for the greater good. She'd see that eventually. She'd come to understand why he had to do what he had to do. It was for them. All for them. He was her one true love. Time would prove this to be true.

As long as Josephine followed the plan, everyone would walk away for the better. It was up to her now. While she had made the wrong choice ten years ago, this time she could rectify it. She could save herself, save him, and save their happiness together. All it would cost was one small life.

Then he set in motion the event that would finally collide their worlds.

*Your daughter is safe. But not for long. There is only one thing I want, and you know what it is. I'll be coming for it soon. But if you refuse, your whole family will pay the price. You know what you have to do.*

# Chapter 26 · June

The roads were slick coming back from Austin's therapy appointment. I'd had to drag all four kids with me, entertaining the other three in the waiting room while Austin threw a tantrum for an hour with his new speech therapist. I couldn't blame him after witnessing her chilly personality firsthand. It didn't help that I wasn't in there helping him navigate through her vague instructions, but with Arabelle, Kiki, and Juliet, I had my hands full breaking up the fights over the scanty toys the facility provided.

In the backseat Juliet cried for her bottle, despite me nursing her for the past hour. Kiki screamed about wanting her seatbelt off, claiming she was a "big girl like Arabelle." Austin made his irritating *eeee-owwwwww* sound while wildly flapping his hands in the air, which set Arabelle to pouting and whining in her corner of the van because I wouldn't take them out for lunch at the McDonald's with a playroom.

Every kid screaming.

Every kid draining what little patience I had left.

Every kid testing my will to endure.

I couldn't take it anymore—the skirmishes over toys, the complaints over what's for dinner, the sulking at being told no, the tantrums I couldn't pull Austin out of, the arm flailing that made strangers gawk, the speech therapy that seemed to be no help, the working too much but getting paid too little, Mike's fruitless job searches, the constant battle for survival, which I was losing …

It was all too much. I was drowning in my own life and I simply wanted to slip under the waves.

A memory rose from the grave of my mind. Back before kids, when Mike and I would spend weekends in bed, making love under the covers and cuddling through the rainy afternoon while we talked about our dreams, planning our future together. I had told him I wanted to backpack through Asia together, riding elephants and shopping at the bazaars in Chiang Mai. Then we'd head to an exotic Malaysian beach where we'd do nothing but sunbathe and sip mixed drinks.

I don't recall *this* being part of that future.

Where had my fantasies gone to die? Why had I chosen this life of chaos and noise and sleep deprivation and stress? I couldn't remember the last time I'd gotten six hours of sleep, let alone the eight I needed. Or when I'd last eaten a hot meal after serving everyone else first and getting up a dozen times during dinner to grab drinks or condiments or clean up spills.

Not once did Mike ever acknowledge what I'd given up. Not once did the kids ever thank me for my servitude. My thanks was four screaming children in the back of my secondhand van whining about dropped sippy cups, grumbling tummies, tight seatbelts, and making noise just for the hell of it.

I. Was. Done.

"Shut up!" Two words that released years of pent-up frustration and anguish over an existence I didn't want anymore. "I can't take it anymore! I am done with all of you!"

And suddenly the car went silent, and I realized I meant it. Life had stripped any desire to live from me.

Maybe it was the patch of water I hit that wrenched the steering wheel from my grasp, or maybe it was the urge to send my family off a cliff at that very moment, but it happened before I could think, before I could stop it, before I could change direction.

Cresting the hill, the road flattened out, but I didn't notice the puddle stretching its watery arms across the concrete until it was too late. Somehow—whether by my own hand or sheer momentum—the tires veered a sharp right, and I felt the car sliding … slipping … heading straight for a drop-off where a thicket of woods met the berm.

The van plummeted crookedly down the short hill. Suddenly the earth flew up and met the passenger-side windows, and I felt myself dangling in my seatbelt, bouncing recklessly. The kids cried out frantically for Mommy, but I was at the mercy of the rolling minivan.

Tipping over didn't seem to slow it down, though, as we plunged into a line of trees. The cries crescendoed—and I realized it was my own voice rising above the kids'. A moment later my body felt like it was pulled apart when my front fender smacked a tree trunk with a grating crunch. The force jarred our bodies forward as the deploying airbag smashed against my face.

The adrenaline masked any pain I should have felt until the voices of weeping children receded in the encroaching blackness. I welcomed it with open arms.

# Chapter 27 - Shayla

"I've been a bad, bad girl ..."

I crooned Fiona Apple's "Criminal," a catchy tune I remembered from my adolescence. About a woman plagued with guilt over using and abusing a man who loved her, it was fitting today—the day I planned to apologize to Kelsey for calling the cops on him and attempted to cut things off as amicably as possible. If that was even possible. I was oddly at ease, considering I had no clue who he really was beneath the charming smile. He'd pulled a complete 180 on me—from agreeable to aggressive. What was he truly capable of?

Then again, he didn't know what I was capable of either. But I had a lot more to lose than he did, a lot more to fight for.

I needed to bury the hatchet with Kelsey, whatever it took. In his thirty-odd messages since our Jim's Tavern scene, he made it clear we had unfinished business, but he still loved me—despite the drama queen that I was. He was a glutton for punishment if he intended to get back together after all the shit I'd pulled.

Back at square one, I'd be breaking two men's hearts today: Kelsey, who was obsessed with having me but couldn't; and Trent, my devoted husband whose heart might never recover from the betrayal. Tonight I would get it all over with, confessing and losing everything all at once.

I deserved whatever I got. My bipolar brain for once understood the nature of the consequences.

My little chat with Bev was only part of what prompted this revelation, though. The other part was growing inside my uterus, a secret that was getting bigger, heavier, harder to hide every day. I still wasn't sure what to do about it. It was early enough that I could terminate the pregnancy and no one would be any the wiser, but could I go through with it? I'd already imagined wiggling fingers and toes. I'd already pictured Trent's penetrating inky eyes and my full lips on this child. And then the image would fade into a looming question mark that sent my worry into overdrive.

I didn't know for sure the baby was Trent's.

And if it wasn't, what then?

No matter who the biological father was, I knew who I wanted the father to be: Trent. He'd done a hell of a job raising Arion and Tenica, and I knew he'd be a good daddy all over again. Hell, he'd probably be thrilled with the news. God forbid I get stuck in a life with Kelsey involved, but would this baby force me into that?

The urge for a cigarette became overwhelming, so with one hand on the steering wheel, I fumbled through my secret stash in my purse and lit up. Pregnant or not, stress was worse on the baby than a couple puffs of nicotine.

Despite the rain pelting the windows, I lowered the passenger-side window to air out any trace of smoke. Trent hated it when I smoked; I didn't need him to find out and add it to my tally of sins against him. A cool haze wafted through the car. The rain's pitter-patter combined with each delicious toke to mellow out my surging mania.

Stopping at a red light, I continued to sing away my anxiety while a car rolled up next to mine. As I sat in my metal and leather cocoon, I suddenly felt a dull thud against my ear, and the spray of something sticky spitting all over my arm. A shriek of laughter later, the car next to me took off, leaving behind the words "Learn how to sing, bitch!" I glanced down to find a half-empty can of soda that had bounced off me and landed in the passenger seat, a pool of liquid staining the cream leather brown as it seeped into the seams.

Seriously? Were people really that immature?

Hitting the gas, I followed the car for the next ten minutes, my tires lapping up the miles as I rode them bumper-to-bumper, swerving up beside them and flipping them off while I lobbed every obscenity I could think of at the punks. I laughed as I scared them shitless. That would be the last time they'd ever toss a Coke in someone's car again.

I was still irritated as I turned onto Oleander Way where Kelsey agreed to meet me. A growl of thunder above resonated with the rumble in my gut. Kelsey vowed that I wouldn't leave unscathed. And what about Trent? How would he react? I imagined him flying into a murder-suicide rage.

Two deadly unknowns.

When I pulled up to my house, Kelsey's car was parked three doors down in case of an emergency flight, something that had only happened once before—and once too many. There would be no need for hiding this time, though, I reminded myself. Arion was at school, Tenica in daycare. Trent was at work, and I only needed a few minutes to speak my piece. Kelsey would resist, try to take back control of the situation, force me into a corner to stay. But I wasn't taking any shit today. I was still too pissed off at the soda incident.

And despite months of dragging this out, I couldn't put it off any longer.

In, out, get it over with. Just like my sex life.

Raindrops stung my face as I ran up the walkway to the front door, signaling Kelsey to follow me. Under the shelter of the porch roof, I hurriedly unlocked the door and waited for him to join me in the entryway.

"Hey, gorgeous," he said, pecking my cheek.

"Seriously?" I replied flatly. "I almost get you jailed and you kiss me?"

"Forgive and forget, ya know. How about we head to the bedroom to dry off?" he suggested with a wink, luring me with a firm hand on my wrist.

I shook my head and pulled my arm free of his grip. "We need to talk."

"In the bedroom." He stalked off toward my room, which instantly pissed me off, as if this was his house, his domain.

By the time I joined him, his belt was already unbuckled, pants dropping, while his fingers hastily unbuttoned his collared shirt.

"What are you doing?" I scoffed.

"What's it look like I'm doing?" Half-undressed, Kelsey dropped onto the bed, then patted the empty space beside him. "Hell, I'll even rub your back. Anything for my girl."

*My girl.* I sighed. This was going to be harder than I thought. "Kelsey, I need to tell you something."

His eyes narrowed. "Don't say what I think you're going to say. I already warned you that you'll regret it."

I already had enough regret to last a lifetime. What was one more?

"I have to do this. I'm sorry. But it's over between us. I plan to tell Trent today, so there's nothing you can do that will change this."

I waited for the yelling, the cursing, the threats. Instead I was met with an unsettling calm. Then he smiled ... and laughed. He laughed until his body shook, and the creepy intensity of it scared me.

"I'm glad you find this so fucking funny," I finally said.

"What I find humorous is that you think it's over between us. I already warned you, but you won't listen. I will make your life a living hell, Shayla. I will leave you with no one and nothing but lonely shame. Is that what you want?"

I had no idea what that meant, and I didn't care. I'd call his bluff and raise him one insanity. I turned on him, pointing my finger in his face, my voice low and full of hate.

"Bring it on, asshole. Make your threats. See if I care. You can't force me to love you. Hell, I don't even *like* you!"

He pushed me away. "You'll like me even less when I take everything you care about away from you, bitch."

Just as Kelsey rose from the bed, I heard footsteps outside in the hallway. A shadow crossed the floor, then stopped. I glanced at the clock and groaned. How could I have been so careless and lost track of time?

"Arion?" I called out.

My son's head slowly peered around the corner. I had no idea what Arion had heard or seen as Kelsey took his sweet time belting his pants, but I needed to clear things up for him before his imagination went wild with scenarios.

"Honey, are you okay?"

I had no idea how a ten-year-old would process this. What could possibly be going through that head full of tight curls?

"Who's this guy?" Arion finally spoke. "And why is he in your bedroom?"

"Well …" I stuttered. I had no idea how to explain this in a way that would make sense to my son. "This is a friend of mine. And we were just talking about something."

"Is he your boyfriend?" Arion asked bluntly.

"What would make you ask that?"

"Because he's in your bedroom showing you his private parts."

I couldn't speak. My throat tightened, and I knew this was bad. Very bad. Traumatizingly bad. My son might never get over seeing this.

I had two choices: I could lie and attempt to cover it up, but Arion would know and he'd call me out on it. He'd always had my nose for smelling bullshit. Or I could simply beg for his forgiveness and hope it would blow over.

Walking over to him, I knelt down in front of him and clasped his small hands in mine, the tears stinging my eyes as I thought through each word. "I made a big mistake. But I'm going to talk to Daddy about it tonight and fix everything. I promise. Can you forgive me?"

Searching my son's hazel eyes for support, all I saw was disgust reflected back at me in his smudged glasses. Ripping his hand away from me, he stepped back, widening the schism between us.

"No, I don't forgive you. You hurt Daddy. You hurt me and Tenica. All you care about is yourself and your boyfriend. Do you even love us—your real family?" Arion glared at Kelsey, who stood there dumbly.

"Of course I love you, sweetie."

"A mom who loves her family doesn't replace them with someone else. I hate you. I wish we were all dead so you could feel what it's like to lose us. You don't care about us anyways, and there's no point living if we don't have a mom who loves us!"

Leaving me no room to reply, he ran off through the living room, and a moment later I heard the front door slam shut. Kelsey was right. I was about to lose everything I cared about, and I'd brought it on myself. Taking a step forward to run after Arion, I felt a hand grip my upper arm, stopping me.

"Let him go," Kelsey said.

I ripped my arm out of his grasp. "Just leave, Kelsey. Haven't you done enough damage already?"

Kelsey shook his head, and I saw pity in his eyes. "You really blame me for your drama? You created this mess. Hell, you thrive on this shit."

"What the hell are you talking about?"

"You know," he said, wagging a finger at me, "I'm starting to realize I dodged a bullet. You're a walking timebomb. You create drama everywhere you go, Shayla. I'm out. Done. I don't need your chaos. Good riddance."

"Fuck you!" My voice box tore as I screamed.

Maybe he was right, but right now I couldn't dwell on what a piece of shit I was. I needed to be with my son. I ran to the door, threw it open, and sprinted through the front yard. Arion had vanished without a trace.

How would I ever explain this to Trent? Could he ever forgive me? Could I forgive myself? One cold, hard word echoed in my mind: no. I didn't deserve mercy. I deserved hell, which was exactly where I already was.

# Chapter 28 - Ellie

*T*oday I believe in miracles. Today I need one.

It appears that things between Denny and his mistress are falling apart, which means that there's a chance I can rescue us, repair our marriage, restore our hope of a future together. It's chilling how I don't see a future unless Denny is in it. Why is that, I wonder? Are all wives linked to their husbands with such stiff cords? Or am I alone in this codependency? I feel like an island and Denny is my ocean. I'm surrounded by him, tamed by him, shrinking slowly in on myself by him. And yet it's the only way of life I know, so it comforts me.

I'm so scared, though. After twelve years of marriage I'm petrified my husband won't end up choosing me in the end.

This vulnerability makes me reflect, take a personal inventory of who I am, who I could be, who I want to be. I've gone from pathetically desperate, to insanely jealous, to bitterly angry, to self-loathing, to a creature I've never seen before. I used to wander through the days in blithe bliss, unfettered by drama or extremes. Now it seems I'm all extremes, from one emotional breakdown to the next. Having to hide it all from the one person I should be able to share everything with. I hate feeling this way. And yet I can't stop. Why can't I stop?

I'm human, that's why. I've spent the better part of my lifetime needing Denny, thus my world revolves around him. My world can't exist without him.

Darla asked me why I was dressing up today. Why I would bother. I told her that sometimes looking pretty for your husband is important. "So I should do whatever will make other people like me more?" she asked. "No, you should be true to yourself," I tried to explain, but I clearly wasn't making my point. "But you're not being true to yourself with Daddy." I didn't want to tell her that being true to myself was what lost him to another woman in the first place.

*I'm not sure what to think of that. Is she right? Has my eleven-year-old daughter grown wiser than her mother already? I'm wondering what kind of example I'm setting for Darla and Logan, teaching them that a woman's job is to make a man happy, and that a man's job is to control his wife or find a new one when he's bored with her. Is this the lesson we're imparting on these impressionable minds?*

*Whoever thought parenting was easy clearly didn't have children. Every decision parents make either sets a precedent, leaves a trauma the kids will discuss in therapy years later, or spoils them rotten. I've accomplished all three of these in a matter of days.*

*God help me. I need a miracle.*

\*\*\*

Candles: check.

Mood music: check.

Something chocolatey: check.

The evening was planned, and it was perfect. An early dinner of macaroni and cheese and hotdogs for the kids while watching *Finding Dory*, followed by a hurried bedtime routine. After a round of goodnight kisses and short stories, I finished the final touches on the chicken cordon bleu and roasted asparagus that warmed in the oven. Two glasses of cheap champagne completed the dinner I'd spent all day looking forward to.

Sure, Denny had cheated on me. Sure, he had lied to me. Sure, he had broken my heart and will to live. But he was coming back to me. We were going to fix everything and go back to being the picture-perfect family we were meant to be. Even if it killed me.

June called it insanity, me returning to my emotionally abusive husband expecting loyalty this time around. But I called it love, forgiveness, endurance.

The only issue was keeping Janyne away, who was making it her mission to stay in touch. I hadn't told Denny about our texts or the note I'd gotten today, and I planned to keep it that way.

Written on kitten cardstock, she'd penned the following message in perfect script, just like her perfect hair and perfect body and perfect teeth:

> *You think you've won, but this is only the beginning. This is your first warning. Don't make threats you can't back up. I know your type—the meek, naïve housewife who fights behind the safety of her cell phone. Learn when to surrender or I will be your worst nightmare.*

In reactionary haste, I burned the note in the kitchen sink, only afterward regretting it. I'd disintegrated any evidence in case she came back for a fight. I couldn't let it spoil the evening, so I shrugged it off and figured what could be the worst that happened? She'd show up at my house and we'd scream it out? I had two obnoxious kids; I could certainly handle the she-devil.

Our dinner and conversation had gone seamlessly, down to the last juicy bite of chicken, as we laughed over Denny's co-worker anecdotes. Everything felt so normal again, and I relished it. I told him to meet me in the bedroom for some *dessert* while I tidied up the kitchen.

As the rain settled down to a drizzle, I remembered that it was garbage night. It was supposed to be Denny's chore, but somewhere along the line it had fallen upon me—and I forgot at least once a month, including last week. My usual reminder was when I saw the boy across the street—Arigon or Arion or some unusual name I could never remember—dragging his can to the curb.

I'd quickly run the garbage out, then resume our night of perfection. Nothing could go wrong.

Until it did.

I hauled the full kitchen garbage bag out the back porch and along the driveway where a thin row of bushes separated my house from the elderly lady's next door. Having forgotten the garbage can on the curb for the past week, I opened the lid and hefted the kitchen bag up, and there it was—sitting right on top of last week's unpicked-up trash, as if taunting me.

A pregnancy test.

And it was positive.

The kitchen bag slipped from my fingers to the ground, spewing garbage along the sidewalk.

No, this couldn't be happening. Was Denny's mistress ... pregnant? And how did it get here, anyways? Was that bitch in *my* house taking a pregnancy test with *my* husband in *my* bathroom? My legs went numb and wobbly as I dropped to the cement, my tailbone taking most of the impact. But I felt no pain. All I felt was despair.

Time passed, but I wasn't aware of it until Denny came walking outside looking for me.

"Whatcha doing out here, El? Come inside. I've been waiting for you."

I couldn't talk about what I'd found ... not yet. The anger was too great for words right now.

"I slipped and fell. I'm going to have to postpone tonight."

"Are you okay?" His eyes widened as he suddenly realized I was sitting on the ground. He rushed toward me, insisting on helping me up despite my waving him off. His touch sickened me, his comforting words made my skin crawl. I wanted nothing to do with this man who had broken me for the very last time.

"I'm fine, I'm fine," I insisted, but I really wasn't fine. The seams that held my sanity together were fraying fast.

I followed him into the house, hating him more than I ever had before, wanting him to feel as devastated as he'd left me. I'd bought into the hope of a new beginning for us. I always clung to false hope, it seemed. It was true—I was the definition of insanity. I'd embraced the lie that we could find love again. And I did that without a single confession, an ounce of repentance, or so much as an apology from him. Another woman was having his child— what did that even mean for us? If he wanted to stay, would he expect me to raise her child with him? Would I have to face her for drop-offs and pick-ups and Little League games and ballet recitals?

No.

I simply couldn't accept that life.

I'd been through enough.

"I'll be back," I said as I headed for the stairs. "I think there's pain medicine in the upstairs bathroom for this." I pulled up my shirt and craned my head around to gaze numbly at the red bruise growing along my tailbone.

"Jeez, El, that looks nasty. How about a massage when you get back?" he offered with a green spark in his eyes.

"We'll see," I tried to say playfully, but my voice fell flat.

I passed by the kids' rooms—first Darla's, then Logan's—and watched them sleep, their blond heads tucked sweetly into the soft folds of down pillows and quilted comforters. I wondered if they'd even care if I was out of the picture. I already knew the answer, though. None of them cared if I was alive or dead. I didn't care at this point either.

# Chapter 29 · Jo

A movie. Popcorn. And chocolate. Three things that I promised Preston and Abby that morning, three things that stole my focus just long enough that I hadn't seen *him* come.

We had just finished a *Harry Potter* movie marathon, the three of us snuggled on the sofa under a heap of Sherpa throw blankets. It was the first time since Amelia's disappearance where I resumed a normal semblance of living. Jay had been right—I'd been neglecting the kids, and I wanted to make up for it. Nothing like a movie to cuddle up to while we shared a bowl of buttery popcorn and licked melted M&Ms off our fingers.

I was lucky enough to lose track of time instead of watching every minute pass, worrying every second away. But during those misplaced minutes, *he* had come and gone, and I'd lost a chance to save my daughter.

A trip to the mailbox would never be so innocuous again.

It was late morning when I caught a glimpse of the white mail truck passing by. The heat of the day hadn't yet peaked as neighbors lounged on their front porches or walked their dogs, always sure to carry a dog waste bag lest they be fined for not picking up after their furry companions.

I told the kids I'd be right back, then headed down our walkway toward the mailbox that I had spent an afternoon decorating with the kids a couple years ago. Preston's handprints in blue and green were the biggest, then Abby's tiny pink and purple handprints with silver polka dots next to his. Amelia's one-year-old palms had been so small that I couldn't hold them still as she wiggled her fingers in the gooey paint, creating a smudged blur of orange. It was messy, but it was beautiful because it was their handiwork.

Everything the kids had created gave me pride, from their colored artistic designs to their scribbled literary endeavors. Drawn pictures of our latest zoo trip, stories about talking animals—I treasured it all as if they were da Vinci's original *Mona Lisa* or a first-edition copy of *Gone with the Wind*.

I peeked inside the mailbox before reaching in. A force of habit, always fearing I'd grab a spider or some other creepy-crawly. After pulling out the stack of ads with some bills tucked into the fold, I noticed a white envelope with one word scribbled on the front:

*Josephine*

Instantly I knew it was from *him*, whoever *him* was. Breathless and frenetic, I ran inside, tossing the mail on the island. Grabbing my dishwashing gloves, I slid them on and carefully tore open the envelope. If there was any chance of a fingerprint or spit, I needed to preserve it.

I unfolded the sole piece of computer paper with one inky paragraph written on it:

> *Your daughter is safe. But not for long. There is only one thing I want, and you know what it is. I'll be coming for it soon. But if you refuse, your whole family will pay the price. You know what you have to do.*

The problem was, I had no idea what he wanted, or who he was. What the hell kind of clue was this? But at least she was alive. There was no reason for him to lie about it … right?

I read the note again, searching for something familiar. I was supposed to know him. He expected me to. Was it possible …? Had my secret from ten years ago come back to haunt me, torment me, strip everything away from me?

That couldn't be right. It was one stupid, regretful night with some random, nameless guy. What kind of man would even remember such a night, let alone hold on to it for a decade? Perhaps a man capable of kidnapping an innocent child.

It didn't make any sense. And yet ... it was the only thing that made sense. This whole kidnapping was about me. It was about someone wanting something from me. I had no enemies I was aware of, no dysfunctional family members, no drama in my life. Only one life-destroying secret that I had thought faded out of existence years ago. Until one month ago when I got that letter.

I needed to know for sure if this was the same person. Heading into the bedroom, I opened my underwear drawer, shuffled my intimates aside, and felt the paper crumple. I pulled it out, then rushed back to the kitchen. Setting the letters side by side, I examined the handwriting. It was hard to tell if they were the same or not.

The letter from J was cursive and scrawled, as if the words poured from an emotional place. The note today was carefully printed, as if the writer had taken his time. But there were enough similarities that it could be the same person. Maybe Detective Cox would be able to tell with more certainty. But if he read the letter, he would know for sure about the affair. The graphic details, the timeline ... J had recounted everything necessary to bury me in my lies. If only I could figure out who J was without handing over the letter.

My phone. I needed to call the detective and Jay. Hopefully Detective Cox could find some trace of DNA or a fingerprint to figure out who was behind this hell. Spotting my hot-pink cell phone case on the end table in the living room, I picked it up to call the detective, whose personal number I had memorized by now.

"Detective Cox," he answered on the first ring.

"Hi, it's Jo Trubeau. I got something in the mail you need to see. Right away."

A beat didn't even pass before he replied, "I'm on my way. And don't touch it."

I hung up feeling a glimmer of hope. Amelia was safe, he had written. My baby was alive. For now.

\*\*\*

Jay was on his way home when Detective Cox arrived. I had bribed Preston and Abby with lollipops then ordered them to play upstairs, not wanting them to distract us while we talked. They had an uncanny ability to know when something important was being discussed and always managed to talk loudly and incessantly during those conversations, much like every time I tried to talk on the phone. I was in no mental shape to be patient with them right now.

I had set aside J's letter, not wanting to bring it up unless absolutely necessary. I still needed to figure out how to explain it without incriminating myself, which seemed impossible given the nature of it.

No one could understand the cost of full disclosure. My life had been built on a certain type of standard. Jay, the loving, dependable husband and provider. Jo, the nurturing homemaker and steadfast wife. Shining examples of the suburbanite dream. These roles were crucial to maintain. One slip and I'd lose my position in my marriage, in the society we'd grown accustomed to, in the world we had created for ourselves.

It wasn't just the threat of divorce that scared me into silence. Even if Jay did forgive me, it was the notion of becoming the neighborhood gossip that I feared. Behind the painted faces on Oleander Way were vultures. They thrived on picking apart the weak. For ten years I had maintained my position at the top, an untouchable, but an indiscretion like this coming to light would put a target on my back, Jay's back, my kids' backs. School rumors would fly, hushed lies would be spread. This place I called home was a den of judgment and cruelty for anyone who didn't fit the mold. I had spent far too much energy reshaping our family identity to fit in with these neighborly imposters to lose it all now.

Hadn't I already lost enough?

I simply couldn't let my affair be known. No matter what. If Jay found out the truth, there would be no point surviving this because my life would be over anyways. He'd take the kids and leave me, and I'd be alone and desolate. But was keeping my secret worth my daughter's life? There had to be a way to give just enough details to catch this guy without every incriminating speck of dirt coming out.

Detective Cox stood at the island, leaning over the note reading it, latex gloves on his hands and a see-through evidence bag already prepped on the counter. He slid the letter into the bag and zipped it shut.

"Well, this is good news. He's here, still in Durham. And Amelia, as far as we know, is okay. Clearly he dropped it off, so I'll ask around to see if any of your neighbors got a look at him. This is a big step, Jo."

He squeezed my shoulder as he spoke. My muscles had tensed so much over the past few days that they felt like rocks had tunneled under my skin.

"Do you think you'll find fingerprints or DNA?"

His lips curled in an uncertain frown. "I doubt it. A pair of gloves and using water to seal the envelope is pretty basic knowledge to avoid leaving identifiers. But I'll still have our forensics guys check it out. Our best bet is if anyone saw him or his car. That would help us a lot."

Silence lapped us before I spoke again. I knew what I was about to do was probably a huge mistake, but if it could lead us to Amelia, it was a necessary sacrifice. This moment felt like the beginning of the end for me, for my marriage, but if losing my marriage saved my daughter, so be it. I couldn't hide anymore. The weight of lies was too heavy a burden.

I had trouble finding the words, but I wanted to bring it up before Jay arrived. "I have something that may be connected to this."

"Okay …" His voice rose with suspicion.

I pulled the letter from J out from under the pile of junk mail where I'd hidden it. "This came about a month ago." I slid the letter across the counter to him. "It's from a guy I knew over ten years ago."

As his eyes pored over it, line by line, I hoped he would leave it at that, no questions asked. How silly of me.

"So you had an affair right before you got married? Is that what this is about?"

How quickly he boiled down a ten-year omission.

"No," I lied a little too quickly. "This isn't what happened."

"Then what happened?"

My brain formulated the words as I went, and I prayed I didn't leave any holes in my story. "I did meet a man at the bar before I got married. But we didn't have sex. He kissed me. That was it. I don't know why he's making so much more out of what happened."

"If he only kissed you, why are you being so secretive about this? Why am I only seeing this now?"

"I didn't think it was related. Plus you can see how this looks— how he made it look. Please don't tell my husband. This would be too much on top of everything else we're going through."

Pursing his lips, Detective Cox gazed right through me. I could feel the skepticism drilling into me.

"Do you remember his name, what he looked like, where the envelope was postmarked from?"

"Only that it came from Pennsylvania. I had thrown out the envelope, so I can't remember. Is it possible to do an inmate search to find him?"

Detective Cox chuckled. "Do you realize how many prisons there are? And if you know nothing about him other than his name begins with a J, that's probably half the inmate population. There's just too many variables to narrow this down. Unless you miraculously remember his name, this won't help us."

He slid the letter back toward me, then turned toward the living room.

"Where are you going?" I asked, following him to the front door.

"I'm going to go door to door asking neighbors if they saw anyone suspicious today. Let's hope you have nosy neighbors."

Flinging open the front door, he paused mid-step and looked back at me.

"Jo, if you're hiding anything, you need to come clean. When we catch this guy—and we will—it will all come out anyways. Better for Jay to find out from you now than from the news later."

As he closed the door behind him, I was left with an unsettling feeling that maybe he was right. Which meant one thing: things were only going to get worse.

# Chapter 30 - June

A *beep beep beep* gently tugged me back to earth from a peaceful place, a place I didn't want to leave. In that place I felt carefree in my sleepy haze. In that place all was calm and quiet. In that place I had no children, no debts, no stress. In that place a sense of ease hugged me. In reality, however, my shattered bones greeted me with stabs of pain and throbbing aches ... and an urgent sense of dread.

Something horrible had happened, but I couldn't remember what. I had no idea where I was or how I'd gotten here. But the deep pulsing in my gut warned me it was bad.

Forcing my eyelids open through the crust that sealed them shut, I found myself lying in a hospital bed with IV tubes snaking around me. Low morning sunlight broke through a sliver between thick pale pink curtains that hung over a window that took up a fourth of the room.

A silhouette moved in the corner where the gray walls met.

"Hey, Juney. You're awake." It was Mike, the only person I wanted to see and yet the one I feared most. He held the power to make me or break me, and lately he seemed to specialize in the latter.

I reminded myself that once upon a time I had loved him deeply—personality flaws and joblessness and laziness and all. I was smitten from the moment I met him at a club where he asked me to join him on the dance floor to Blackstreet's "No Diggity." After enduring a broken heart from the only other person I had ever loved, I had accepted Mike's offer, and we made musical love together that night. It was love at first song, and I was charmed by his dance moves and humor. He was the balm my shredded heart needed, though he was never quite enough. But I didn't see that back then.

We dove headfirst into a whirlwind romance, both of us ignorant of who the other truly was. I interpreted his job-hopping as self-discovery; he interpreted my control-freak nature as just being super-organized. Apart we were complementary opposites; together we were madness.

Over the years I realized he had never completed me, and perhaps I had never completed him. Only one person had made me whole, but it was a forbidden long-lost love that I buried eons ago. At least I had thought it was buried. Lately the memories clawed at me like a zombie hand reaching out of the grave.

"How you feeling, hon?" Mike's voice was mellow and soothing, and as he stepped closer, the red veins in his eyes told me he'd been crying. I wondered for how long.

"Hey," I replied, my throat coarse like I'd swallowed sand.

"Have some water." He lifted the straw to my lips and I sucked a small mouthful.

"Thanks," I said, then gulped some more. "What happened?"

"You were in a car accident."

And this was when total recall slammed into me. The kids—they weren't here. They had been in the van with me—as it dropped down the bank, rolled onto its side, slammed into the tree. No, no, no, no. I couldn't hear what came next. But I had to know.

"The kids—?" I asked, choking on a sob. I was afraid to finish the question. A breath caught in my throat.

"They're all okay," Mike said quickly.

I exhaled relief … and guilt. "I'm so sorry!" I began babbling, covering my face with my hands in shame. I couldn't face Mike with the remorse of what I'd done. How could he ever forgive that I'd almost killed the kids?

"Hey, babe, it's okay. They're okay," he soothed, rubbing circles on my shoulder as I shook with forceful sobs. "Everyone's fine. It was an accident, sweetie. The roads were slick. Don't blame yourself."

But that wasn't the truth. I knew the truth, and it wasn't that simple. I didn't know how to put it into words.

"But it is my fault."

"Juney, stop. I know life has been rough. With Austin's autism, and four kids and working, and me not pulling my weight—it's too much for you to carry. I haven't supported you, but I promise to do better from now on."

I touched his cheek with my hand, rubbing the scruff that I'd always found so attractive about him.

"Honey, I don't know how to say this …" I began. How could I tell him what I was thinking about before the accident? He'd throw me in the nuthouse for sure. Which was where I deserved to be.

Mike placed his finger on my lips. "Shhh. Babe, you're exhausted. That's all that happened. You were tired and the roads were wet. You can't fault yourself for that. But we're all okay, and that's what matters."

"You don't understand," I muttered between snuffles. I looked up at him, the face of the man I adored, into the caring, gentle eyes of the one person I knew accepted me. What I was about to say would change that look forever into one of fear and revulsion.

"Mike, it wasn't an accident." I couldn't meet his eyes, not with this nasty secret. I gazed down at my fingers as I fidgeted with the corner of my sheet. His disgust at the monster I'd become wasn't something I could handle. "I did it on purpose. I tried to kill us all."

# Chapter 31 - Shayla

A gun shook in Arion's tiny hands, the barrel quivering at my chest when I opened his bedroom door hours later. Amid Avenger posters and Spider-Man bedding, my ten-year-old son stood there holding a deadly weapon, a contrast to the childish action figures and Legos scattered in the background.

After telling Trent to come home and calling the only place Arion would have escaped to, I located him at Drew's house, the one friend he had. I'd let him process the disturbing scene he'd witnessed in his own way before coming home. I had heard Arion slip in through the back door, heard his footsteps rumble up the stairs, and I had wanted to give him time, but too much had already passed.

Watching his finger wrap around the trigger, I had expected an angry little boy, but not a murderous one.

"Oh my God! Arion, what the hell are you doing?" I took a step over the threshold, but my son stopped me with a single word.

"Don't!"

His arms locked and his legs shifted into a firm stance. A firing stance.

"Sweetie, that is very dangerous. Please put it down."

"I know it's dangerous. I'm not stupid. That's why I have it."

"Honey," I drew the word out slowly, "where did you get that?"

"Drew."

I vaguely remembered his best friend Drew, who lived down the street, bragging to Arion about going to the shooting range with his parents pre-divorce, but I was certain this wasn't what he meant.

"I stole it out of his mom's bedroom."

"Arion, you're scaring me. Please put it down before someone gets hurt … or killed."

"That's the whole point—that's why I took it, Mom! To hurt *you*!" His chubby cheeks reddened and his eyes watered. He wiped at a trickle of snot with his sleeve and clenched his jaw.

"Is this because of what you think you saw?"

"I *know* what I saw. Don't try lying to me. You're leaving Dad for another man."

"It's not like that." I wanted to explain, but not like this. Not with a gun pointed at me by my traumatized son.

"I'm not stupid, Mom. I'm stopping you before you hurt Dad and ruin our family. You're gonna tear us apart, like what happened to Drew's family. I can't let you do that. I'd rather be dead. I'd rather *you* be dead."

Drew's parents' divorce had left a hole in Arion's social life when he suddenly became friendless every other week during the time Drew lived with his father across town. I hadn't realized how much the change impacted my son until now.

"Honey, no one is going anywhere. I'm going to talk to Daddy tonight and fix things. We'll be okay. We'll get through this together. I promise, sweetie."

"No more lies! You can't promise that. No one can. Drew's parents told him they'd fix things, and look at them. They hate each other, are always fighting. I hear it every time I'm there."

"We're not the same as Drew's parents. It's not fair to compare us to them."

"Tell me what's fair, Mom. Is it fair that I have no friends at school? That I'm constantly made fun of? And now I don't even have a family anymore. That was the one good thing I had, and you're ripping it away from us."

"Arion …" I tried to soothe, but he only grew louder.

"You're so selfish. I hate you!"

His rage blocked my assurances. I couldn't get through to him. His heart was unreachable.

"Please, give me a chance to make things right."

"You can't fix this! Don't you see that? Dad will be crushed. I hate what you've done to us. We'll never be okay, Mom. I'll never be okay. Drew's gone half the time, I have no one, nothing I'm good at, and ... and ... there's no point to living."

Tears rolled down his face, dripping to the carpet below. His arms shook violently, then with a split-second glance at me, he turned the gun on himself, bent his finger, and a deafening shot echoed along with my blood-curdling scream as I reached him too late.

# Chapter 32 - Jo

I sensed it was coming. Another letter. Another clue. But this time I would be ready for him.

After asking every neighbor up and down Oleander Way if they had seen anyone suspicious, or noticed an unfamiliar car, Detective Cox returned to my doorstep empty-handed. No one had noticed anything, which put us back at square one, no closer to finding Amelia's kidnapper than the day before.

"But we have information now," the detective tried to encourage me before he left. "We know he's got an agenda, we know Amelia is alive, and we know he's still here in town. He's going to reach out again. We just need to be prepared for it."

That's when Jay had gone out to Best Buy to shop for security cameras to place around the exterior of the house. The best that money could buy, I instructed him. If this bastard was coming back, which the detective seemed assured of, we'd catch him on camera in the highest digital clarity they sold.

I glanced out the window for the umpteenth time while a pot of water boiled for that evening's spaghetti dinner. I had settled on jarred marinara because the kids preferred it to my homemade sauce anyways, and I felt too wired to peel tomatoes all afternoon. Funny how children enjoyed the blandness of an assembly-line recipe over the painstakingly combined flavors of my culinary flair. Normally it would have irritated me, but today it simplified my life a little as I emptied the jar into a pan to simmer.

A semblance of normal had returned little by little with each passing day. It wasn't any easier to drag myself out of bed each morning as my hope dimmed with the rising sun. But I had no other choice but to adjust or mope in my bedroom, and Jay had made it clear that moping was taken off the table. So I forced myself along, doing my best to busy my hands with cooking or cleaning or making rounds posting more flyers.

Shayla had even gotten creative with the search by sponsoring an ad on social media with a picture of Amelia and a bold HAVE YOU SEEN ME? heading. Along with the police's original Amber Alert, her cherubic face was spreading like wildfire after a drought. Eventually someone would see her, I kept telling myself. Her abductor would slip up, and the world would be watching.

It had been my fourth trip to the window in the past thirty minutes, when something drew my attention. A car across the street from my house. A black sedan. Possibly an Oldsmobile, though I didn't have a good enough angle to know for sure. Old and beat up, with tinted windows in the back. The car had been there for too long, at least twenty minutes.

The driver was definitely a man and appeared to be middle-aged, like Abby had described. Wearing sunglasses, I couldn't get a good look at his face, but as I watched him sit there, unmoving, his eyes scanning the street for several more minutes, I sensed something was off about him.

Why would someone just sit in their car, clearly not talking on the phone or waiting for someone, unless he was up to no good? The whole thing felt stalker-ish, arousing my curiosity to check it out. A swell of adrenaline mixed with justified rage gave me the courage I wouldn't have otherwise had to approach him.

The kids were playing on their iPads upstairs—I had removed my usual one-hour time limit and couldn't care less if they gamed all day since it gave me more time to worry in secret—so I headed outside. The closer I got, the creepier he looked. A picture-perfect child molester hiding behind a baseball cap and large sunglasses, sitting in plain sight as if taunting me.

When I caught sight of a tuft of brown hair poking out under his hat, my primal instincts screamed that this was him. This was the man who took my daughter.

With bold steps I approached, by chin sternly lifted and my eyes glaring. Once he saw me, he acted confused, like he suddenly had somewhere to be but couldn't remember where. His window was closed, so I tapped it with my knuckles. A moment later he rolled it down just a crack, enough that he could hear me.

"Can I help you?" My voice was no-nonsense but wary. I didn't know what he was capable of.

"Um," he fidgeted with his seatbelt, then tapped the steering wheel, "Nope. I'm just waiting for someone."

"I don't recognize you. You don't live on this street. I know everyone who lives here." I would be showing no mercy to this creepy pervert.

"I live further down." He waved to somewhere in the distance.

"Oh really? What number?"

Turning his head, he looked away, clearly hiding something. "I gotta go."

"How about you stay put so I can have the cops sort this out?"

Only now did he look at me with pleading eyes. "C'mon, lady. That's totally unnecessary. I'm not doing anything wrong but sitting in my car. There's nothing illegal about it."

"Then you can explain that to the police when they get here." I pulled out my phone, about to dial Detective Cox.

"You know what? Go to hell! Call the friggin' cops, you psycho. I'm outta here."

As he yelled, he rolled up the window and revved the car, flipping me off as he shifted gears. But I wasn't about to let him get away. Raising my fists, I pounded on the driver's side glass, punching it in a blind craze. As the car started to glide forward, I jumped onto the hood, gripping the edge to hoist myself up. Once securely sprawled across the hood, I continued banging the windshield with my fist.

"Get off my car!" he yelled loud enough for me to hear through the glass.

I was swept too far into the ire to hear Jay behind me, screaming for me to get down. It wasn't until I felt two arms circle around me, pulling me backward, then setting me on the concrete, when I realized it was him.

"Jo, what's going on? Why are you attacking Elliot's car?"

I was too enraged to hear what Jay was saying at first, unable to put meaning to the words. Then slowly the sentence starting coming together. Elliot? Who was Elliot?

"Is this your psycho-ass wife, Jay? She needs to be committed. Out of nowhere she started attacking me. Stay the hell away from me." He sped off, leaving a trail of rubber behind him.

"What happened?" Jay asked, folding me into his arms. "Are you okay?"

No, I wasn't okay. I had just made a huge fool of myself, verbally and physically assaulting a completely innocent person. How could I have been so stupid to think Amelia's abductor would make catching that easy?

"I'm so sorry," I blubbered. "I don't know why ... I thought that was Amelia's kidnapper. He was ... sitting there watching the street. I just thought ... Oh God, Jay. I'm so mortified."

Smoothing my hair back, he lifted my face to meet his. "Hey, it's okay. The guy shouldn't be smoking pot down here anyways. That's what he does—parks down the street from his house and lights up so his wife won't find out. You didn't do anything wrong."

"I was punching his car, Jay!"

"Hey, think of it as keeping our streets clean, sweetie." He smiled at me, and I couldn't help but laugh at the ludicrousness of the whole situation.

Soon Jay started chuckling, which spurred us both into laughing fits the entire walk back to the house. It was only then when I felt the bruising on my knuckles. I shook my hand, as if shaking off the pain, which did nothing to help.

"I think I broke something." I lifted my hand for Jay to examine. He kissed the tender bones, then opened the door for me.

"How about you ice your paw, Rocky, while I get us some wine. I think we could both use a glass."

Or a whole bottle.

# Chapter 33 - June

"Remember this one, when we kissed on Valentine's Day at that frat party?"

Despite the sharp pain in my abdomen, Ellie and I laughed at the decade-old photograph of us in our prime—young and beautiful, single and in college, sharing a drunken kiss at a party. We had showed up dateless and dressed to impress, but we ended up leaving early for a night of pizza, beer, and chick flicks. Although I had never told Ellie, it was one of my fondest memories with her out of the hundreds we shared because of its simplicity.

No drama. No tears. No responsibilities. No children. No husbands. No bills. No struggles. Just us, living it up, dancing and feeling free, enjoying something intimate and meaningful that only we understood. It was our secret life, a precious moment captured in time, forever locked away in my memory to get me through the tough times.

I'd always have that moment with the one person I could count on, the one person who loved me as much as I loved her.

I hugged my side, which was covered in bandages that did little to ease the ache in my cracked ribs. As soon as Ellie got the news of my accident, she showed up on my doorstep carrying a casserole and soup, insisting on nursing me and the kids back to health. Of course, no meal was complete without some cheap Merlot, which we sipped straight from the bottle. I could never turn her down, even if I wanted to spare her the trouble.

"The good old days," Ellie said, her voice soft and nostalgic. "How did life get so bad after this? Why couldn't life have stayed this good?"

Ellie turned to me, serious. She wanted an answer, but I had none. After hearing about Denny's love child with another woman, I had no hope to offer. The truth of the matter was that he didn't deserve her, but she'd never leave him. She'd just take his crap and eat it with a smile. Didn't she know how much more valuable she was than that?

I spent our entire friendship trying to show her, but she was a glutton for punishment. The typical hapless wife who sucked up the emotional abuse she was fed. But who was I to talk? I was doing the same damn thing—trapped in a Mobius strip of disappointment, unwilling to change things or fight for myself. Maybe it was time to take control. Only, my methods of control nearly killed my entire family, because I knew what Mike and Ellie wouldn't believe. I knew the accident was indeed no accident. What was wrong with me? Had I snapped? Was I losing it? Was my sanity too far gone to salvage?

"Yeah, those were the best days of my life. I miss that sense of feeling free, happy, hopeful. It's so long gone now, isn't it?" I drowned the thought with a gulp of wine.

"But why does it have to be?" Ellie asked, taking the bottle from me. "Why can't we get back to that?"

I laughed, not because it was funny but because it wasn't. "We can't because we chose to have husbands and kids instead. Maybe if we had stayed single with jobs that allowed us to travel and blow our money on cute clothes, cute boys, alcohol, and fine dining … I don't know. It seems like everyone who settles down is miserable. They're either broke or stressed or plagued with a sense of duty to someone who doesn't appreciate them. Maybe that's just life."

Ellie groaned. "That can't be the way it is. There's no point to it if it only makes you miserable."

"I'm sure there are a lucky few who are happy in their marriages, but we're not among them. We chose poorly."

"Aw, is Mike really that bad?"

I shrugged, rolling my eyes. "He's got his moments where I'm reminded why I fell in love with him, but the constant letdowns, job losses, laziness … eventually it wears on you. I've lost that loving feeling."

As soon as I said it I knew what was coming. Off-key and pitchy, Ellie belted out the lyrics to "You've Lost That Lovin' Feelin'," which made me wonder just how much Ellie had to drink. A couple lines in I joined her, both of us teary with laughter.

When our loudly obnoxious rendition ended, Ellie touched my hand, penetrating me with wet eyes. "Do you think life can get better?"

"I don't know. Without a complete restart, I just don't know. Maybe we missed our chance. Picked the wrong path with the wrong people."

I hadn't intended to be cryptic, but I could never tell Ellie about my lost love. No one knew, not even Mike. Besides, she would never understand. To her love was a man's provision for his family; to me love was a soul connection. I had found it once, then lost it because I was too afraid to reach for it. I ended up settling for Mike, whom I loved, but never in the same way.

"A restart?" Ellie asked.

"You know, a complete do-over. Getting a clean start in life."

"How's that possible when you have kids and a mortgage?"

"I dunno. Turning back time?" I held up my finger to Ellie's lips in a playful warning. "And don't you dare start singing Cher or I'll have to join in and my lungs will literally explode!"

Smiling at me, Ellie mimed zipping her lips. "I promise no more breaking into song." Then her smile faded. I watched the twinkle in her eyes flicker and die. "So if a restart is the only way to be happy, I'll have to lose everything. Maybe that's what I need."

She paused, her lower lip trembling. "I don't think I can handle watching Denny father another woman's child. And my own kids have no respect for me. Heck, I don't even have respect for me. I'm miserable, June. And my only option is to leave it all behind and go it alone."

A tear slid down her cheek. The strongest woman I knew had become a wilted rose right before my eyes.

"You don't need someone else to carry you, El. You can walk on your own two feet."

Ellie shook her head at me, fiddling with the blanket's unhemmed edge that fell off the side of the sofa where we sat. "I don't know if I can. I'm not that courageous. I've always relied on others—boyfriends all through high school, you during college, Denny throughout my entire adult life. When have I ever stood on my own?"

"What are you talking about? You're tough, forged in steel, girl. Don't sell yourself short. You're a genius, you're incredibly good at helping Austin, you have your PhD, you're gorgeous … I mean, you're perfect. How can you possibly think you couldn't survive—no, *thrive*—without your idiot husband? You don't need him. In fact, he's probably holding you back."

Ellie chuckled humbly. "I don't know about any of that, but thank you. I love you so much, Juney. I don't know how I'd get through this without you."

"We've been through a lot together, haven't we?"

I grinned. "We sure have. And there's lots more to come."

I had reached the end of my college photo album, the last page a close-up we had taken with my disposable camera in my college dorm. Behind us in the photo was my Justin Timberlake poster—why I faked a crush on him, I have no idea. I never needed to fake it with Ellie. I wore my favorite pink velour sweatsuit with a Juicy butt logo, and Ellie wore her classic cargo pants and tank top. I admired how courageous we were back then, savoring every ounce of life.

"How about a selfie for old times' sake?" I suggested.

"Definitely. Screw my bad hair day and bags under my eyes. Let's do it!" Ellie agreed with a giggle, holding up the bottle of wine.

I held my phone's camera out with my good arm—the other one had limited mobility—and snapped a picture of us with piles of unfolded laundry and children's toys in the background. The living room, which opened into the dining room, had become a dumping ground for clothes, shoes, and junk that climbed up the walls, leaned against the furniture, and smothered the tables. Junk engulfed us. I would have kept the *Hoarders'* crew busy for days. Had it been anyone but Ellie in my house, I would have ushered them out the door in a horrified hurry. But after living together in college, Ellie knew how I was and accepted me unconditionally.

"Send me a copy of that," Ellie said, eyes on the picture. "Gotta put it in my family photo album, since you're my sister from another mister."

It'd been a running phrase we'd used over the years, since Ellie had been like another sister to me, only better, without the sibling rivalry or petty fights.

I pulled up the picture and texted it to her, then began leafing back through my latest photos out of habit. Scrolling through pictures of the kids at the park playing and laughing, it seemed like we could be happy at times. So why did I feel so miserable and my life so pointless?

"Aw, cute. Are those from the park?"

"Yeah. I'll send you the good pictures." I selected a picture and texted it to her.

"Did you hear about the child that was abducted last week— most likely when we were there?" Ellie asked. "She lives on my street."

"Yeah, scary, huh? I met the mother the other day. She was asking around to see if anyone remembered anything. It's just awful." While it was indeed awful, no emotions clung to the words. Maybe it was because I was tapped out. Or maybe it was because only a day ago I had driven my own kids off the road, attempting to murder us all.

"I can't even imagine what she's going through … just heartbreaking." Ellie's voice trailed away. I wondered if her empathy was as forced as mine.

After nearly killing mine in the wreck, such news should have felt tragic. It should have sent chills of horror up my spine to even think of something happening to one of my kids. But for some perplexing reason, it didn't. Detachment watered down any emotional maternal response I should have had over the suffering of a fellow mother. What was wrong with me? Was I truly so damaged that I wouldn't care if my kids disappeared off the face of the earth?

Of course, my accident raised an alarm with my attending physician. When I'd talked to him at the hospital about it, covering over the truth with a vague explanation about being tired and losing control in the rain, he sat down on the edge of the bed and rested his hand on my knee. I could see the worry in his face, the way his white eyebrows knitted together, how the creases around his eyes deepened. He went on to tell me postpartum depression could go undetected for years, mentally tormenting thousands of mothers well after giving birth. It could cause anything from mild depression to suicidal urges. Was that all it was—a delayed case of postpartum depression? Could my demons be easily scared away with a simple pill? Mother's little helper? For some reason I didn't think so, because only I knew the pang of dread that wakened me every morning as I faced another day of sleepwalking through it.

I'd read about mothers who drove their children into lakes, cooked them in an oven, duct taped them to walls, stabbed them to death. All seemingly normal people. Then suddenly they weren't. These women gave in to an impulse and morphed from mom to monster. I now understood the progression in a real way. I was one of them, only I hadn't succeeded. Yet. I had stood on that same step, jumping into something unforgiveable, irreparable. Like those child killers, I couldn't endure the daily chip at my soul— the constant sacrifice, the endless responsibility, the battered self-confidence, the social deterioration into isolation.

Ellie shattered the wave of thoughts with a gentle pat on my leg. "Juney, I better get home. I'm trying to maintain life like usual until I know what to do about Denny and—well, you know."

"Yeah, I understand. We'll talk later this week, okay?"

"If I don't kill myself or Denny by then." Ellie grinned as she said it, but I saw the gnash between those white teeth.

"I'm always here for you."

"I know. You're the only one who is."

After a long hug, she walked out the door, shoulders hunched as if facing the outside world was too heavy a burden to bear. She needed my help, and I had no idea what to do for her. I couldn't save my own life; how could I save hers? I had become useless.

A mother who couldn't stand her children. A wife who felt apathetic toward her husband. And a friend who couldn't shoulder the burden of her friend's pain. I had to be better than this. I had to prove that I was capable of caring, of serving a greater good in this world.

On my end table was the flyer Jo Trubeau had given me—a picture of her little girl, the one who was kidnapped. Three-year-old Amelia Trubeau with a dimpled smile and innocent blue eyes. Last seen wearing a pink short-sleeved shirt and jeans. Her face seemed familiar, so I grabbed my phone and started scrolling through the pictures from the park, this time slower, looking for something. What, I wasn't sure of yet.

At the kids' request I had captured random accomplishments. Pictures of Austin on the monkey bars, Kiki falling off the bottom of the slide, Juliet picking a fluffy dandelion. Then further along my camera roll I saw it—in the background a hot-pink top and a pigtailed little girl being led away by a brown-haired man into a red car. On the back I could make out part of the license plate number—TY6—and the word Camry stretched across the trunk.

The girl was facing away from me, but her clothes matched the description.

This had to be him. It was a gift from God above to make up for all my failings. I could do something important for the greater good, help reunite a mother who would have died for her children. I could be the me I wanted to be.

I held the flyer in my hands, my fingers trembling with excitement, and called the number listed, hoping against hope that it wasn't too late.

"Hi, my name is June Merrigan, and I think I found your daughter's abductor."

# Chapter 34 - Ellie

*oes Life live to torment me? To offer me a morsel of hope, only to sour it a moment later with vinegar? Finally I thought Denny and I would work things out, fall back in love, end up together. Save our family. But it just doesn't seem that way anymore. He's lost himself somewhere along our marriage, and I can't find him. I don't know who he is.*

*I thought he was the man who would take care of his wife and children no matter what, who would make everything okay during the hard times. He was my for-better-or-worse guy, my till death do us part companion. How could I have been so blind and stupid? How could I have been so disillusioned to think that any man was capable of such devotion? The only things men care about are beauty and sex. If you can't offer both of those things, then screw you. You get kicked to the curb.*

*Here I go whining about my cheating husband when other people have it so much worse. A woman in my very own neighborhood, on Oleander Way, is missing her daughter right now. Kidnapped. Possibly murdered. And yet I'm too self-absorbed with my own pain to care. Sure, I can say the same pity-filled condolences everyone else offers: "How horrible! My heart breaks for that family. I can't imagine what they're going through." But do I really truly care? No, because I'm too obsessed with Denny and his pregnant mistress and my spiteful children to notice the suffering of others.*

*I really am a monster.*

*It's no wonder Denny fell out of love with me.*

*As long as my life is perfect I'm okay, but the moment it gets rocky my seams tear open and my heart falls out on the floor where Denny tramples it all over again.*

\*\*\*

There was only one Janyne W listed in Durham—a Janyne Wilson—in my many online searches, making my quest for the home-wrecker much easier. I didn't care that I looked like I'd just crawled out of bed, with my hair a tangled mess, no makeup to cover the angry zits on my chin, and my rumpled loungewear. I wasn't there for a beauty contest. I was there to say my part before bitch-slapping the whore into next week.

The house—no, it was more of a mansion, I realized as I climbed the porch steps—was an impressive restored Colonial, with four white pillars and a wraparound porch lined with handcrafted rocking chairs and gorgeous, expensive-looking furniture. It was clearly a million-dollar home, which I didn't know even existed in this part of town. Suddenly I felt self-conscious showing up here looking like a homeless person. The woman had money, which irritated me more. Beautiful and wealthy—a deadly combo.

Reminding myself why I was there, I shrugged it off and searched for a doorbell. Instead I noticed a cylinder holding a key that, when twisted, rung the old-fashioned doorbell inside. I did this a couple times, hearing the echo it made in the lofty rooms within. I wandered down the porch, resentfully admiring the decorative eaves. Cupping my face, I peered into a massive window that opened up a view into an enormous living room with incredible woodwork, from the ornate baseboards to the intricate beams that crossed the ceiling.

A few moments later the door—which was easily nine feet tall—swung open and Janyne Wilson appeared. I recognized her by the luxurious chestnut brown hair that framed a face way too beautiful for my husband. Honestly, what would a woman who looked like this and lived like this want with my husband, who was neither rich nor remarkably handsome?

A sinking feeling told me perhaps it was indeed love after all.

"I figured you'd wind up on my doorstep one day," she said, cocking her hip and resting polished fingers on her jutting hipbone. I imagined her stuffing salads and fish into her kewpie-doll mouth, afraid to eat anything heartier for fear it might put a couple pounds on her skeletal frame. I stared jealously at her and banished from my mind a fleeting image of her bee-stung lips on my husband's body.

"You guessed right. So you know who I am and why I'm here?"

She nodded, her runway model hair shining under the entryway lighting behind her. I hated her even more for it.

"To talk me out of stealing your husband, I expect."

I laughed, and her confused frown creased her perfect skin. "Oh, no, you can have him. I'm done with him."

"Really?" She pursed her lips as if skeptical. "So that's it? You're not going to make this difficult for us?"

"Well, don't expect me to come to the wedding. But I don't want a man who will leave a marriage of twelve years on a whim. And just so you know, he'll do it to you too. You'll find out soon enough when your boobs deflate and your ass flattens."

"I doubt that will ever happen."

"Oh, you have no idea what pregnancy will do to your body. Congratulations on the baby, by the way."

"Pregnancy? What pregnancy?"

"You're having a baby with Denny, aren't you?"

She flipped her hair over her shoulder and narrowed her blazing blue eyes at me. "You've clearly gone off your meds. And you need to refine your investigative skills, Nancy Drew. I'm not pregnant. Do you think I'd want to ruin this perfect body with a baby? Uh, no."

If the pregnancy test I'd found wasn't Janyne's, then whose was it? Did that mean Denny was serious about breaking it off with her and staying with me? At this point I realized I'd made a huge mistake in my assumption—and in coming here. Mortified, I just wanted to leave and keep a shred of my dignity on the way out.

"Oh, that explains a lot."

She humphed. "What's that supposed to mean?"

"Just that it's no wonder Denny doesn't want you. You're a coldhearted bitch who hates children. Good luck finding any decent guy who'll want more than a good screw with you."

"I'd rather be a good screw than an old hag," she spat back.

My whole body began to react, my fists clenching, my arms quaking, my jaw tightening. This little girl needed a lesson, and clearly God had sent me to deliver it. With her painted lips in focus, I threw my arm back, then thrust it forward so quickly neither of us saw it coming. My knuckles crunched against her perfect nose, none of which I felt until she fell back, clutching her face. Blood began to seep through her fingers as she screamed and shuffled backward, her eyes wide with fear. I shook my hand, rubbing the now tender spot where I had made contact. It hurt, but boy was it worth it.

"Who's gonna screw you now with your jacked-up face?"

With that I turned on my tennis-shoed heel and sauntered down the porch steps, proud of myself for my uncharacteristically good aim. My first chick fight, and I'd kicked ass. As I reached the bottom step, I turned around, flipping my hair behind my shoulder with a mocking smirk. "Oh, and on second thought, I think I'll keep him after all."

It felt so good watching her cry as I sashayed away with an exaggerated hip sway.

# Chapter 35 - Shayla

A shot rang out, blending with my screams, its deadly crack ringing in my ears. Then the gun fell from his fingertips as Arion's body dropped to the floor a moment later. I ran to him and hugged him to my chest, searching for blood. In my panic I couldn't find the wound or any blood. Then he looked up at me with teary eyes and cried. Had he missed?

My fingers searched his body as I kissed every inch of his face, his cheeks, his eyes, his nose. He seemed untouched by the bullet, but not unscathed by the trauma. Thank God for the kickback of a gun!

"You're okay, honey. You're okay."

I rocked him against me, the motion frenzied yet soothing. For several strung-out minutes we cried together, my firstborn and I, mother and son, bonding over our shared suffering and vulnerability.

Our moment together lasted until I heard a panicked voice behind me.

"What's going on? Is everything okay?"

The air shifted as a warm body knelt beside me, the heat of Trent's form washing over me.

"No, everything isn't okay. Arion almost shot himself in the head, Trent. And it's all my fault."

"What? What are you talking about, Shay?" The gun, lying on the floor next to Arion, must have caught Trent's eye, for he immediately picked it up and engaged the safety. "What the hell happened?"

But Arion was speechless, too terrified to respond.

Trent rushed to Arion's side, holding him alongside me. "Arion, what were you thinking?"

Arion whimpered and continued swaying in my arms, too shocked to speak.

"Trent, it's because of me that he did this."

Trent sat back, watching me. "What do you mean?"

I closed my eyes, shutting out his intense gaze. I heaved a rattling sigh and confessed the truth. "He found out I've been cheating on you and he was afraid we were going to split up. I've wanted to tell you, but I just didn't know how. So there it is. You can decide what you want me to do—if you want me to move out, or whatever you want. I won't fight back."

When Trent didn't speak, I peeked at him. He was still there, kneeling beside me in stunned silence. I was afraid to meet his eyes, but I needed to know what he was thinking. A trickle of tears left damp stains on his cheeks, and he looked away from me, unable to meet my gaze. We were in a no-man's land of pain where relationships went to die. I had hurt him beyond repair.

Finally he shifted and rose to his feet. He paced to the window, his carpet-muffled footsteps the only sound. While gazing out of the window, his voice split the silence.

"Is it over?"

"Yes, I've ended it."

What felt like an eternity passed as he continued to just stand there, staring out the window. "Please, say something!" I pleaded.

"I can't believe you cheated on me. God, Shayla!" he groaned. "What do you want me to say? I do everything for you, for our family." His voice broke, then resumed forcefully. "Why? Why'd you do it?"

"I-I don't know," I stuttered.

He turned angrily toward me. "Don't say you don't know, damn it! You know why. Just spit it out."

I exhaled the breath I hadn't known I was holding in. "Maybe because I need more passion. Maybe because we never spend any quality time together. But it doesn't matter, because you're not the problem. I am."

"You sure as hell are! I'm not sure we should even bother trying to come back from this."

Trent was silent for an uncomfortably long time, staring out the window while I stared at him, silently praying that I hadn't shattered us beyond repair.

"Do you want out of this marriage?" The terse question caught me off-guard.

"No, of course not! I love you," I exclaimed. It was the first honest thing I'd said to him in a long time. "What about you—do you want out?"

He was silent. A minute passed. Then another. This couldn't be good, too much thinking.

"I really am sorry," I finally said, "and I do love you more than anything, you know."

"This sure as hell doesn't feel like love." I felt the breach between us widen. "How could you do this to me, to our family, and say you love me?"

"I made a mistake, Trent. I was selfish. I hope you can forgive me someday."

"You want forgiveness?" He forced an awkward laugh. "Why?"

"I wanted attention, I guess. You work so much, we never spend time together, and I just wanted to feel loved. It took one kind word from a man to undo me. I don't know what else to say other than I'm sorry. And I love you, I really do, even though I know I haven't shown it."

Trent's eyes returned to the windowpane sprinkled with rain droplets. His eyes stared firmly at something far beyond, beyond me, beyond this room, beyond the many questions he had bottled up that were ready to explode. Then he walked across the room and sat down on the other side of Arion, who burrowed against me.

"Look, Shay, I don't want to split up our family. I just don't know how to move forward from this. Right now I hate you. To be honest, it's taking everything in me not to wrap my fingers around your neck and strangle you. But somehow I still love you. If you're willing to fix the damage you've done, I'm willing to try to stay together."

"You—you forgive me?" *Please, God, say yes.*

"Not yet. I'm not there yet. But give me time and maybe someday I can."

His forgiveness was all that I had wanted, even the outside chance of it, but not like this. Not with a lie still in hiding. There was something I hadn't told him yet. Something that would possibly destroy every lingering ounce of hope he had in our future. I needed to tell him everything.

"There's more." I paused.

"God, Shayla. I can't take more!"

"I don't want your forgiveness until you've heard everything." I had to go on, no matter what it cost me. "I'm pregnant."

I had never seen Trent get furious. Frustrated, yes. Worked up, yes. But full of rage? Never. Until now. After his bewildered calm, he jumped up and slammed his fist into the drywall. The gypsum crumbled as he removed his hand from the almost perfectly round hole and rubbed his reddened knuckles.

"Is it his?" He heaved.

"N-n-no," I lied, afraid of saying more.

"Is it his?" he yelled this time. "Tell me the damn truth!"

"I-I don't know yet. I won't find out until the baby's born and take a paternity test."

He rolled his eyes and let out a bizarre cackle. "Wow, Shayla, you sure know how to surprise a guy, don't you?"

"I'm so sorry."

"Fuck your sorrys. They're worth shit," Trent spat.

I felt Arion shift in my arms, then squirm. "It's okay, buddy," I whispered against his cheek as I kissed him and let him scamper out of the room, clearly afraid to witness this. On my knees I crawled to Trent's feet, grasping his legs, pulling him down to me. I needed him at eye level so he could see the sorrow in my eyes, know my regret. "Trent, I want this baby with you. I want a future with you. You're the only person I've ever loved, and I want to spend a lifetime making it up to you. Proving to you that I can be the perfect wife."

"I never asked for a perfect wife—just a loyal one, Shay."

"I promise. I'll do whatever you ask, whatever you need, if you'll just give me a chance to be that woman. Please. Please, honey, don't give up on me."

"I was never the one who gave up. You did that."

"I know, but I won't ever give up again. Please, just consider sticking it out, being an amazing father to this baby like you've been to Arion and Tenica."

"So you want me to raise this child, even if it's not mine?"

"There's no one else I'd rather raise a child with, Trent. I haven't told Kels—" I stopped short, unwilling to put a name to the man I'd been sleeping with for fear of changing Trent's mind, "—anyone I'm pregnant. No one knows but you. I wasn't even sure I was keeping it. Please have this baby with me. Or if you want to get rid of it, I'll do that for you. Whatever you want I'll do, honey. We can get through this stronger than ever, I promise. Please."

He couldn't look at me, searching the walls, the bed, the toys for answers. Then finally his answer came.

"Like hell you're not keeping it!" Trent grabbed my hand, traced my palm, linking his fingers with mine. "You're my weakness, y'know. You're who I am. I'll support and take care of you and the baby. I always have and always will. But if you do this to me again, Shay—I will never forgive you. Look at the damage you've done to your son. It'll only get worse if you don't start being faithful and honest. I love you, Shay, but not enough to go through this again."

Cupping his face, I kissed his cheeks, his lips, his neck—every exposed area of skin, until he kissed me back.

That day I vowed to Trent, to my kids, and to myself to be the woman I was meant to be. Selflessly devoted. It'd be hard, especially when the manic days came, when the self-loathing attacked, when I needed a high to survive. Trent didn't understand the impulses that my bipolar brain drove me to surrender to. But I'd be faithful, I promised him.

I'd live it out, or die trying.

# Chapter 36

"Mother, mother, I am sick
Send for the doctor quick, quick, quick.
How many days shall I live?"

Together they chanted the morbid counting rhyme, him and Amelia, slapping their hands together to carry the beat. They'd just finished eating a lunch of hotdogs and popcorn while watching *Shrek*. Now days into the kidnapping, he'd run out of ideas for entertaining a three-year-old. It wasn't as easy as he expected it to be. The girl was demanding, particular, exhausting.

He was downright sick of the little brat.

Two slices of cheese in her grilled cheese sandwich, she insisted. Don't cut it. Apple juice, not orange juice, she whined. Hot cocoa, not cold chocolate milk with dinner, but don't stir it. You need to shake it like Mommy does. How the hell Mommy shook hot chocolate without splashing the scalding drink everywhere was beyond him. One thing after another; she was impossible to please. He almost doubted if it was worth all the trouble. But once Josephine was in his arms, he'd have everything he ever wanted or needed. Ready for the next step in his plan, he'd penned his first ransom note, waiting for just the right time to drop it off:

*Time is up. Amelia's life for yours, Josephine. I'll give you back your daughter safe and sound in exchange for your heart. If you agree, tie a red ribbon on your mailbox and I'll contact you with further instructions. If you don't agree, tie a black ribbon and say goodbye to your daughter.*

Considering this was his first—and only—kidnapping, he had no idea what he was doing. His demands would be simple: Josephine must run away with him, and Amelia wouldn't be hurt. A simple request, and even more simply executed. He would lock Amelia in the bedroom he had set up for her and only disclose her location once he and Josephine had safely fled the country. After this unsatisfying taste of parenthood, he had no intention of keeping the child. His Plan B, however, was still a question mark. If things went awry, he'd need to get rid of Amelia, though what he would do with her and how, he wasn't sure yet. Killing her would be tough to stomach, for sure, since he wasn't a murderer. A little violent, maybe, but he only dished out what was deserved. But with the girl's constant fussing and complaining and need for entertainment, the thought of smothering her grew easier to stomach by the hour.

There was always the other option, to keep his hands clean and make a little cash on the side. Thanks to his time on the inside, he'd met certain people that dealt in this kind of trade. After a few phone calls, he got the name and number he needed. George Battan. A man who paid for children—and paid well. Where the child went after being sold wasn't his concern.

The line trilled. Voicemail.

"Hi, George, my name is … well, never mind that. I may have certain merchandise I was told you may be interested in. Call me back at this number to discuss terms."

That was as good a Plan B as any, though unlikely he'd really need it. He was sure Josephine would comply. She had to. This all had to work the way he dreamed it would.

Unfortunately, he found himself winging this whole thing, and it was a prickly thought just how deep he was digging himself into this mess. All he wanted was to rush forward to the outcome of this whole ordeal. He had enough money to pay for two economy class airfare tickets to London—Josephine had mentioned it being the top place she wanted to visit one day—and a list of cheap hostels where he and Josephine could stay until they found jobs and a flat to live in. That, along with the two fake passports a buddy from prison had hooked him up with, would get them safely out of the country and into their new life.

He expected Josephine would be reticent about running away with him, but he hoped the life of her daughter weighed more heavily than her urge to flee him. The looming threat of what his prison inmate friends—and their friends on the outside—would do to her children might be convincing enough to keep Josephine in check. Regardless, he sensed that in time he would win her over, remind her of the passion they once had, if even for a night. And if it didn't work … well, then he'd discard her like the trash that she was. Like the garbage all women proved to be. He hoped Josephine was the rare exception.

"I'm tired of this game," Amelia grumbled, wiping her eyes sleepily. "When can I see Mommy?"

"Soon, little one. I promise, I want you to go home just as much as you do."

"I'm hungry."

The child's voice grated on him. How did parents deal with this day in and day out? He reconsidered the idea of building a new family with Josephine. Maybe just the two of them would be idyllic enough. Who needed kids when you had an epic love?

"How about a snack?" he offered stiffly, ready to toss the twerp in bed and smother her with a pillow.

"Okay. I want ice cream. With hot fudge."

He closed his eyes and counted to calm himself. By the number five he felt composed enough to appease the spoiled brat. "You got it. Want to watch *Shrek* again?"

She made a face. "No, something else."

"I'll see what I have."

As he headed to the kitchen to prepare an ice cream sundae, she trailed behind me chattering.

"I don't want ice cream now. I want chicken strips."

"Chicken strips?"

"With ketchup. Lots of ketchup."

Another demand he couldn't meet.

"How about fish sticks? They're practically the same."

"No! I want chicken strips!" she belted out.

An urge to strangle her piercing voice swept over him. Picking her up a little too roughly, he held her in the air, pressing his face up against hers and sneered.

"You will eat fish sticks or you will eat nothing, little girl. What will it be?"

Her eyes were wide, a mixture of shock and fear. Then she melted into a puddle of tears and even louder screams. He pressed a hand over her mouth, stifling the sound as best he could. But the wailing continued at a higher pitch.

His urge to squeeze her neck was interrupted by a knock on the door. No one knew he lived here. He'd used a fake name and paid with cash. And the neighbors weren't exactly friendly. Had someone heard her cries and decided to check on it? Certainly no one in this part of town would give two thoughts to a shrieking child.

Whatever waited for him on the other side of the door could be nothing but bad news.

# Chapter 37 - Jo

It had been four hours since I'd received June Merrigan's phone call identifying the partial license plate number of the man in the picture holding hands with my daughter. Four hours since I gave this information to Detective Tristan Cox. Four hours and still I'd heard nothing. Four hours of torture waiting, wondering, worrying.

Did they find Amelia? Was she hungry and dirty but okay? Had she been raped or molested or beaten? Was all that was left of her a rotting corpse? I wondered grimly if I'd be planning a reunion or a funeral for my daughter today. I knew that since her kidnapper was negotiating with me, and that I was his true objective, not sadistic pleasures with a child, it was likely she was still alive and unharmed, but I couldn't stop my mind from venturing into extremes.

Pacing the living room floor, I was sure I was wearing out my sneakers on the hardwood floor. But what irritated me most was how casually Jay sat there, legs crossed on the sofa, playing on his phone, doing God knows what while we waited for the cops to bring us news. Detective Cox assured me we'd know something more today. With a partial license plate number and the make and model of the vehicle, he was confident a suspect would be brought in for questioning. And that someone was most likely "our guy," as Detective Cox had put it.

I headed to the kitchen to make some coffee—I needed a caffeine boost to stay alert and awake tonight. I wouldn't sleep until Amelia came home, no matter how much Jay chastised me for it. He, on the other hand, didn't miss a wink, snoring so loudly at night that it shook the bed. And I despised him for it. I didn't know what to do about the anger I felt, since I knew Jay hadn't done anything wrong—I was to blame for everything, after all. I had lost our daughter, but his recent laissez-faire attitude poked me like a scalding iron.

"Are you just going to sit there all night?" I asked, biting back the tension in my voice.

Jay glared at me. "What else am I supposed to be doing, Jo? Wearing a path in the floor like you?"

"No, but it seems like you don't even care."

"Why would you assume that? Because I'm not constantly speculating over it?"

"Well, yeah." That was exactly the case.

"Just because that's how you process this whole thing doesn't mean that's how I process it. Do you think I want to dwell on what may have happened to Amelia? Do you think I want to imagine all the horrors she might have experienced? Just because I'm not losing sleep doesn't mean I'm not thinking about my baby girl every minute of every day. Maybe sleep is the only respite I get from my worry. Maybe my phone is the only distraction that will keep me sane, keep me from breaking down and losing it. I'm sorry that I'm not dealing with my suffering the same way you are, but don't you dare question if I care about our daughter. I'm feeling every terror she's enduring and then some. So don't tell me I don't care."

Apologetic silence was the only way I could respond. He was mourning with me, worrying with me, hoping with me. I simply hadn't noticed. Maybe his calm was the only way I could get through it.

"Thank you for being you, Jay."

He offered me a sad grin. "I love you, Jo. I just hope we don't have to survive without our baby girl."

"I know …" I whispered. "Me too."

With my back to Jay, I clutched the edge of the sink. I didn't know how to survive anymore. As I busied my hands scrubbing the coffee pot, the warmth of Jay's chest pressed up against my back.

His arms circled my waist, and I couldn't help but lean into the comfort of his body. He squeezed me tenderly, kissed my cheek, then whispered against my hair, "I love you more than anything, Jo. No matter what happens, I'll always be there for you. I'll always adore you. Don't give up on us, honey."

My throat tightened with the unspoken words that dangled between us. We had gone through too much, and yet he still loved me, still wanted me. My knees weakened, shaking and ready to drop me to the floor. After all I'd done, Jay still loved me. But I hadn't loved him enough to tell him the truth.

Even if Amelia was okay, even if our family was restored, the lie I'd buried for my entire marriage wrapped itself around me like a strangling grip. The weight of my affair was a burden I could no longer carry.

I turned around in his arms, gazing up at him. His brown eyes searched mine knowingly, as if he'd already forgiven me for my sin against him. But what if I was wrong? What if he couldn't forgive me?

"Jay, I have to tell you something," I began, forcing a courage I didn't have.

Before I could speak the words I dreaded ever having to say, a knock rattled the door. Pushing out of Jay's arms, I ran toward it with Jay close behind, flinging the door open. And there she was, standing hand in hand with Detective Cox, the same sweet little girl I'd lost, her pigtails swinging, her eyes sparkling, her baby teeth gleaming as she smiled up at me.

"Mommy!"

Amelia was finally home and in my arms. And everything else—the fear, the past, the confession—melted away.

# Chapter 38

**N**o one could ever understand love like I did. The sacrifice you make as it takes everything from you. The passion you feel as it gives much more back to you. The pain you endure when it's stripped bare. This is love. And love makes you do crazy things.

Like kill.

I'm not a killer. When I catch a spider in the house, I let it go outside. When my daughter lost her first tooth and it bled, my knees trembled like jelly. I can barely tolerate a paper cut.

But something changes inside you when day after day you feel hopeless against life. When you're dragged down into the depths of nothingness and no one cares if you ever surface … except for one person, the one that you love. To my husband and children I was nothing but a caretaker, a baby maker, a cook, a maid, a therapist. I could fall off the face of the Earth and their only concern would be who was going to make dinner tonight.

Then there was the constant screaming. Screaming for food. Screaming over toys. Screaming because I hadn't laundered the outfit they wanted to wear today. Screaming about our financial problems. Screaming just for the heck of it. There's only so much verbal assault one can take before they crack.

And I had cracked.

I had seen her slow demise, much like my own. Once upon a time she had been a beautiful person—full of vibrant dreams and hopes. She had wanted a career, she wanted to serve a bigger purpose, she had dared to do great things. I saw all of this in her.

I supported her. I encouraged her to grab those reins and ride that horse all the way to the finish line. I even envied her drive, so opposite from my own apathy for—well, everything.

I guess she was my *idée fixe*—the only thing I wanted out of life.

Then she met her soon-to-be husband. Although he didn't nurture her dreams like I would have, he didn't suffocate them altogether … right away, at least. He entertained her passions for a brief time. Just until the wedding bells rang and she was his.

It was all downhill from there.

Baby number one came and canceled out any chance of a career. Held captive to her kitchen and laundry room, she served her masters—her family—and became a silent slave. I would have never done that to her, stifling who she was. Had we had children, we could have worked together as a team—me nurturing her dreams, her fulfilling mine simply with her love. She would have lived the amazing, exciting life she deserved.

But she chose him over me. Not that I had ever really made known my intentions. When I first met her, the only label I had for what I felt was deep friendship, a soul mate kind of bond. It was only with time that I realized I loved her in a not-so-platonic way. I was *in* love with her—with who she was, who she wanted to be, and who she saw me as. And my love was reciprocated in its own unique way.

I wasn't a doormat with her. I wasn't a maid or a cook or a sex slave. I was a person with feelings, a woman with value, a friend with something interesting to say. With her I was words, thoughts, creativity, beauty, importance, contemplation, fears, silliness. I was so much more than this empty shell I've become.

Because of her love I owed her this. I owed her a real life, free from the chains that bound her: her self-absorbed husband and ungrateful children.

She'd complained enough about how horrible they all were to her. Her husband took what he wanted from her and then left her to rot in her own self-loathing. He stole her youth then betrayed her, unwilling to give her lifelong devotion in exchange. And her kids treated her like garbage, sassing her with harsh words, sucking every last morsel of good out of her. They were just as bad as he was. Truly his progeny.

I didn't want to hurt them. I didn't want to manipulate my way into the house with the intention of killing them. I didn't want to, but I *had* to.

The letter was written and in hand when I rang the doorbell. Tears streamed down my face and I mourned the loss of this family I had grown to care about for so many years. While I hated them for what they'd done to her, I wept at the memories. Memories of birthday parties and backyard barbeques and shared meals and milestones. They were like family to me—and right now I resented them almost as much as I resented my own.

"Hey, is everything okay?" he asked me upon opening the door.

"I know she's not home, but mind if I come in?" I asked timidly.

He opened the door wider. "Of course. Have a seat." He waved me to the living room, a gesture I'd been offered many times over the years.

That was his first mistake.

"What's going on?"

I handed him the letter. As he bent his head to read my scribbled prose, I reached into the purse slung over my shoulder and grabbed the knife I had hidden in it. It was a typical butcher knife—a quiet weapon of choice that wouldn't alarm all of Oleander Way—and as I clutched it, the indelible shower scene from *Psycho* flitted through my mind.

Blinking it away, I pulled the knife discreetly out of my bag, ready to thrust it into his gut.

"What is this?" he mumbled, his eyes still on the page.

"It's a goodbye."

Just as he glanced up, I inhaled a deep breath and stepped forward, thrusting the blade into his throat. I leaned upward, pushing the tip in up to the hilt, then stood there, both petrified and fascinated. A moment later a jab to my chest pushed me backward as he staggered toward me. I stumbled a few steps into the sofa as he pulled the knife out and tossed it to the hardwood floor. It clattered a few feet, then came to rest beside my feet.

That was his second mistake.

Blood seeped into his collar, spreading through the fabric, then trickled down the front of his shirt. He grabbed his neck, stared at his blood-soaked hands, then looked up at me.

"What the hell? Why would you …?" His words were wet and raspy, then wobbly as he swayed woozily. At last he slumped into an unconscious heap.

His gurgles faded moments later.

But the job wasn't done yet.

After picking up the knife, I headed upstairs, where the racket of a kiddie program grew louder with each step. Whatever the show was, the theme song was annoying and loud—deafening enough to cover what had just transpired downstairs. When I arrived at the playroom door, neither glanced back as I greeted them with a chipper "hi."

I walked in front of the sofa between the kids and the television, hiding the knife behind my back.

"I said hi. You should acknowledge it when someone speaks to you."

"Move, freak." The girl had always been *strong-willed*, her parents preferred to call it, as long as I could remember, shoving my kids on the playground and starting fights at every opportunity. I ignored it all those years, hoping she'd grow out of it, but clearly I was wrong.

"That's not polite to talk to an adult that way—or another peer, for that matter." My voice remained cool and calm, but my annoyance bubbled under the surface.

"Do I look like I care about being polite? What are you doing here, anyways? I hope you didn't bring your retarded kid with you."

The boy laughed from his seat on the other end of the sofa, and I turned sharply toward him.

"Is that funny to you—calling other kids retarded?"

"Well he is, isn't he?"

And that was it. Conversation over. They'd sealed their fate and marked their graves, the insolent little brats.

Assuming the boy would be faster and stronger, I lunged at him first, hefting my body on top of his as I stabbed him once, twice, in the gut. He screamed, and the girl shrieked and scrambled to get away. But the coffee table blocked her exit, giving me enough time to heave myself across the sofa cushions, arm extended, as I sliced at her. I made contact at least once when I felt the blade get stuck in her abdomen, then I ripped it back and jabbed again, connecting with more tissue. She cried and dropped to the carpet, scurrying away on her knees. I watched her make progress halfway across the room before the injury caught up with her and she sank face-first into the carpet with a muffled *thud*.

Wiping the blade off on my pant leg, I stood there, numb to their spurting blood, deaf to their wheezing breaths, blind to the death encircling me.

In a daze I walked back downstairs, dropping the knife on my way through the living room to ensure Ellie's innocence. My slow shuffle left a trail of crimson behind me through the front door.

I didn't know what would happen after this—whether my letter would give my identity away, or a witness would place me at the crime. My prints were all over the weapon, so there was that. By this time tomorrow I would be in a jail cell. Oddly enough, I didn't care. It didn't matter what I left behind, because I had nothing to begin with. All I wanted was to do one selfless act for the one I loved. I'd carried out my purpose, and I hoped that with my sacrifice she would get the wonderful life she deserved, with or without me.

This was love at its fullest. Maybe it was a twisted kind of love, a love only I could understand. I knew what a woman needed but would never get if she stayed in an emotionally abusive marriage with hateful children: her *identity*. Her passion in life. Her beautiful soul. Yes, I loved her enough to give her back her soul.

# Chapter 39 - Ellie

You never expect to come home from a confrontation with your husband's mistress to find your family murdered, sprawled out in pools of their own blood. You never expect to go from wife and mother to widow and childless in a single earth-shaking moment.

But here I was, living this nightmare. While cops swarmed the house, paramedics packed up their bags, and CSIs collected evidence, I sat stoic and stunned, unable to process what surrounded me. My initial response was to tend to Denny and the kids. My brain knew they were dead, but my heart couldn't accept it. I wanted to hold Darla to my chest, stroke Logan's head, kiss Denny's lips. But instead I just sat there like an invalid, unable to move or speak.

I was in complete, utter shock. My feet felt nailed to the floor. An indescribable weight hung on my shoulders. After the dust settled from my mental explosion, I pieced together what had happened.

Only one tiny thought flickered in my mind: why?

With my heart ruptured by the one person I trusted, I suspected who did it, and then I knew why.

This wasn't about vengeance. This wasn't an act of terror. It was a message, an attempt to give me a clean slate … but my slate was now covered in blood, and I couldn't push the images out. My stomach clenched and I thrust forward, vomiting on the floor.

A hand patted my back. "Are you okay, Mrs. Harper?"

I shook my head, spitting out the lingering taste of bile. I would never be okay again.

"I know this is a terrifying experience you're going through, but we want to help find out who did this to your family. Do you know of any enemies your husband might have had?"

It'd only been a little more than thirty minutes ago when I had walked in the door, four shopping bags packed with tonight's makeup dinner, and found Denny facedown on the floor. Dropping my bags, I ran to him, afraid to touch him. Pressing my hands against his neck, his skin had the chill of death.

I'd just finished recounting to Detective Cox the panicked silence that greeted me when I called for the kids and got no response. After running upstairs and finding them both dead, I couldn't make sense of it. Who would want to kill my family? I admit that over the past few days I'd played around with scenarios of taking Denny's life, but my children? They were innocents in all of this.

It wasn't until I found the bloodstained letter lying next to Denny that I realized the reason for it all. It was supposed to be a gift of freedom to me—but instead she had ripped away everything I cared about.

In my pocket was the folded up letter with her confession and Denny's blood. I touched my hip where the letter was hidden, fingering it with uncertainty.

"I had found out my husband was cheating on me with a woman named Janyne Wilson," I explained. "He had tried to break it off, so I'm sure she was pissed off about it."

"And I'm guessing you were pretty upset, too," Detective Cox said, the accusation tinting his question.

"At him, yes. At my children, no. I would never hurt my kids, if that's what you're implying."

"I'm not implying anything, Mrs. Harper. I'm just trying to figure out what happened and why." The detective glanced down at my bruised knuckles. "Did you take up boxing recently?"

I rubbed the achy joints where a black and blue tinge spread across the top of my hand.

"No. I paid the mistress a visit. It didn't end well."

"Ah, payback, right?" I shrugged as he continued. "So other than his mistress, do you know of anyone else who would want to hurt your family?"

"No, not that I can think of."

And yet the truth itched to come out. Maybe it was best I come clean with the letter. If I didn't, she would walk free and hurt someone else. I couldn't watch that happen. The scariest part, as I waited in the aftermath, was that I had never seen the warning signs. All mothers felt it at one point or another—the breaking point. That moment you snap. I knew what that was like. But to follow through and take the life of a child ... that part I couldn't digest.

What if she did this to her own family next? And chances were high she'd come after me. I imagined a modern-day Romeo and Juliet death scene playing out as she tried to entangle me in a murder-suicide plot, the same as I'd tried to do with Denny. The difference was, I'd chickened out. This was a whole new level of crazy.

I deliberated, my fingertips playing with the corner of the paper sticking up out of my jeans. I realized now how much she loved me, and I loved her, too. I loved her enough not to condemn her to a guilt-ridden life.

I'd free her soul to own up to her sins. I'd stand by her side through whatever came; I'd forgive her and do whatever it took to carry her through the coming consequences. But I couldn't turn away from this.

"Here." The paper crinkled as I pulled it out and opened it up, handing it to the detective. "I found this next to my husband's body. I know who wrote it."

I had memorized the poignant words, both appalled and honored that someone would do something of this twisted magnitude for me:

*Sorry isn't enough anymore. Sorry can't fix what's broken. Sometimes a sacrifice is the only way to start over again. This is one of those times.*
*We've shared many years and many memories together. We've exchanged dreams and jokes and sorrows and judgments*

and advice. But what I've never shared with you is the truth about how I feel about you.

I love you.

I love you with a love that sees through your smile into the pain you hide behind it. I see your fear of losing everything, when the reality is that you've lost yourself because of it. I see the way Denny looks through you, and the way your kids don't even notice you except for when they want something. They all take from you, and you keep giving without getting. You've suffered too long. You deserve more. So I'm giving you more.

It will cost me my life, and I'm okay with that. I lost my sanity long ago when I should have confessed my love for you and I didn't. Instead I settled into a life of mediocrity and misery, whoring myself out to a thankless husband and raising his children. It's too late for me to change my life for the better. And I'm sorry I never stood up for you sooner, but it's not too late for you.

This is my hello and goodbye. It's a hello to a new life for you where you can become the speech therapist you always talked about being when we were in college. And it's a goodbye to the crappy hand you've been dealt.

Don't worry about me. This was the greatest thing I could do with my life—a noble sacrifice in the name of love. I'll take the punishment I'm dealt with pride, knowing I could suffer for you.

I love you, Ellie, my sister from another mister.

Detective Cox read the note, then fixed his eyes on mine. "Do you know who wrote this?"

I nodded, my chest aching and throat suddenly sore.

"My best friend, June Merrigan, killed my family."

# Chapter 40 - Jo

### Three-Year-Old Returns Home After Manhunt

*D*urham, North Carolina
    *After a terrifying four days, police located the abducted daughter of Jay and Josephine Trubeau, 3-year-old Amelia Trubeau, who went missing from Forest Hills Park early last week. Search parties and a media blitz failed to turn up any viable information. A park-goer's chance cell phone photo showing the kidnapper, Jude Simmons, walking away with the child, provided the crucial lead in solving the case.*

*A partial license plate number for the vehicle used in the abduction, a red Toyota Camry, led investigators to Simmons' residence, where Amelia was found unharmed and returned to her family by Detective Tristan Cox, one of the lead detectives in the investigation.*

*Under interrogation, Simmons admitted to abducting Amelia in a bizarre act of retaliation after being spurned years earlier by the child's mother. "Jo and I were lovers long ago," Simmons explained to police. "She broke my heart and I just wanted her back."*

*After serving a seven-year sentence in Pennsylvania for assault, Simmons was released last month. He is currently being held on a $500,000 bond while awaiting trial. The court date is set for next month.*

I set the *News and Observer* on the dining room table, glaring at Jude's mug shot, wondering how someone like Jude Simmons could steal a child. Yet because it was someone like Jude Simmons, and not a sadistic serial killer or child molester, my daughter came home unscathed. The night she walked through the door she recounted four days of ice cream, candy dinners, board games, and cartoons. I was thankful Jude was simply disturbed and obsessed, not perverted. It was an odd gratitude to feel.

Jay never asked for the details about who Jude was; I couldn't understand his desire for ignorance and I didn't want to understand. Had it been Jay's infidelity, I'd want every last heartbreaking, excruciating detail. Not that it would have helped, but I would have needed to know. Maybe out of morbid curiosity, maybe because human nature was a glutton for punishment. Or maybe my imagination would have made it far worse than the reality, and I would need to hear that it was just meaningless sex.

Not Jay. How I knew Jude wasn't important to him.

"I'm so sorry," I had begun the conversation the night before, after Amelia came home as we sat on the sofa talking things out into the early morning hours. With Amelia tucked in on the love seat between us, I was too wired to sleep. So Jay and I drank coffee and hugged and watched our daughter sleep. It'd be a long while before I'd let her sleep in her own bed without me there. "There's something I didn't tell you, Jay. Something that at the time didn't seem important, or relevant to Amelia going missing, but looking back on it, apparently it was."

He had squeezed me tighter to him.

"What is it, honey?"

I swallowed the thickness that swelled in my throat. I hadn't wanted to hurt Jay any more than he'd already suffered. But I couldn't harbor anymore secrets. "A letter Jude had sent me about a month ago. I never told the police about it because I didn't think it was relevant to the case. It was so vague, and it didn't even have a name or anything useful to the case in it. I just feel like if I would have handed it over, maybe Amelia would have been found sooner."

He had kissed my head, sensing my apology. "Don't sweat it. It's over."

"Is it? Until the trial is over, he's not technically guilty. Maybe I should give it to the police."

"Is there a reason you don't want to?" He had asked it so casually that I was certain he had no idea of the contents of this letter … or the nature of my past with Jude.

"I don't want the details going public. It's kind of a personal letter that I really would rather stay private. Unless you want to read it."

I had looked up at him, my eyes sore from crying tears of relief all evening. He had cupped my chin and pressed his lips to mine.

"I don't know, don't care. As long as Jude was in the past and he's gone for good, which he will be, that's all I need to know," he had told me. I was lucky that I didn't have to share such life-shattering details with the man I loved. As far as Jay knew or cared to know, Jude was a fling from the past—the timeline wasn't important to him. I guess ignorance was bliss for Jay.

I wasn't granted the luxury of ignorance when it came to Jude Simmons. I'd spent the morning with Detective Cox unearthing every detail, scouring through my past like he was panning for gold. I purged myself of every horrible memory while sipping bitter police station coffee. Every detail came out except for the letter, which I withheld not for me, but for Jay. I didn't care how bad the intimate details would made me look; I didn't want Jay to be forced to hear words he could never unhear about my doubts in him, in us. But things change, hearts change. That's the part that Jude didn't understand. After making it through the trenches with Jay, I knew I would never doubt us again.

As the police interview unfolded my secret, Jude's motives likewise unraveled. After our one-night stand, he had committed my name to memory, while his name was lost in a blur of drunken regret. He'd apparently fallen for me that night, though a week later when he read about my marriage in the local newspaper, he'd attempted to move on. Apparently to a mirror image of me he'd found online—a blonde, blue-eyed, freckled girl living with her parents in Pennsylvania. They'd even lived together, until he beat the shit out of her one day, almost to the point of death, I'm guessing for burning dinner or not folding his socks properly.

At least that's the kind of innocent act I imagined would set off a psycho like Jude.

Fast-forward seven years as he recycled long-lost fantasies about me during those long, lonely nights in prison. Upon his release, all it took was an online search to find my address, a few days of stalking to figure out my schedule, and a twisted plan to steal my daughter in some insane hope that it'd bring us together. Why me? While a small part of me wanted to know how his deranged brain ticked, why all the effort without any guarantee of it working, it was probably best I'd never know. No one could truly comprehend the mind of another or why people do what they do.

I pushed today's newspaper across the table and reached for my mug of chai. Running my fingers through my washed and air-dried hair, I savored its silky texture. It was refreshing being human again, doing mundane things like taking showers and brewing tea. But while my life had regained a semblance of normalcy, chaos ruled beyond the feeble security of my home.

I'd just read about a family that was murdered by their friend—happened on my very own street, 15 Oleander Way. What kind of woman—a normal mother like me—can stomach killing innocent children? But it happens all the time. The news is chockfull of perfectly sane moms and dads who go off the rails on a crazy train on a really bad day and do something unforgiveable. Something breaks them. Reality cracks. People snap. The same mothers that tuck their children into bed at night drive into lakes, drowning their children with them. No one really knows the thoughts that torment them. To the world at large they might appear merely stressed out, but their demons attack them relentlessly when no one's watching.

After losing Amelia I sort of got it—the reflex. The compulsion. You act without thinking. Our desperation can change us, mold us, turn us into something warped and unrecognizable. In my own survival mode I neglected Preston and Abby for the sake of finding Amelia. I sacrificed my own children out of fear, panic.

I had even verbally attacked a neighbor and physically assaulted a car. I'd done things I wasn't proud of, things beyond my control. The rage had taken the reins from me, leaving me helpless to my urges until I learned how to tame it.

Maybe I was no different than the monsters out there. Maybe we all had a little bit of monster inside us.

# Chapter 41 · June

*Six months later …*

The inmate who shared a cell with me wandered the halls like a ghost. I was pretty sure she was dead inside, the way her vacant eyes never moved, how her lips trembled with no words, her slow shuffle heading nowhere. Only once did I ever see her alive, and I'll never forget that day …

By the slant of the sun through my one-foot-by-one-foot barred window, I could tell it was late afternoon. My legs splayed out on my stiff cot, I was trying to get comfortable, which was impossible on a mattress as firm as a concrete slab. I was halfway through the pile of books Ellie had mailed me, all of them with broken binding from a guard haphazardly inspecting them. I was one of the lucky few who got regular care packages and visitors.

Casey was my roommate's name, though don't let the term *roommate* fool you. *Roommate* implied living together; we barely existed together. Two passersby who eyed each other warily. I was pretty sure she was going to shiv me in my sleep.

Sitting upright on her bed next to mine, I felt her watching me with a dull expression. I lifted my eyes to meet hers, and for the first time since I'd been there we made a brief connection.

"Hey," I said. A simple word not intended to break into conversation, but an acknowledgement of her presence, mostly. I had been meaning to break the ice with her for weeks, but to be honest, I was petrified of her.

Casey looked like she belonged on the cast of *The Ring*. Her long, black hair hung in front of her face, greasy and knotted. She never bothered to push the tangled mess out of her eyes as she instead peered through it with beady black eyes. Everyone avoided this creepy character that I had the misfortune of bunking with.

It was only now that I realized her eyes weren't black at all, rather a spring green with yellow flecks.

"I'm Casey," she replied. It was the first time I'd heard her voice. A husky drawl, like it was tinged with years of tobacco and farming. It sounded like far too old of a voice for a woman her age.

"June." I held out my hand to shake and she limply touched it and released.

"Why you here?" she asked me.

"I did something horrible."

"Haven't we all?"

I didn't want to explain that amid a psychological breakdown I had killed my best friend's husband and children because I couldn't kill my own. It wasn't fueled by hatred or revenge. It was the culmination of years of exhaustion, frustration, stress, and depression that suddenly awakened an urge to end it all. When I couldn't carry that out against my own family, it popped up like a Whack-a-Mole against Ellie's family. I never saw the darkness coming. To me, it looked like justice.

It was a distorted sense of virtue driving me, this urge to prove my love for Ellie by freeing her. I knew *why* I did it; what I had yet to understand was how I got to that point. In my cracked psyche, how did murder wear the guise of a solution?

I couldn't begin to explain the mental torment that drowned out any moral compass or logic. I didn't want to explain it, because I couldn't possibly justify it.

Like being stuck in a house of mirrors, everywhere I turned I saw what I did—my hands covered in blood, crimson spatters on my clothes, the knife reaching out and getting caught in flesh. I still relived every moment, but over time it grew remote, like a disembodied version of me doing it until I became just a spectator. My only mercy was that with each day, I put more distance between me and that monster I had become.

We were silent, Casey and I, neither of us knowing how to navigate the worst moments of our lives. Then she spoke, her voice hoarse and crackling.

"I did it for love, y'know."

"Did what for love?"

"Let my boyfriend rape my baby girl. Ended up killin' 'er. I s'pose it's best she didn't live through it, though. I never wanted 'er to grow up like I did. Constantly strugglin' to survive. I like to think she's in heaven with the angels playin' with blocks." She paused, then said wistfully, "She loved blocks."

I imagined Casey was right. Perhaps her baby was better off gone from this insufferable earth. She'd spend eternity frolicking in heaven's sunshine, all pain wiped from her memory, in endless bliss while her mother rotted down below.

"I don't understand. What do you mean you did it for love?"

"I let 'im take her 'cuz he asked and I loved 'im too much to say no. He was the only man who ever loved me. I mean, we was messed up together, 'im and me. Both of us high all the time. Always broke. But he made me feel special. Before 'im, I never had no one care whether I was alive or dead. I was whorin' myself, livin' in the streets, eatin' garbage. Then he rescued me. Gave me his trailer and food and told me I was pretty. Didn' judge me no matter what I done in my past … or what was done to me. I woulda given 'im anythin' he asked … even my baby."

Her confession left me mute. Although we had come from different worlds—my middle-class privileged suburbia and her impoverished trailer park roots—we were more alike than I wanted to admit. The same motivation lurked behind every injustice: love. We either love ourselves too little, or we love ourselves too much.

Addicts used because they loved their high more than they loved those they hurt. Abusers victimized because they loved control, feeding their beast with the tears of others. Mothers hurt their own children because they loved their freedom or uninterrupted television or full night's sleep or boyfriend's approval more than they loved their offspring. Tragic choices, all rooted in a twisted, disfigured need for love.

Just like how I loved Ellie too much, and myself not enough. I sought Ellie's happiness at the cost of my own. I hated how such a perfect soul suffered at the hands of a selfish husband and ungrateful children. Combined with my own depression and dissatisfaction with life, it turned out to be lethal.

I still didn't understand how the train flew off the tracks, other than it was a momentary thing. One horribly insane moment where I simply couldn't take it anymore and mentally exploded. All because of a blind love for her that overpowered any love for my family or hers. I knew I'd get caught, be torn from my children, leave them motherless and Mike wifeless, and yet I still did it without blinking. Without a second thought … until it was done.

"Have you ever loved someone so much you'd give up everythin' for 'em?" Casey asked, her eyes burrowing into mine.

"Yes. I guess that's why I'm here too. But love should never require that kind of sacrifice."

She snorted at me then, her chuckle growing into an unsettling cackle.

"You're more naïve than ya' look. Love always demands sacrifice. Ain't no one loved another without givin' something up. It's all part of the deal—if ya want love, somethin's gotta give. Some love takes a little, some love takes a lot. You gotta be willin' to pay the price is all. 'parently our love took a lot. That's why we here."

Such basic wisdom that I had never understood. I had wanted love, but from the wrong person. I had never bothered to consider the cost. Now I had life in prison to make up for it. I didn't know how, exactly, but I'd figure it out.

# Epilogue Ellie

*One year later ...*

*I*t's a redemptive day, the kind of day that reminds me life isn't so bad after all. When the sun kisses my face and the cloudless sky brightens everything. I wonder if June is able to see the sky from her prison cell. We all need a little bit of blue sky to lighten our dark days.

I once thought that my world revolved around Denny, I couldn't exist without him. My purpose was being Mom, Cook, Maid, Wife. I'm glad to discover how wrong I was about myself. There is so much more to me than I imagined. June was the only one who saw this potential in me. And she lost her freedom trying to show me the truth.

The Greeks believed in a mythical creature called a Chimera—a fire-breathing she-monster with a lion's head, goat's body, and snake's tail. All incongruous parts, all part of the same woman. I understood this monster, having spent years feeling like the pieces of my life were strangely juxtaposed. I was a contradiction of parts, until a horrible blow shattered the illusion of my life. Then suddenly behind the fantasy I found something much better. June had exposed me to my true self.

The self who loved to write. The self who loved to dance. The self who loved to sing. The self who loved to help others. It still hurts that I'll never see Logan or Darla or Denny on this earth again. I miss them every day. I long to run my fingers through Darla's platinum blond hair, to tussle Logan's golden bedhead. And Denny's lips I'll miss the most. But day by day I'm unearthing more good memories and clutching them close to my heart.

"Auntie Ellie!"

The familiar call drew my gaze upward from my leather-bound journal. I capped my pen and slid it, along with my journal, into my purse. My solitary moment was gone, and I was perfectly happy with that.

Austin came running toward me holding something covered in dirt and grass.

"Look what he found, Auntie Ellie." Austin shoved his hand up to my face, his fingertips brushing my chin.

"Look what *I* found," I corrected.

"Look what I found, Auntie Ellie," he amended.

In his palm a black and gold insect slithered through the clump of earth. With a huge grin, his pride shined through at his latest treasure.

"Cool. Do you know what kind of bug it is?"

"He look it up—" then a pause, "*I* look it up."

"Yes, we'll do that when we get home. Okay?"

"Thank you, Auntie Ellie."

"You're welcome, sweetie." As he scampered off to find more creepy-crawlies, I called out to him, "I love you, bud."

Stopping mid-stride, he turned around and smiled, affection reaching his eyes. "I love you, Auntie Ellie."

I had never been more proud of anyone than I was right then. I'd learned to love more, feel more, appreciate more because of the trials I'd suffered. No ribbon of words could articulate how much the flames had forged me, shaped me into something stronger than I knew I was. I felt the tremor of life around me now. No longer was life cruel and waspish, but gentle and nurturing. The mother in me hadn't forgotten how to love.

You can't play in the rain without getting muddy. It had taken a downpour to awaken my soul, but in the process I learned to love both the rain and the mud. Where one soiled and stained, the other washed it all away. Following my family's murder, my broken heart had been stitched up and ripped open again and again with each memory. My recovery became a story with lots of chapters, each day a new page of rebellion, religion, healing, self-affliction, and surrender. I was no longer myself. Maybe I was a better version. Maybe I wasn't.

Birds pecked at the crumbs Juliet tossed to them from her seat next to me on the park bench. On the playground I watched Arabelle and Kiki play a game of tag, weaving in and out and around the colorful assortment of slides and ramps. In my lap was a copy of Arabelle's latest literary creation, *The Girl Who Got Kidnapped,* a story about the little girl in the news who was abducted, the one who had lived on my very own Oleander Way. I shivered at the thought of how close to home the horrors can be— one in my own house, another just down the street. How could I have been surrounded by so much suffering and not have noticed?

After her mother's conviction, Arabelle had begun writing at my suggestion, something I found therapeutic that released the weight of my thoughts. While I journaled about real life, Arabelle wove tales about things she observed, heard, or imagined. I was glad to have imparted some useful advice on a child who had lost so much because of me. I hoped she found comfort in writing the way I had. Perhaps it would be her salvation.

Mike Merrigan was supposed to meet me almost thirty minutes ago to pick up the kids for the weekend, but he was late like usual. I didn't mind, though. Against all odds he was getting his life back together, had found a good job, and was making strides toward being a better father in his wife's permanent jail-time absence.

After being charged with murder in the first degree, June had received a lenient sentence of life in prison—which was better than death row, I suppose, though living with the guilt of what she'd done to her family and mine was a fate worse than death. June wasn't a hardened criminal. She was simply a mother who snapped. With too big a heart and too heavy a burden, the ache of watching us both drown in misery had become too much for her to bear. I loved her and yet hated her for it, because in the end, she destroyed us both with her version of justice and freedom. Only one of us would survive the aftermath.

June would be serving time while Mike's life fell apart. I'd kept my promise to foster their kids until Mike could handle single parenthood of four young kids, particularly his autistic son, who needed more attention than Mike could give right now. Despite all the pain, in the end things were getting closer to okay one day at a time.

Thanks to our daily sessions, Austin's speech and behavior had improved by leaps and bounds, and he even had a friend in his kindergarten class. Drawing upon my college studies, I'd figured out how to work through the tantrums, and while it wasn't easy, we had a connection. I understood him, and in his own unique way he understood me. We relied on positive reinforcement to encourage good behavior, and I picked my battles. When he listened and obeyed, he earned a reward. When he calmed down during a tantrum, he earned a reward. I dealt out a lot more hugs than threats, and it seemed to work for him. It also worked for me. I'd become the parent I always wanted to be. It helped me through my guilt and regret.

Over the past few months Austin grew into a happier kid, and I got to be a part of it. For the first time in a long time I made a difference in a life, and it felt good.

My last morsel of closure happened when Janyne Wilson contacted me out of the blue to express her condolences for my loss. She never outright apologized for what she'd done to my family, but her guilt fell between the lines. The domino effect of Denny's infidelity and my reaction had led to this conclusion. I blamed her for her part in my family's murder, but I also blamed myself. It was a complicated emotion I couldn't pinpoint.

While Juliet's legs swung back and forth wildly, another mother sat down next to me, hugging her newborn to her chest as she released her other two children off to the playground. Without being obvious, I looked her up and down. Something about her seemed familiar behind her oversized sunglasses. I recognized her from somewhere. Her brown poker-straight hair was pulled up in a neat ponytail, and her full lips were colored with a muted shimmery lipstick.

While I was racking my brain about who she was, her husband—I could tell from their matching wedding bands—sat down next to her. One close look and I instantly knew who he was. My neighbor back on Oleander Way before I sold it at a loss—taking the first and only offer I'd gotten for the home now dubbed "the Triple Murder House."

"Trent and Shayla Kensington?" I asked. I couldn't believe I remembered their names after so long, but odd things tended to tunnel into my memory bank.

The woman looked up from her baby. "Yeah? You know me?"

"It's Ellie Harper. I used to live across from you on Oleander Way."

"Oh, yeah!" Shayla chirped. She instantly exchanged her grin of recognition for a sympathetic "I'm so sorry about what happened with your family."

"Yeah, well, it was hell trying to sell the house," I joked, trying to lighten the mood. "Hope I didn't bring down everyone else's real estate values."

The couple grinned stiffly, unsure how to respond. Most people had no idea how to navigate the waters of pity. "I feel bad I didn't get to know you better when you were living there. Did you move far away?"

"Not too far. I'm actually fostering four kids right now, and their dad lives nearby, so I wanted to stay close by for now."

"Four kids? Sounds like you're pretty busy ... or losing your mind," Shayla said, smiling sincerely.

"Sanity is overrated. Kids are worth the sacrifice." And I meant it.

June had thought that I needed to be freed from these chains of marriage and children. But they had never been chains to me. They were a choice. They had given me purpose, joy, pain, suffering, sleeplessness, endurance, and strength. What is pleasure if we've never felt anguish? What is courage if we've never been tested?

If only June had understood that. If only she'd realized sooner that sacrifice could teach us how to live fuller, that being true to oneself wasn't about temporary happiness, but about enduring the hardships and finding strength within. Even I learned that lesson too late.

The baby cooed, and as Shayla unwrapped him from his swaddle, a shock of black hair just like his daddy's poked out.

"Congratulations on your little one."

"Thanks. This little guy saved my life." Shayla kissed him on his fist-sized head, then turned to her husband. I didn't know their story, but whatever it was, it had a honey-sweet ending.

My isolated little bench soon became a hub of activity when another woman approached, waving at Shayla.

"Hey, Jo." Shayla stood and greeted her with a hug. "I'm glad you could make it. I wasn't sure if you'd be able to handle coming back here."

"Baby steps, Shay. But we can't stop living just because something bad happens, right?"

No truer words … and from a stranger.

"Jay keeps telling me to face my fears, so here I am," Jo added. "All I know is that one stupid secret from ten years ago almost cost me my daughter. No more skeletons."

All of us carried our own secrets, buried our lies, and hid our ugly pasts. But we also grew more beautiful from it—overcoming pain, starting anew, and venturing out past our discomfort to challenge ourselves. Fire could burn us or temper us: the choice was ours. Some stumbled through their pain and crumbled like ash. Others walked through the flames stronger, courageous, with renewed empathy. I chose to live. It was the only life I had and I wanted to make the most of it. Clearly the two other moms chatting next to me had made the same decision.

We each shared the labor pains of life, but we birthed something new: hope for a better tomorrow. And tomorrow looked pretty damn good.

*\*\*\**

# The Girl Who Got Kidnapped
## By Talia C.

While Arabelle Merrigan didn't actually write this story, my real-life seven-year-old daughter, Talia, did. Much like her thriller-writer mother, my firstborn has a passion for crafting mysteries of her own. I hope you enjoy this short story that she's written for your enjoyment, depicting what she thinks actually happened to Amelia Trubeau …

\*\*\*

*Once a little girl did not want to listen to her parents. She'd rather go to a family who always listened to her, so one day she was at the park wondering what family she could run away with. But she did not hear a small creeping of a man, and she got kidnapped by the man!*

*Soon she fell asleep right in his arms. She thought that man was a nice man, but he was not, and the man put her in his home and got ready to kill her. So when she woke up, she acted nice because she still thought he was nice. And then she noticed that he was a mean man, so she acted even nicer so that he wouldn't hurt her.*

*The next morning after he woke up she asked, "What's for dinner?"*

*The man went out to catch some worms for dinner. The little girl knew something was wrong but she ate the worms anyways. Then she wanted dessert, and the man went out to find some dead birds, and again the little girl knew this was strange. But she still ate the dead birds to make him happy.*

*Then the man had a brilliant idea. When the little girl fell asleep, he was going to put her on the stove and put some vegetable and fruit on her—since he knew how healthy fruits and veggies were—and he would cook her for a feast for Thanksgiving.*

*At this point it was in the middle of the day, so he got the vegetables and fruit out, and he put together a medley of celery, pineapple, apples, oranges, tomatoes, carrots, and beans.*

*"What are you making?" the girl asked when she saw this.*

*"I am making fruit salad," he said.*

*"Yay!" said the girl, thinking he was nice after all.*

*So she danced around with her dolly while he made fruit salad. Until she saw something was very wrong with it. The man had put poison in the salad. The man asked her to eat it, and because she was afraid of him, she did.*

*Eventually she fell asleep, and she woke up to find herself in the oven, being prepared for dinner. As she closed her eyes to say goodbye to her mommy and daddy in her head, she realized that her mommy was always right.*

*Just as she was about to be cooked to a golden color, the police broke down the door and rescued her. She never wanted a new family ever again.*

*The lesson is to always listen to your parents and that just because someone eats vegetables and fruit doesn't make them a good person.*

## The End

# Acknowledgments

Every time I get to this part I don't know where to begin. My superhero husband who takes on kid duty so that I can write. My four amazing children for cheering me on, whether in words or baby babble. My friends and family and fans who buy my books, leave positive reviews, and remind me that sleep is overrated. And of course my editorial team at Proofed to Perfection, who polishes my prose and fixes my "oops," as my youngest daughter calls them. Then there's my publisher extraordinaire, Bloodhound Books, whose amazing team helped me through the final birthing stages of *Pretty Ugly Lies*. They produced a book I'm so proud to call my own. Though, for those authors who compare publishing a book to child labor, I'll give you the honor of carrying and birthing my next child (wink)— writing a book is way more fun than labor!

There are so many people who contribute and support this dream of mine to be an author—thank you, all of you.

But ultimately all of this is for you, my readers. All these words, characters, plots swimming around in my head—it's for my fans. Those incredible minds all over the planet who purchase a copy, invest in my characters, enter my world, and embark on the thrills I spent countless hours creating, plotting, planning, living.

If only I had enough pages to list every person who has left an imprint on me, encouraged me, and supported me. But we'd be talking about a book of Bible-length proportions. Thank you, all, for reading this.